Legacy Girls

Jennifer Vaughn

Published by Waldorf Publishing
2140 Hall Johnson Road
#102-345
Grapevine, Texas 76051
www.WaldorfPublishing.com

Legacy Girls
The Jaycee Wilder Series, Book 2

ISBN: 978-1-944782-76-4

Library of Congress Control Number: 2016956997
Copyright © 2017

Dedication

For all the exceptional young women in my life. From the soccer field to the classroom and beyond, always find the light in yourselves and follow it. I can't wait to see what you become.

CHAPTER ONE

Moonlight filtered through sheer curtains cast long silvery lines upon Eve Levesque's naked thighs. They reminded her of piano keys, bone-colored planks of white interrupted by dusky jutted nubs. If his swollen, arthritically deformed fingers arched over the keyboard of her leg could emit a sound, it would be woeful, in B-flat minor, that melancholy flavor featured in several arrangements by her favorite composer, Tchaikovsky. Eve blinked sharply to pull her gaze away from the grotesque hands climbing upward over her well-defined quad muscle. She blinked again, opting for the blackness behind her lids, the safe place where she would retreat to for the remainder of this encounter.

There had been strict instructions not to cower, wince, or show any emotion at all that might disrupt the passion of The Messiah. Those were the rules. As a Legacy Virgin, Eve had agreed to abide by them, but at the time, they were merely words. She had no context of what they meant, or how they felt beneath her skin. Her Mother had never discussed what to do if her body betrayed her with nerves that rattled her teeth and clamped her legs so tightly together sweat was dampening the lavish Victoria's Secret black lace underwear he'd provided her.

They weren't hers. No, she had never liked the overpriced and itchy scraps of fabric that barely covered her butt cheeks. Eve had no reason to impress anyone with her undergarments, so she had always opted for the comfortable Hanes Her Way bikini cut sold at the Kmart near her house. They fit nice and snug under the compression shorts she wore beneath her soccer uniform. The scratchy lace gave her another sensation to focus her senses on, because if she let herself feel The Messiah's prickly tongue assaulting her upper bicep like it was a salt lick, she just might heave up the tuna fish onion roll she'd had for lunch.

"Relax, Number 14," he moaned. Even his voice was old and weathered, as she remembered her grandpa's had been after decades of smoking menthol cigarettes. She wondered if this decrepit being slobbering his way across her collarbone was someone's grandfather. *Great* grandfather? Had he walked a daughter down the aisle at her wedding? Did he have a wife at home? A woman with equally gnarled hands and white hair who had once been lovely and idealistic? Had she pledged to love him for the rest of her days? Had he promised to love her back? Who in his life was he betraying? There was always someone. Entry into Fantasyland was only granted at the expense of an innocent. Eve had already sacrificed that part of herself. She wasn't the victim here, just a willing partner in a business arrangement.

Modern advances and technology that rewarded instantaneous solutions would never blunt the power of the oldest business known to man. It never changed. Simple, pure, and untainted by time, it remained the root of all pleasure, the ultimate victory, the symbiotic win-win human beings were built for. So, when a Legacy Girl accepted the deal from her Messiah, she was taken care of for life. She would know what it felt like to jet off for a weekend of shopping in Paris, or to build a house from the foundation up with all the upgrades included. A Legacy Girl lived out her days surrounded by all fine things. An American Express Centurion Card would bear her name and there was never a spending limit to worry about. She would travel the world on someone else's dime, sit in first class, and dine upon the tastiest cuts of Kobe beef as she sipped Cristal champagne on the French Riviera. She would have it all. Eve had never wanted it all, she just wanted better.

With considerable effort, she forced her breath to come faster, harder, and more sensuous-sounding. Eve knew she had to prove herself worthy of The Messiah's long-term investment. She was the stock before the IPO. Messiahs only bet on the ones guaranteed to take off.

She had to show him she was about to soar.

It had started easily enough. Eve had been coached to believe *she* could control this—it would not control her. The drive out to this barren northern New Hampshire estate was quiet, peaceful even, as the supple leather passenger seat of her Mother's Range Rover wrapped her up like a present. It was flashy and red, hard to miss. Boys in cars traveling along I-93 to the mountains with snowboards hanging from their roofs nodded their approval through the tinted windows. Her Mother preened. Unlike the Legacy Virgin she was in the process of nurturing, Mother was luxurious in every way. Her Messiah made sure the Rover had its oil changed every four thousand miles, was always gassed up, and had her most current playlist loaded into its onboard sound system. Its shiny exterior was free of winter road gunk. Mother's world rotated around a number plugged into her iPhone that she texted often. No name, just a series of numbers. Within a half hour, theater tickets appeared for a new show on Broadway, or a square envelope encasing the signature blue Tiffany box popped up in the mailroom at school. Whatever the whim, no matter the request, the text activated action. Eve didn't ask where all that shit came from, but she was certain this grandiose vehicle with a comical sticker price had been delivered without hesitation. Her Mother had every aspect of her life taken care of. She was a kept woman, and loving every minute of it.   Despite being dumb as fuck, Mother had already been accepted at Harvard and her Messiah had booked a graduation trip to Dubai. She had a bevy of admirers at their school who assumed she came from old money.

In a way, she did.

Eve was Number 14 on her Mother's side, the fourteenth generation of the Legacy Girls. She would never have a name in this family. She would never have a say, or be valued for the vibrancy of her brain. She would never again own the right to say no. After tonight, if she maintained good Legacy standing, she could count on guaranteed acceptance into the college of her choice. Did she want a career? That would be a sure thing, too. Messiahs had connections and strings to pull in boardrooms and corporate headquarters across the globe. She had been told of past Legacy Girls from several other exalted boarding schools who had gone on to medical school, become hedge fund managers, international beauty pageant winners, and stay-at-home moms. Rumor had it one of them was an Academy Award-winning actress! They were everywhere. Across every walk of life. Legacy Girls represented a deep and unblemished tradition seamlessly carried out for a very long time. Every member of the inner circle played his or her role with the utmost discretion.

Their secret was to be protected at all costs. Even if real love brought marriage and children, Legacy Girls remained committed to their Messiahs. In their very late years, many Messiahs called upon their girls merely for companionship. When the body could no longer perform, the fondness and familiarity became the lasting connections.

They lived otherwise normal lives with every financial whim covered. A Legacy Girl was beholden to her Messiah until he decided she was free—or until either of them stopped drawing breath. The contract was for life. No Legacy Girl came to her decision for the same reason. Many of them, like Eve herself, had known a simpler, no-frills kind of childhood. They likely resented their hand-me-down wardrobes, and the pockets of rust that decorated their dads' old Camrys or Civics. Maybe a few of them felt underserved by fate. And, perhaps some were just immature and wanted a music video life full of yachts, beachside bungalows, and G6s stuffed with professional athletes and boy bands. Eve figured some of them had signed on solely for the adventure.

It is the Mother's responsibility to find, nurture, and prepare her Legacy Virgin to assume her role in their tribe. Her Mother had befriended her during freshman orientation. Eve remembered how hot that early June day had been, an uncharacteristically humid morning for late spring in New Hampshire. She sat in the crowd of well-heeled young adults and their chaperones all by herself, no one in her own family could take a day off from work to attend. The kind of parents who sent their kids to a boarding school with this level of exclusivity also sent someone else to deal with the paperwork and the swampy heat. She wore her finest white sweater and a fitted black skirt on loan from her neighbor. Her straight brown hair with sun streaks of golden blonde hung down her back in a neat ponytail, and she had applied a light coating of mascara on her eyelashes. In spite of her youth, Eve's hazel eyes reflected wisdom and patience, but her insides churned with a neurotic stamina that was never off duty. Her friends told her she was beautiful and appealing but she knew it was more like sturdy. She had a muscular body honed by years of grueling soccer sprints and endless conditioning. Hours of practice and studious attention to her grades had earned her both academic and athletic standout status in her woodsy hometown about an hour south of the co-ed Episcopal school that welcomed all faiths, and encouraged its campus dwellers to forge a path through their lives that was solidly built upon a common devotion to their fellow man. Lovely in thought and marketing purposes, but in practicality the tony school was an historic cash cow and king-maker. It boasted graduates that ranged from a former president, to two secretaries of state, and one Arabian prince. Eve had slipped through the elegant gates by being nominated for scholarship status. Her family committed without hesitation, even though they would be responsible for the supplementation of her education and housing. Soccer travel, books, and expensive apps on their school-issued iPads ran these kids several thousand dollars a semester. Both her parents, and her very pissed-off twenty-year-old brother, were now logging extra hours at menial jobs to pay her way. It was a humiliating feeling that tugged at Eve's indomitable desire to be self-sufficient. She worried the weight of her debt might one day kill her. Wasn't there a better way?

Mother sure thought so.

Eventually, she realized the attention of her Mother that began that day had been part of the grooming process. She never asked why she had been marked—it would have been painful to hear that she presented to the world as an easy target, a woebegone but feisty come-from-nothing go-getter with a chip on her shoulder and a slanted view of society. She was guarded and quiet at first during the Get to Know You BBQ on the sprawling front lawn of the Academy. Her Mother was insistent, forcing chit-chat that felt ridiculous and stilted. She couldn't figure out why this gorgeous light-haired creature, who moved with the silky body awareness of a dancer, was wasting her time on inane banter with a lowly incoming freshman. Below her sweat-sticky eyelashes, Eve watched Mother's glossy lips stretch and strain with overblown animation as she gushed about campus life, some sweet little candy store with homemade chocolates, and the low water pressure in Dawson Dorm. She was exotic and alluring, the kind of imposing presence who would hashtag her selfies with #nofilter. She didn't need one. In spite of knowing they were hardly BFF material, the sturdy girl and the goddess became friends.

About six months later, over café mochas at a brick-faced coffee shop a short walk away from campus, Mother brought up Eve's drawn and tired-looking eyes. She was so conscientious of her *real* family's sacrifices to pay her way that she was working herself ragged to maintain a 4.0 GPA with all honors classes. She was bone-weary, had lost weight because there was no time for a full meal, and had started leaving handfuls of her hair behind in the shower drain. Her body was taxed and it was starting to show.

Her bright-eyed teenaged Mother was disturbed about stress and the toll it takes on a young person. "You're still growing, for fuck's sake!" she'd fuss, sniveling at Eve's heavy chin bobbing with exhaustion upon her open palm. She was double-booked as a student athlete, the starting striker on the soccer team, and year-round three-day-a-week practice often ran late into the night. Her coach was pushing and her teachers were pulling; she was caught in an exhausting game of tug of war and the rope was slipping right through her overworked fingers.

"There's a way to make it all stop," she said finally.

"Make what stop?" Eve asked, sipping on her skim mocha latte and giving her head a quick shake to wake up.

"The madness," Mother stated firmly. "This crazy assault on your body and mind. The stupid rat race. All the ridiculous scholarship crap you're trying to keep up with. Getting straight A's in boring classes that mean nothing in the real world." Her angular face was vivid with expectancy. Eve squinted at her. What the hell was she talking about? "I'm trying to tell you it doesn't have to be like this for you. It isn't for me. I can teach you how to get so much more."

Eve huffed. A new way? So much more? Seriously. At the time, it sounded ludicrous. There was no such thing. To be truly exceptional, there was no gain without pain. She knew she had only just begun paying off her portion of life's sweat equity requirement. Mother's intense eyes glistened. She wanted to take away the agony and get straight to the trophy.

All Eve had to do was believe.

"I'm about to share with you a secret that's been protected by generations of women just like us," she crooned.

"Are you punking me? For real? What the ..." Eve wasn't following.

"You're special," Mother interrupted. "And you deserve a life full of adventures and country club memberships. *Honey*, famous designers have my measurements on file. I snap my fingers and they start sewing." Eve peered into her eyes. People sewed for this girl? The bewilderment must've been sorely apparent. "I'm going to teach you how to make the ultimate investment in your own future." Eve smirked at the obscurity. Mother sounded just like the Scientologists on that HBO special Eve had recently watched. How they worked a new recruit with promises of community and acceptability. It was just a smoke screen. Totally not real.

As she leaned her perky chest over the square wooden table between them, Eve's eyes dropped to the iron breasts stuffed inside a white button-down shirt. They never even budged. She chuckled on the realization that those perfect mounds were artificially fabricated, but felt dismay that some surgeon out there would agree to supplement someone so young.

"Sounds great, sign me up," she trilled, still assuming they were merely mocking the absurdity of the rich as only the poor can.

"Actually, I already have," Mother told her, ignoring her attempt at humor. "And all you have to do is …"

The rest of it sounded so surreal Eve left the coffee shop in a daze.

She tossed and turned in her tiny dorm-sized bed that night, asking herself impossible questions. What would her legacy truly be? Was hers to be a life spent trying to measure up? Would she be mortgaging her future before she even had one? How would she carve out time to be a mother someday if she was holding down three jobs, managing housework, and hating herself for settling? How would she ever pay back her family for what it was sacrificing for her? She would be forever indebted to *so many people!*

Was that the life she wanted?

No.

Mother told her the first time was the hardest.

She was so right.

Her Messiah had left a rectangular pink box on the bed at The Heights, the hulking stone mansion where Legacy Girls and their Messiahs shuttered away for weekends at a time. Tucked deep inside an obscure town with more moose than residents, southwest of the Canadian border, The Heights was an architectural beast with a medieval old-world facade and gleaming marble floors. Library-like in its stillness. The soaring wooden ceiling spun intermittent sound into echoes that swirled a melodic hum through the cavernous foyer. Eve and her Mother arrived early to set up and get settled. Mother led her to a room on the second floor and turned the glass knob of the heavy wooden door.

"There will be a box on the bed. Inside will be either a costume of your Messiah's choice, or lingerie."

"So I'm either a naughty nurse, French maid, or a porn star?" Eve snipped.

"Yes," Mother said sharply. She grabbed her tightly, spun her around and placed her palm on Eve's back. With an elbow against her spine, she thrust her across the threshold into her new life.

Eve looked around the dimly lit space. She approached the box on the bed. With a heavy sigh, she tore off the lid, preparing for dirty flight attendant but coming up with a slightly racier version of a suburban housewife. Mother told her she could keep the garments once the encounter was over but Eve planned to feed them to the lapping flames in the fireplace across from the ornate mahogany bed with striped sheets and a blood red comforter. She tugged and pulled the ridiculous black lingerie into place, squirming at the way it hugged the private nooks and crannies of her curves. The sideshow was about to begin. The door swung open and a tiny man with a negative balance of body fat appeared.

"Number 14," her Messiah pronounced boldly upon sweeping into the room for the first time. Eve could sense he wrapped a bawdy persona around his diminutive stature to overcompensate for being a scrawny puke. He liked acting big because he had money and had taken merciless heat his entire life. Eve felt her mouth tighten and her legs pulse with a nearly irresistible urge to front kick her foot straight into his pompous ass.

She declined to speak to him as her large inquisitive eyes followed his trajectory toward her. Her Messiah was wrapped in a thick white terry cloth robe that displayed a narrow torso and knobby knees. He had bristly gray hair and eyebrows with a light scattering of stubble upon his chin. As he scanned her from top to bottom, Messiah gripped her firmly by the shoulders to brush each cheek with his dry mouth. His breath smelled of peppermint Lifesavers but as he grinned Eve became fairly certain his teeth were either implants or dentures.

The introduction swiftly moved into the next phase of their rendezvous.

He wanted to touch and feel. There was no time to inquire about who she was, and he displayed zero interest in seduction.

A residual medicinal odor reached her nose every time he opened his thin, dry lips. His hands moved up. Squiggly blue veins connected the skin atop spongy fingers. They were soft. Not at all like the calloused hands of the boyish hockey player she'd already gone all the way with. No, those had stroked her with sweet and hesitant curiosity. These hands were incessant and informal, heavy yet swift. They moved high and then low, a rhythmic back and forth that Eve knew was strictly to entice himself at her expense.

Her pleasure was not a concern. It never would be. It was in the contract.

"Look at me, 14." His voice was bated by desire. Before he indulged in her intimacy, he needed to authenticate the tie that would bind them, to not just seal their union but burn it into her marrow.

He was so close his features were blurred. Hard brown eyes sunken deep into their sockets stared impatiently into her own. Old age had stolen so many of his eyelashes that only a few hung on in wispy disarray. Eve felt her ab muscles quiver in desperate revolt of what her mind was forcing them to do.

This isn't real, she told herself. *This is Mrs. Dwyer's Honors Creative Writing class*. Just write the scene.

Okay, let's do this.

13

Eve put herself on the train from her favorite movie, *Risky Business*. She was a cool and sophisticated provocateur prepared for the ultra-elegant sexual sequence with her leading man. She wrote her script in her imagination, swapping out parched and cracked lips for the pliant, youthful ones of Tom Cruise. His touch was electric, a charge that sizzled her skin and lit her on fire from the inside out. Mrs. Dwyer asked for more tone and texture in her scene so Eve added a haunting soundtrack.

I can feel it coming in the air tonight.

Yes, she was on the train and it was moving. She and Tom were writhing on the ripped leather seats and the iconic strains of Phil Collins' eerie revenge anthem rolled over them like brackish water.

I was there and I saw what you did ... saw it with my own two eyes ...

Thank you, Tom. Thank you, Phil. Eve thought with their help, she could see this train ride through to her final destination.

We can do this!

Wipe off that grin ... I know where you've been and it's all been a pack of lies.

Skeletal fingers grabbed at her chin. Tom skittered away into the shadows of the ceiling, taking poor Phil with him. Eve was back at The Heights. Her train ride was over and the pinched mouth of her Messiah was close. Too close. She blurred her eyes to further obscure his face; the intensity of his expectant glare was repugnant.

"Look at me, Number 14," he drawled. "Look *into* me."

Eve cracked her eyes in a lazy peek-a-boo, but then slammed them closed again. The raw aversion was palpable.

Messiahs were like bloodhounds, especially when it came to money. A true capitalist could always sniff out a fake.

Eventually, he dropped his head and began to engage in the motions of satisfying himself. The shift was subtle yet clear enough that the Messiah had made his decision.

Number 14 had held back. He had demanded all of her but she wasn't willing to part with the one thing she had left: her soul.

No, Number 14 would have to go.

* * * *

The next morning, Mother bid farewell to her own Messiah and went downstairs to wait on a soft velvet couch in the empty foyer. Flush with a fistful of hundred-dollar bills, she tapped her toes to an imaginary beat and glanced at the calendar on her phone to figure out what day of the week she had open to shop. There was a new boutique in Portsmouth she'd heard about. Maybe she'd take her new Legacy with her to celebrate.

She checked Twitter and Instagram, waited impatiently on a wavering Wi-Fi connection, and couldn't suppress a smug giggle when images of her old "friends" eventually popped up. Losers, she thought, with their shitty cars and impending student loans. How grateful she was to her

Mother for saving her from a life of bad credit and an off-the-rack wardrobe. She smiled as she thought of her new Legacy. She'd been careful with her choice. Eve would be an epic Legacy Girl and she would take all the credit for finding her. She couldn't wait to hear about her first night at The Heights.

She checked the time again. Eve should've come down by now.

Finally, heavy footsteps on the marble signaled she was on her way. Mother collected her things and prepared to leave. Instead, a formally dressed butler appeared. Mother gasped, she had never seen anyone else at The Heights, it had always functioned silently from some deep unseen headquarters.

"Number 13, you are excused," the butler told her, puckering the "u" on a proper English accent.

Should she respond? Was she allowed to speak? Mother was unsure what to do.

"Uh," she sputtered and moved back, feeling the soft edge of the couch connect with the sensitive skin spread over the flatness behind her knees. "I'm waiting for, um, for, my friend." She noticed the butler seemed to be expecting that.

"Number 14 will not be joining you."

Mother felt like hot tar had just been poured through her digestive tract. What was going on here? Something wasn't right. She couldn't just leave Eve here by herself, could she?

"Do you understand?" the butler pushed. "Number 13?"

Clearly, she had a choice to make. So she did. Mother straightened her back as her brain shredded her conscience. She hadn't fucked up, Eve had. This wasn't her fault. She pretended that she had never heard of the rare occasions when Messiahs would enact their own punishment on a Legacy who wasn't a good fit for the family.

As she left The Heights, Mother decided on Wednesday.

Wednesday would be the best day of the week for a shopping trip.

CHAPTER TWO

Skin had a funny way of healing. It wanted to. It really tried to. But the ravages of disease or trauma always got the last word. In Van's case, there were a lot of words.

Jaycee Wilder watched her boyfriend's back as it bent sideways to absorb a small swell near the shore. Even from her towel on the sand she could still make out angry red grooves of puckered skin where stitches and staples had closed ragged and ripped flesh. As she watched Van dive into the cool water, Jaycee's pointer finger gently traced the crescent-shaped crease halfway between her ear and chin. It still hurt whenever she rolled onto her back at night, and most especially when she accidentally got too close to the raw patch when brushing her hair.

Constant reminders.

Six months ago she almost lost Van. She nearly lost herself. Apparently time and fate had gotten together and made some sort of deal in the afterlife to spare them both, because there was no other explanation for the pieces fitting together just so. In the hours and days after both of them were left for dead in the bowels of a den specially designed for the criminal minded, it could have gone either way.

Her one-time best friend, turned homicidal serial killer, was still out there. Samuel Greene, or Ben Roderick, as she knew him, her obscenely brilliant videographer, had taken so many innocent lives in the most brutal of ways. Because she had been crafty enough to root him out, he'd decided she was an unacceptable risk. Van was simply the handy stand-in to sell his story of innocence.

But that was *so* six months ago.

Jaycee had changed. In the most cliché of ways, she did admit to that oft-spoken of near death clarity that had survivors seeing colors more vividly, and breathing air that had miraculously become fresher and more intoxicating. But at her badass core, she knew that life had just become a battlefield. A girl who had cheated death once owed it to herself to buttress her shit up. She had been fully cleared by the doctors and was working herself back up to warrior princess status with her trainer five days a week at the gym. Her news director, Clare, was forcing her to stay away while some short-term disability bullshit ran its course. Fine, sure, she'd go along with it because she had to, but Jaycee couldn't wait to get back to her reporting job at Los Angeles' highest-rated TV news station.

Van, however, was taking a more indirect route to full recovery. His lungs had been seriously damaged, his brain was still healing, which meant lots of memory issues and odd misplacement of certain words, and his blood pressure often dipped too low. Van's bartending job at a bustling West Hollywood nightclub would hold until his stamina returned, but his agent was growing impatient to throw him back into the acting arena. Suddenly, juicy roles for a scarred leading man with a dark past were plentiful. Mid-level movie producers wanted him, while one well-known director had taken him to lunch at The Polo Lounge. Van was being wooed by both old-school Hollywood, and new age writers who needed a moody, brooding actor for their upcoming Netflix series. Jaycee's favorite approach had been made by an aging yet still relevant actress who had sent her panties in the mail with a note about some sexy script she wanted Van to consider. By almost dying, Van achieved the ultimate Hollywood goal: he had created buzz.

Otherwise, they were trying to get back to their lives. The victim's advocate they were working with called it their new normal. When true horror parks itself in your living room it does take some time to think, act, and plan like the person you used to be. Until Ben was caught, Jaycee would spend each day stepping around the worry and fear that he'd show up to finish their story with the ending he had preferred. In her heart, she knew Ben wouldn't go after Van again. If he came, it would be for her.

Jaycee heard her cell buzz from inside her beach bag. Her new normal should override her Type-A need to know everything that was going on at all times. She bit her tongue to discourage her overactive curiosity. By the time it buzzed again, her finger was already on the answer button and that curiosity was zinging. A 603 area code. New Hampshire was calling. The only people she knew there were the ones related to her.

"Hello," she said tentatively.

"Jaycee, is that you?" asked a meek-sounding voice she recognized as a throwback to her childhood—her mother's sister, Marcy, who Jaycee wasn't sure she'd even seen in this present decade. How'd she even get her number?

"Yes, it's me. Aunt Marcy?" she wanted to confirm.

"Oh, thank God. Yes, it's me and I need your help."

I'm fine, Aunt Marcy, thanks for asking. Jaycee sighed. Not a single member of her family ever called simply to say hello and see how she was. Even when she was nearly killed, only her father's wife had sent flowers. Marcy probably had no idea she'd recently returned from the combat zone.

"What can I do?" she started, because she couldn't help herself. If someone was in trouble, relative or not, Jaycee wanted in on the rescue mission. It was just who she was.

"It's Evie," she said through loud wails. "She's missing."

"Missing?" Jaycee repeated.

"Yes, she's away at boarding school because you know she got all the brains in the family…" Jaycee rolled her eyes. Of course her successful career as an award-winning television reporter didn't count. "… and her roommate says she hasn't been there since last week."

"Did you call her? Text? Track her phone?" Most parents didn't allow their kids the opportunity to go missing anymore. Their whereabouts could now be handled by satellites and apps.

"She doesn't have an iPhone, Jaycee; the one she has is from Walmart and is dead half the time."

Jaycee did some quick thinking. No iPhone because they lived poor, just as she had. Eve was Marcy's daughter, Jaycee's cousin. She hadn't seen Eve since she was a little kid flying through the air on a backyard swing set during a family barbecue. Marcy was slightly brighter than her sister, Jaycee's mother, but still dim enough to marry some fool who worked third shift and drank gin straight from the bottle. Maybe Eve had just bolted, figuring the world at large had to be better than that.

"Okay, no phone. But you must have been in touch with the police? The school? Surely, someone has been in contact with you?" she asked her aunt.

"Well, yes, but they're not doing squat to find her, Jay Jay! They keep telling me that boarding school kids become very independent, and they're looking into it, but I know they're not. Days are going by and she's still not here! I don't know, maybe this happens all the time and the kids always come back. But Lord almighty, Jay Jay, my stomach is in knots here! That's my baby!"

Jaycee considered the breadth of this situation. She'd seen it go both ways. Elizabeth Smart, snatched from her own bedroom. Those three girls locked into a shithole basement in Cleveland, treated to nothing but barely edible scraps of food and twisted sexual abuse for a decade. But more often, there were happier resolutions to the panicked calls and emails that came into the newsroom all the time. Little Joey didn't come home from school today. Or, Molly went to get an ice cream and then promptly disappeared. Now, ninety-nine point nine percent of the time the Joeys and Mollys of the world turned up without even knowing they were being pursued. The basic question here was whether Eve was really gone. Logically, if neither the school nor the police were alarmed, maybe Eve was just taking a mini break at a friend's house. Jaycee rolled her name around her mouth. Eve Levesque. She tried to remember what her younger cousin even looked like. She had been a cute little girl with long brown ponytails who loved to run and jump, but that's all she knew of her. She must be in the neighborhood of fifteen or sixteen years old by now, and didn't she have an older brother.

"Let's back up. You said she's been at boarding school?" Jaycee asked, closing her eyes to begin her mental puzzle. It was how she told her stories on TV. Move the lead piece into the middle and build the rest around it. Eve's school was the lead.

"Yes," Marcy confirmed. "She's a student at Holy United Academy."

Huh? Wow. *Holy* was right! Jaycee knew of at least one U.S. Senator who was a graduate of this ritzy New England boarding school swaddled in majestic pine trees and black wrought iron fences. How was Marcy and Uncle … *Uncle* … Uncle whoever-he-was paying for this?

Shit, what was her uncle's name?

"How is she there?" Jaycee asked. "I know that's quite expensive." It sounded horribly insensitive but Jaycee couldn't concern herself with being delicate. She had to know what she was dealing with. Had Marcy won Powerball without telling anyone? Was she in a gang?

23

Selling heroin? Maybe she was keeping her newfound wealth on the down-low to ward off Jaycee's mother. She was a notorious troll when it came to sniffing out loose cash.

"Almost a full scholarship, Jay Jay," Marcy said. "I told you she was smart. I mean super smart. Gifted. She's also a remarkable soccer player. We are helping as much as we can but she works so hard …" her pride was evident as her voice trailed off. Eve was obviously the best of their bunch.

"I'm sure she does," Jaycee said kindly. "When was the last time you spoke with her?"

"Last Thursday," Marcy said. "I asked her to come home for the weekend but she said she had too much studying to do."

"So that's not unusual for her?" Jaycee probed.

"Honestly, it would've been more unusual for her to come home," Marcy replied. "Sometimes she doesn't even call me back for days because she's so busy. She's also on the school's soccer team and they practice all the time."

Funny, Jaycee thought. Eve sounded eerily similar to her. A driven, determined young girl sprinting her way out of a subpar starting block.

"Boyfriend?" Jaycee asked.

"Not that I know of," Marcy told her. "But I can't be sure. I have not met any of her classmates or friends either. The school discourages us from contacting the teachers directly. They've only had one parent weekend and both Teddy and I had to work."

24

Teddy! That was it, Uncle Teddy.

Van sauntered back from the water and eased himself down into a sitting position next to Jaycee on the towel. She made room for him and then playfully swatted at his abdomen as he sprinkled seawater droplets down her spine. *Stop*, she mouthed. *Give me a minute.*

Despite their unique near-death experience, Jaycee retained alpha dog position in their relationship. Van was too good-natured and easygoing to give a shit.

She peppered Marcy with a few more questions but her reporter's curiosity was stirring and her mind was already made up. By the time she hung up she was already onto a mental to-do list that included plane tickets and hotel reservations.

"Who was that?" Van asked as he slathered on a new layer of the special sunblock his dermatologist had recommended, paying extra attention to each raised line of recovering skin that wasn't yet well enough for sun exposure.

"My aunt," she told him.

"You have an aunt, Jay Jay?" he feigned surprise.

"Yeah, several of them in fact."

"No shit," Van laughed. "How about that. A family. Here I was all this time thinking you had given birth to yourself."

"You are so funny," she tried to hide the grin. He really was funny sometimes.

"Don't forget devastatingly handsome."

"Well, that's the only reason I like you."

25

"Figured. So, about that aunt. What does she want?"

"Nothing much," Jaycee skirted the red zone.

"Really? We're going to play this game?"

Jaycee sighed. She was supposed to be lying low, building back her strength and all that. Van would try to stop her, or worse, want to come. She wanted to avoid both. She had to go, and he wasn't strong enough yet to take on a baby llama at a petting zoo, let alone whatever dark force could be involved in Eve's potential disappearance.

"I would prefer if you sat this one out," she told him, softening the blow with a sultry smile. "I need all of this to remain as intact as possible." She ran a fingertip down his defined chest, stopping at the drawstring of his bathing suit.

"Will you at least tell me what's happening?" Van brushed back his wet hair with both hands. He knew better than to argue with Jaycee once her steel trap mind was at work.

"Long story short, I guess my little cousin has gone missing. I'm not sure yet if that's 'real missing' or 'moody teenager missing.' She goes to this fancy boarding school in New Hampshire and her roommate says it's been days since she saw her last. No help from police or the school. Her mom is freaking out a little."

Van's face tilted in surprise. "New Hampshire!" he scoffed, like the small east coast state was really on a Third World continent. "And since when can your family pay for fancy?" he asked, wrinkling his nose in surprise. Van knew Jaycee was an entirely self-made superwoman.

"Yes, New Hampshire, Van. It's nice there, you know. Remember, we considered going there to help you rest and recoup?"

"That's when I was still concussed," he reminded her. She laughed.

"There are actually people who *choose* to put down roots there. It's a wholesome, understated existence," she noted. Van couldn't understand why anyone would take farmland and deer ticks over beach volleyball and neighborhood Botox clinics, but who was he to suggest New Hampshire was a frozen tundra barely able to sustain life. He shrugged and gave Jaycee's shoulder a soft kiss.

"Sorry, my queen," he muttered. "I'm sure New Hampshire is … splendid."

"You're an ass," she barked.

"Yes, I have a nice ass," he joked back. That was how they worked best. Van played an important role as the jester to provide a break from the tension convention in which Jaycee voluntarily immersed herself. She couldn't help it; she lived like she was on constant standby. Hers was a world of deadlines, deadbeats, and sometimes, dead ends.

"Anyway," she continued. "That's the thing. Apparently my cousin Eve is a brilliant and athletic prodigy who earned her way into this private school. She must have gotten all that awesomeness from me," Jaycee smirked, and leaned into Van's shoulder.

"No doubt," he replied but his mind was bogged down with loose threads. Before his squash had gotten in the way of Ben's evil plot, Van had been masterful at building real life scenarios from television crime dramas. Jaycee could tell he was trying to find the perfect episode in the fog of his memory. It was there. She watched him crunch his way through the empty space of what used to be filled by personal experiences and connections. She willed him to close the gaps.

"So, you're going to New Hampshire?" he sniffed. "For how long?"

She shook her head. "Yes, I'm going, just in case I can help at all. I won't be there long." She bit her lip, suddenly caught up in an odd feeling. She'd left home so long ago it was difficult to remember if she had ever belonged there at all. New Hampshire was more mystique than sentiment. Encased by natural elements like granite and water, and loaded with remarkable physical artistry, Jaycee saw her former home more than she felt it.

"Do you have any old boyfriends I need to worry about?" he asked, pulling her head in for a kiss.

"Yes," she told him playfully. "About two dozen. I wonder if Eve taking off has anything to do with a guy. I used to stay weekends at this one boyfriend's house and never bothered to tell my parents. Of course, they didn't ask."

"Season Two, *The Blacklist*..." he was trying so hard.

"Yes," she encouraged. "Remember how much we love James Spader." She entwined her fingers through his. It was fading. The vague flashback was petering out.

"It's okay, Van. You'll get there. Season Two, *The Blacklist*. Russian billionaire …"

"… kidnaps a tiny gymnast …"

"A ballet dancer," Jaycee corrected.

"Tiny dancer, of course. Kidnaps a tiny dancer and, oh fuck, who cares. Let's eat!"

"Can I get an amen," Jaycee stated firmly with a jut of her chin to cover the sprig of an emotional twitch. She pulled the cooler onto her lap and dispersed sandwiches and bottles of Diet Coke.

Van was never one to stay down for very long.

CHAPTER THREE

"So, it's a cousin?" Los Angeles Detective James Barton asked during their weekly phone check-in. They also had dinner together at least once a month. Barton's ex-wife, and soon-to-be new fiancée, Debra, was an excellent cook and their little son, Mason, adored both Jaycee and Van. Barton had become like a foul-mouthed father figure to Jaycee, cementing his role in her life after helping unravel the murders of young women in fetish nightclubs. Barton's investigative insight and provocative willingness to act as her source during the intense death probe that eventually revealed Ben as the prime suspect had planted a deep trust between savvy reporter and seasoned police officer. Not to mention the macabre on-the-job injury to his right hand that almost destroyed him, had ended up saving her by fitting just so around a wound that otherwise would have drained the blood content of her battered body. They were now like family, which was why Barton had serious concerns about Jaycee's travel plans.

"Yes, Eve is my cousin," Jaycee told him.

"Interesting," Barton quipped. "How is it you never told me you had family back east?" Barton's injury had come during what had been a rat's nest of a career in Boston law enforcement. Both heroic and horrific. Los Angeles was affording him the opportunity to rebuild what alcohol and that one tortuous crime scene had almost decimated.

"I didn't think it mattered," Jaycee fired back. "Seriously, Barton. As we were discussing the blood and guts of Throw Away Girls I was supposed to inject the logistical branches of my family tree just to make happy chat with you? Come on now."

She could feel his resistance building. Barton was no longer simply a work source. He had become invested in her life and safety and Jaycee could understand why he would be less than pleased to hear she was back on the hunt for another feral human who may be disappearing young girls. It sounded too close to what she had just narrowly survived.

"You two are tight?" he asked, ignoring her sarcasm. "You feel as though she could be in real trouble here?"

"If you ask the school, she's just taking a little hiatus from the rigors of her schedule. My aunt, however, is worried. Eve's a hustler, a good girl, Barton. A really smart kid on scholarship at one of those hoity-toity New England boarding schools. She isn't a party hound who needs a week to sleep off a bender. She's legit." At least *I think she is,* Jaycee thought as Barton was working up his objection to her risking her ass again on a girl, cousin or not, that she barely knew. Hadn't the nightclub murders taught her anything about the perils of dancing too close to a bonfire?

"What boarding school?" Barton wanted to know.

"Holy United Academy," Jaycee answered. "It's pretty highbrow, like a Stepford City for the spawns of the world's elite class."

"No shit," he whistled long and low. He was more serious when he came back. "You do know boarding schools are like sewers, right?"

"Sewers, Barton?"

"Ya, sewers. They got a lot of shit going on under the pretty cover on the cobblestone street. Sewers. In fact, I can smell the stank from here. Think now. These fucking creepy boarding schools that put little girls in short skirts in the same living space as horny men. Boundaries have a way of disappearing when some professor-type works a girl into thinking a physical relationship is equivalent to a transformative education, 'scuse my mouth." Barton had a love-hate dependency on the "f" word. "They lose the social rules of what's decent. Happens all the fucking time. If I were an investigative reporter, I'd start there," he told her. "You start with the aging intellectual who thinks it's his obligation to indoctrinate the next generation of existential thinkers. Love the one you're with, and all that."

Gross! "Barton, these are children we're talking about here. Why are you going all Mary Kay Letourneau here? I did ask about a boyfriend. My aunt doesn't think she has one."

"Doesn't matter," he sniffed back. "That was a simple case of boy getting too hot for teacher, and frankly, I don't think of this in the same category."

"Figures, that's sexist."

"Whatever," Barton dismissed her. "It's true. And, didn't Barbara Walters just do a special on them? They're still married, you know. She popped out a couple kids with

32

the horny boy before her ovaries got too old and shrunk up into her gut. Besides, randy middle-aged dudes don't get all caught up in the romance. It's whammin' and bammin' and movin' on to the next class of fresh meat."

"Barton, that's enough," Jaycee interrupted, shaking her head on a smile. Barton was both investigative guru and inappropriate uncle rolled into one.

"So back to these *children* you mentioned. Remember, the sweet little tykes have grown up with nannies and Snapchat. Their best friends are the cast of *Gossip Girl*. Their hormones are screaming by middle school with all the antibiotics slipped into their chicken tenders. Throw them into a vat of togetherness, cell phone cameras, and skimpy school uniforms and voila, it's like Paradise Cove, in the snow. You know how fast dirty sidewalk snow drips into the sewer system?"

Jaycee rubbed her left eyebrow as a dull headache built from concentration.

"Let me understand this. You're telling me you think my cousin's sudden departure from an exclusive boarding school she can't afford and is working her ass off to stay at, is all about sex? That Eve is enrolled at a playground for child molesters?"

"No, not exactly," Barton clarified. "I never said all of them were a Chester the Molester, but isn't one enough?" He always left the conclusions for her to draw but Barton walked the hard line because experience had taught him to start with the most depraved possibility and work his way back.

"I'd bet a tuition payment this all comes down to that, Jay Jay. Either little Evie gave it up to the wrong guy, or she didn't give it up at all and the wrong guy is bullshit. In the light of rejection, powerful men who aren't used to being shut down are capable of all kinds of things. And, you said it yourself, they're just children. Too young or too stupid to fight back."

"Okay, okay," Jaycee told him, nodding into the phone, and feeling her puzzle start to shift on a sickening chance that her cousin had become entrenched in a web from which she wasn't wily enough yet to escape. Maybe Marcy was right and Eve was in danger. Or maybe the school was right and she just cut out for a few days to shake off the stress. Was this a schoolgirl fling gone bad or was Eve fighting off unwanted advances from a powerful man quite used to engaging in the "transformative education" campus culture? Either way, Barton had her scrambling again with his hastily crafted profile of a vastly different landscape than the one she had expected. This could get dirty.

"Okay, Barton. I'll start there."

"How about I put in a call to a few friends—"

She abruptly cut him off. "Absolutely not," Jaycee told him. She didn't want him having to reconnect to the east coast law enforcement community he'd been forced to detach from.

"Not yet," she corrected. Barton didn't do well with being entirely shut down.

"Okay," he said. He'd let her have this one. "But I will. If I have to. If this gets out of hand or too hot."

"Fair enough." She promised to be in touch.

Jaycee closed her eyes and pictured the tantalizing tranquility of a New Hampshire snowfall. It was blissfully peaceful as it fell in delicate fluffs of silent white that rolled like marshmallow waves over hills and valleys.

By the next day, plows and people had turned it to shit-brown slop.

The sewers then swallowed the runoff, keeping the offensive sludge hidden below.

I can smell the stank from here.

Jaycee would pry the lid off the sewer if that's where she had to go to find Eve. She could do dirty if that's what it took.

She already had.

Hello, darkness, my old friend.

CHAPTER FOUR

The Levesque home in small town New Hampshire was little more than four rooms, an oddly shaped add-on that probably broke at least one building code, and a brittle deck off the kitchen slider permanently fogged up by cold air outside. A wood stove mounted on a layer of crumbling bricks coughed out hot wafts on a narrow path that failed to reach either Jaycee's feet or nose. Her pelvis though, was snug as a bug. Maybe Jaycee had spent an Easter Sunday here once or twice, but she could barely conjure up a single memory of family togetherness in these tight quarters. Holidays were mostly held at her old house two towns over, with the larger back yard, and a narrow creek they pulled frogs from on warm summer nights.

She shifted her UGGs beneath the poker table set atop square patterns on the kitchen linoleum. She and Aunt Marcy held two coffee mugs filled with foamy instant Sanka. Uncle Teddy and Teddy Jr. were both at work. Neither could afford chit-chat time with the niece and cousin who hadn't come around in a hundred years. Marcy told Jaycee both her husband and son believed Eve would show up any minute and there was nothing to worry about. Apparently, the miniscule family home had little room left for their affection.

Marcy had pictures spread across the kitchen table that showcased a pretty, brown-haired girl with a preoccupied-looking smile. In her younger years that could be a sentimental preciousness similar to what made Miley Cyrus

36

so lovable during her Hannah Montana days. As Eve grew, that curious spark had darkened, even when she was forcing herself to carve a grin into her stony features for family photos. Eve had all the trappings of a person who had developed an early awareness that life would be what she could make it. Good or bad, it would be up to her. A lot of pressure for a little kid.

"She has always been … umm … different from us," Marcy's hands fluttered as she tried to explain. "Better. Smarter. It's almost as if she lives on a different plane, you know? Like she came out of me knowing this wasn't the right place for her. That we …" Marcy looked away as her eyes filled with moisture. "… that we weren't right for her." At least her mother appeared to love Eve. Maybe she hadn't given her that whole hearth and home childhood, but Marcy seemed to be genuinely distressed.

"Just because Eve is smart doesn't mean she feels that way," Jaycee tried to comfort her aunt, but she understood exactly what she was saying. She had grown up with that same preoccupied smile plastered on her face, too. Maybe she and Eve were, in fact, different than what they came from. It didn't make them bad people, just … more suited to the real world.

"Tell me about this school," Jaycee turned the topic to Holy United Academy.

"Oh, goodness, it's like a dream," Marcy wiped at her eyes and then wrapped her thin fingers around a coffee mug that displayed a yellow flag and the phrase Don't Tread On Me.

"A recruiter came to one of Evie's middle school soccer games last spring," she explained. "He was impressed with her talent and focus. He told her coach there was room for a player like her at The Academy."

"And because of her academics, she qualified for some assistance," Jaycee offered.

"Yes. We couldn't do it otherwise. Teddy thinks it's silly. He went to public high school, Teddy Jr. did, too, and it was just fine for them," she wearily went on. "I went to bat for Eve on this one. Again, because I already knew she was ready."

"I understand." Jaycee smiled at her aunt. She had always had that tired tightness across her eyes, but now they were *old* and tired. She didn't much resemble her mother at all. They were five years apart, but Marcy looked like time had decided it would punish her more. Both sisters were slender, but Jaycee's mother was taller and curvier around the hips and ass. Marcy looked like her frame was routinely assaulted by her body's constant demand for energy. She not only opened the Dunkin Donuts down the road every morning, she managed the entire gas station it was connected to. Between keeping the place staffed and full of product, and then racing home to run a household for two hungry grown men, Marcy's khaki uniform slacks looked like they were about to slide right off.

"I always wanted better for both Eve and Teddy. He's more like us, but Eve has been ready to fly for a while. She is everything Holy United Academy wants. The rest of us

are public high school people. Do you see what I mean?"
Marcy stared across the compact table at a niece she had
never taken the time to know. She was suddenly struck by
her remarkable beauty. Jaycee was fresh off a six-hour
plane ride, followed by an hour journey in a rental car over
slushy back roads, but her golden good looks were
startling. Even with her hair pulled back into a braid that
fell over her left shoulder, her California sun-kissed cheeks
and supple lips defied the tiredness she felt. These were the
times when she was reminded of the injuries Ben had
inflicted, and the stubbornly roundabout process of
recovery. Some days were good, while others had her
feeling like roadkill. It wasn't too long ago that Jaycee had
the stamina of a pancake.

"Sorry," she told Marcy, noticing she was looking at
her a bit too intently. "You can tell I'm a little worn out.
Long flight."

"No, that's not it," Marcy smiled shyly, "I just can't
believe how beautiful you are. I mean you always were, but
I haven't seen you in so long."

"Oh, thank you, that's very kind," Jaycee said
formally, for she and Marcy were practically meeting for
the first time. She could tell her long lost aunt was seeing
something in her that reminded her of the deadbeat sister
she didn't keep track of anymore.

"I know I look like her," she supplied generously.
"When my mom was young. My father used to tell me that,
too."

"How is your father?" Marcy asked. "He was nice enough to pass along your number," she said sheepishly. Jaycee smiled thinly, not bothering to wonder why—if her father indeed had her cell number—he never chose to use it.

"Fine, I guess. He has that whole other family thing going on," Jaycee laughed again, surprising herself with how uncomfortable it was discussing her parents. Her father seemed happiest when she was far away from the Utah neighborhood where he and his new wife were raising their children. A brother and sister she had only met once. She cleared her throat and took a sip of the lukewarm froth in her mug. Funny, she never gave her parents power over her emotions. Maybe it was the jet lag.

"And her?" Marcy looked down at her hands and plucked at the edges of her short thumbnail. "She is doing well?"

Jaycee noticed something else in the inquiry. A sadness perhaps, an existential longing for what Marcy had never known but desperately wanted. She had been starved for love her entire life. Shunned first by her only sister, then by the brute of a man she had married, and now, by a daughter whose excellence was the very force driving her away.

Jaycee would spare her the truth. She would withhold the fact that her mother only called when she was flat broke and in between boyfriends. Marcy needed hope, not more heartbreak. She needed to believe that happy endings weren't just for Disney movies and the Harlequin romance novels she tortured herself with at night. She needed someone to swoop in and shake the cobwebs off her dingy, overworked, strung-out life.

"Yeah, she's doing well." Jaycee noticed a slight bob in Marcy's head, acknowledgment that her sister was a scrappy survivor who was likely more 'hanging in there,' than 'doing well.'

"Good," she said with a plastic smile, a signal she was done with that portion of their conversation.

"Thank you for dropping everything and flying out here," she said sincerely. "I reached out because I had heard you were involved with police work out in Los Angeles, some sort of investigative or research something or other that could help me."

Jaycee should have been crushed that a first-degree relative had been passed bad information about her life and career, but she wasn't. It didn't matter. Marcy wasn't in the position to feel pride about her achievements. Jaycee had developed a steely reaction to potential hurt or emotional injury: she shut it down completely by stripping away its potency. Ben had called it a pathetic disconnect, but it kept Jaycee away from medication and expensive therapy bills.

"I work in television, actually," she clarified. "But I know a lot of people in law enforcement, so I've picked up a few skills along the way. I took the liberty to inquire with the police department already. It's a small town, with three or four officers on staff, and apparently no one is enterprising enough to even call me back yet. But I've learned how to push at that a little."

41

"They won't call you back," Marcy said sadly. "I keep waiting for them to call me back, and I'm her mother!"

Marcy's voice quivered. She was all alone, desperate to cling to any scrap of hope Jaycee could produce.

"Plus, I like to solve mysteries that others aren't smart enough to figure out," she gave Marcy a campy wink. "If someone thinks he can hurt Eve, or take her away from you, trust me … I'll figure it out."

Marcy's shoulders fell. She nodded in silence as the fear she kept locked out of her busy existence seized her heart and squeezed. Finally, someone stronger and more capable had joined her team. It was the only time in her life Marcy had felt like she could rely on hardy hands other than her own to accomplish a task. She could feel the goodness radiating off her niece. There was a confidence deep within her that had guided her to find the right path. Exactly what she had sensed in her own child since the day she was born.

If anyone could find her daughter, it would be a woman who was just like her.

CHAPTER FIVE

From across the street, Jaycee sat in her rental car watching young bodies in all stages of development skitter around on plowed and salted walkways that directed them from one towering brick building to another. Slim, black lamplights lined their paths with a sallow, twenty-four-hour-a-day glow that flickered off the snow pack. A safe, brightly lit campus alleged to foster cheerfulness and camaraderie between students and faculty. At least that's what the brochure said, anyway. *Come join us*, it lured, *our environment nurtures both the mind and spirit of our inhabitants.*

Jaycee shuddered at the uppity mind-meld some overpaid PR executive was selling to families with too much money to see through the smokescreen. Come on, people, she thought. Why was it that so many moms and dads gave away the privilege of raising their own kids to total strangers?

Flags with the bold blue and red school colors fluttered in the frosty breeze. New Hampshire's winds were fierce in the dead of winter, notoriously brutal for even the natives to withstand. It had been awhile since Jaycee had felt the season's vengeance in person. The small car's heater remained on level ten as she rubbed her hands together in front of the vent.

Mostly, the students walked in small packs, or side by side with another. Many of them had two hands wrapped around dark brown paper coffee cups. They wore thick, puffy parkas over their cardigans and regulation plaid. Skirts for the girls; ties for the boys. Most of the girls sported black leggings below their knee-length pleated skirts, a necessary climate adjustment cleared by the school's strict attire and etiquette police. They moved swiftly on L.L.Bean rubber-soled boots, their weighted backpacks slung across shoulders or crooked around elbows. Upper classmen boys mature enough to grow facial hair were clean-shaven with high and tight haircuts one step below bare-scalped. The girls with straight hair were fortunate enough to call that neat enough, while the ones who battled frizz or curls had to tame that shit into submission with tight ponytails or ballerina buns.

Jaycee squinted at the student-bots passing nearby. She pulled her New England Patriots pom-pom hat low over her finely arched eyebrows and slunk down in the seat. She assumed no one here would recognize her as that blonde newswoman from California who got caught in a serial killer's crosshairs, but she didn't want to risk getting noticed. Immature voices were immersed in the airflow around her car, but none of them seemed focused on the driver parked outside the gates.

She watched them disappear into buildings and eventually, the campus grew quiet again. Jaycee moved her car over one block, closer to the smaller of the campus gyms and a line of dorms. A paddock and stable sat off in the distance, housing the agriculture department and training rings for horse riders. White-tipped mountain peaks poked through the low cloud layer, their magnificent and dignified presence standing guard like an ever-present overlord.

Jaycee wasn't sure yet what she was looking for; this was more of a reconnaissance mission to set her markers and coordinate her way around the schoolyard laid out across a thousand acres protected by elm trees and a smattering of thin, distressed white birches. She could see how the picturesque, quaint, quintessential New Hampshire feel showed well to city dwellers buried in smog and humanity, or international families soothed by a visual similarity to the *Sound of Music* and its crackling muesli mural. Willow trees held limbs like umbrellas, with branches arched in sheets that fed long, flowing shadows to the brick paths below. Carefully placed granite resting benches were empty, but Jaycee pictured them full of students squirming together to gossip or relax with one another during warmer days.

Did Eve fit in here? Did the Mean Girls discount her as an unfortunate creature huddled like a matchstick girl in the admissions office begging for her financial aid package? Jaycee moved puzzle pieces into position. Holy United Academy still filled the middle. Unlike the public school philosophy where societal norms were shifting and uptight, demanding parents were rising up to protest everything from standardized testing to gender-neutral bathrooms, boarding school traditions held firm. No makeup on the girls, no facial hair on the boys. No earrings except for tiny studs, no nail polish or jewelry on the wrists beyond a watch. Make that a *hell no* on tattoos. A student at

Holy United must not be unique from the rest. Jaycee suspected she could line up yearbooks from 1927, 1995, and 2016, and the images would be identical. Time stood still here. No one came to Holy United Academy with the hopes of being her true self, if that meant purple hair, t-shirts, or metal hoops in her eyebrow. Puritanical custom still had enough influence to force emerging liberalism to bow down and kiss the ring of scholarly mythos.

Do it our way, or be gone. We build champions to maintain the world order, not change it.

Jaycee pulled over again and watched a tall girl emerge from one of the dorms. She moved briskly, with her chin tucked into her heavy coat, and a scarf wrapped up to her nose. She was slim and carried both a backpack and a gym bag. She hurried into the building housing the gym used by the volleyball team that also boasted a heated pool and a few classrooms. Jaycee shifted her car into drive and moved around to the back of the gym. Giant square heating and cooling units attached to hoses controlling the climate inside the building poured thick white exhaust into the air. No one was around and there wasn't a fence keeping her vehicle off school grounds. She could drive right up.

Risking it for the chance to look inside, Jaycee got out of the car and walked over to a ground-level window. The glass was freezing and frosted up white around the edges. She used her sleeve to wipe a circle to peer through. The room was empty but the door was open into the hallway. She could see students milling around. She shirked backwards and slid onto her butt when a girl and an older man rounded the corner of the doorway and stood just inside the unoccupied classroom.

Shit! Shit! Shit! she muttered under her breath, praying they hadn't seen her. Her back was touching the arctic block of brick wall, so cold it felt like freezer burn on her skin despite several layers of clothing. She counted to twenty, half expecting a keystone campus cop to appear and bark at her for trespassing. When no one materialized, she risked another peek. Coming up to a half-squat, Jaycee lifted her chin high to gain visual access. The window was fogging again but she could make out the two figures in the room. They were discussing something written inside the female student's notebook. Jaycee could see the girl pointing to what she wanted the man to see. Was he her teacher? Her coach? He was clad in black pleated pants and a polo shirt with some embossing near his left pectoral muscle. *Must be someone on staff,* Jaycee assumed. They peered into her notebook, their faces intimately sharing close space. What was she showing him? Jaycee watched them intently, squinting in an effort to read their lips and body language, immensely pissed off she couldn't hear exactly what was being discussed. The girl leaned in with her chest, coy and giggly, in typical pre-pubescent tease mode. Jaycee thought of Barton.

I can smell it from here, he'd told her.

She was starting to get a whiff now herself. That mouthwatering scent of allurement sprinkled like sugar over a bowlful of forbidden fruit few men were strong enough to resist.

Only takes one Chester the Molester. Barton was in her head as she watched the older man standing just a hair too close to a teenage girl inside a deserted room. Was this how it started with Eve? She couldn't picture her intellectually gifted cousin posing like a baby porn star, but then again, stranger things have happened when opportunity or fortune were in play.

Jaycee's mouth turned down as she watched the brief exchange come to an end. The girl slipped back out into the hallway, but not before the man laid one hand just above the waistband of her plaid skirt. His hand didn't linger there, and it may have just been a friendly send-off, but Jaycee was disturbed nonetheless. Male staff members had no business touching a kid not even old enough to drive or buy cigarettes at the local 7/11. Teacher or not, it was a boundary that upstanding professionals were careful not to cross. No one wanted a field trip to human resources, and hadn't he sat through that mandatory online course in sexual harassment?

Your co-worker wears a lovely suit to the office. Do you A. Tell her she looks hot. B. Whistle at her when she walks by. Or C. Put your head down like the peasant you are. Jaycee had clicked through her own training program and then printed out her certificate for her work file. Everyone who held a job these days knew about the corporate perils of inappropriate touching, commenting, or ogling while on the clock.

He had definitely touched that girl. Through a frosted window from a healthy distance, Jaycee would also conclude they had been flirtier with one another than was proper. The whole thing stunk.

Like a sewer.

Jaycee slunk back to her rental car. She knew she had to find a way in. To truly figure out if there was a sexual undercurrent running below the classic veneer of Holy United Academy, she had to experience it herself.

CHAPTER SIX

"She lives in Cushing Hall," Marcy told her, brushing off stray hairs from Jaycee's shoulders. "It's the dorm closest to that little pond in the back where they ice skate on weekends." Her hands fluttered around, pulling on the hem of the skirt. "You're taller than Eve, this isn't regulation length on you," she fretted. "It's just not sitting right."

Jaycee shifted her hips. If she pulled the waistband lower, the material landed just above her knee. Unless a proctor approached her with a ruler, she figured she could make it work.

"It's fine," she said, gently pushing away Marcy's nervous fingers before they got too close to the still sensitive puckered skin on her neck. "Trust me."

"Ramona will buzz you in," Marcy told her, stepping back to take a long view of Eve's school uniform draped over her taller and older cousin. "At 6:45 sharp, that gives you time to get to Chapel at 7. I guess after that, you'll just … um … you'll take it from there." The two had agreed their best option at this point was for Jaycee to infiltrate Eve's life, starting with a quick tour of her dorm room and an introduction to the roommate who had called Marcy to report her absence. Jaycee arrived at her aunt's house before dawn to prepare. Every Holy United Academy student was given two full uniforms to start the school year. One remained with Eve at school, while Marcy kept the other in her room at home, pressed and wrapped in a plastic dry cleaning bag. It fit snug across Jaycee's chest, but drooped through the waist. Eve had more of a square athletic build, while Jaycee was fuller up top with a slim, California beach bunny behind. With her blonde hair pulled into a low bun and no makeup on her face, Jaycee's youthfulness could pull off a girl in her late teens, if no one looked at her too closely.

"You look good, Jaycee," Marcy assessed. Her mouth tightened into an awkward half-grin.

Jaycee nodded. "Yeah, I think it'll do. Fresh as a New Hampshire farm girl." She shrugged her shoulders forward to tame her cleavage. "Or, backup dancer for a Britney Spears video." She frowned. Buttoning the cardigan all the way up, she evaluated her look. "Better, right? I think I'll just keep the sweater on," she said, offering a smile to make Marcy relax. Her aunt was expressionless, staring at her with worried eyes. Her daughter was missing, her school wanted to believe her return was imminent, and now, the unconventional niece she had brought in to help was telling her the best way to find Eve was to role play. It all felt hopeless, and Marcy had never had cause to trust in the naïve belief that everything would work out. Because in her case, it rarely had.

Jaycee had convinced her aunt to allow her to borrow Eve's uniform and sniff around campus as inconspicuously as she could. She explained to Marcy that she needed to become one of them; it would be the only way she could access rumors and supposition on Eve's level. The roommate who had notified Marcy of Eve's absence would meet with Jaycee, but she was unaware that Eve's cousin would be moonlighting as a buxom co-ed. Jaycee talked Marcy into believing that was an element of surprise she didn't want to squander. She also didn't want to tip her hand and give the roommate reason to back out of their meeting. Girls can be fickle when it came to keeping secrets.

"I'll be in touch," she told Marcy. "Hopefully today we are one step closer to bringing Eve home."

Marcy nodded. She pressed two fingers to her lips to stop them from quivering. No words were necessary; Jaycee felt the desperation radiating through the small bedroom that held trophies and medals on a three-tiered shelf, and old stuffed animals that sat atop an empty twin bed. They locked eyes in the dusty, scallop-shaped mirror over Eve's bureau. In that moment they both felt the weight of Jaycee daring to enter the arena with very little armor.

* * * *

Asian eyes hidden beneath wisps of longish bangs squinted at Jaycee through the glass panes of the door that kept residents of Cushing Hall safely locked inside. She smiled at the girl she assumed to be Ramona. Marcy had told Jaycee Ramona was from a wealthy Japanese family that split time between San Francisco and Tokyo. A metallic click was followed by a buzz and the heavy door clanked open.

"Ramona?" Jaycee inquired quickly as she slid through into the foyer of the dorm and shut it behind her with a thud as the lock re-engaged. It was still quiet but she could hear

52

water running through pipes. Students were starting to shower and get ready for their days. A bulletin board was on the wall, splashed with colorful notices reminding residents of Chocolate Chip Cookie Day, a Coffee Breakfast Social, and the upcoming Popcorn and Movie Weekend in the lounge. Student life was bustling here at Holy United Academy.

"Yes," she told her. "Hi, come on, we'll head to my room so I can fill you in."

"Okay," Jaycee smiled, noticing Ramona spoke without a trace of an accent. She followed behind Eve's roommate, who walked briskly toward the elevator on solid legs protruding out from a green and white polka dot bathrobe. She wasn't freshman-fifteen territory, but this girl didn't miss meals, that was for sure. Her feet were wrapped in brown fuzzy slippers with bobbing monkey heads on the toes. She held her hand over the door of the opened elevator and motioned for Jaycee to step in. She smiled at her and then punched the number eight and the doors rolled back together. The elevator creaked and moaned as it began its upward trajectory.

"I'm a gymnast," she explained over the sound of the pulleys. Her face was fresh, with no makeup or acne and she smelled like Ivory soap. "My parents call me a spider monkey. Every Christmas I get a new pair of these stupid things," she told Jaycee, angling her ankle over her knee to display the cartoonish animal head. "I feel bad if I don't wear them."

"They're cute," Jaycee smiled. Ramona was compact but hardy-looking. Even on cumbersome monkey slippers she was agile. "And I'm hardly one to comment about attire, wouldn't you say?" she unzipped her Patagonia ski jacket to display the taut sweater above her plaid skirt and black leggings tucked into North Face boots.

"Surprise!" she singsonged. "This is my creative way of moving around campus freely." She gave Ramona a strong look that suggested she wouldn't be swayed.

Ramona chuckled rather than argue with her logic. "*Damn*. Hit me baby one more time," she drawled with a fast finger snap. "Malibu Barbie goes to boarding school."

"That's why I wore the sweater," Jaycee explained, nodding in agreement. "To tone down the fact that I'm already fully grown."

Ramona nodded. "Truth," she said, her tone protracted into one indicating respect. "You sure are. But honestly, you'll be fine. No one will notice. There are a few slutty girls around here who order their uniforms one size too small. They can't quite pull off what you're bringing, but…" she trailed off.

"Oh, good," Jaycee said. "I'll fit in just fine with the sluts."

"No, you're cool. It's like, when the characters on *The Walking Dead* get all, like, bloodied up and float around with the zombies," Ramona said with a straight face. "Their guts throw off the human scent. Like the uniform. It'll totally throw them off, even the sluts who aren't all that bright anyway."

"Well, they're sluts, so ..." Jaycee mumbled.

The elevator dinged. They had arrived at the eighth floor. The doors parted and Ramona led Jaycee to the right, down a long hallway with maroon paisley carpet that looked like it had been installed back when the Titanic set sail. The air smelled of honeyed body spray and Febreze.

"We're 809," Ramona told her, keeping her voice down as they passed several locked doors with quiet occupants behind them. The low whirl of a hairdryer could be heard as they passed 807 and 808. 809 was on the left. Ramona slid her key into the door handle and twisted. The door opened into an orderly square with two beds, two short dressers, and two narrow desks that faced one window. From the eighth floor, a spectacular citrus-colored sunrise was just beginning to kiss the mountain range in the distance.

"My gosh," Jaycee peered out. "Fall foliage must be glorious from here."

"I guess," Ramona agreed. "But only the environmentalists give a shit about the view," she scoffed. "I'd gladly trade the freakin' pretty leaves for a closet of my own." She plopped down onto her unmade bed. The one across the room, Eve's, was neatly arranged with the comforter folded back to display two plush purple pillows. Jaycee walked over and reached down to touch the soft bedding. Her cousin slept here. A girl she didn't know but was already starting to care about. She did a slow circle to take in the room. She approached everything like the reporter she was—her eyes were like a shark's, forever on

55

patrol. Back when Ben was her dependable and talented photographer, she counted on him to follow with his camera rolling, spouting his crafty mix of profanity and creative nicknames. With Ben, she was Jay Bird, mostly, a silly, babyish moniker she could no longer even bear to think about, it hurt her so deeply. She could almost feel him behind her in Eve's room. She closed her eyes and breathed. At times, Ben still snuck into her heart in affectionate and familiar ways. She would hear his smartass comebacks and remember the thrill of seeing the video he captured for their stories. *Holy shit, how did you see that?* She would marvel at the scope of his creativity. Ordinary images of everyday life became kaleidoscopes of exploding color and edgy angles. His talent was limitless.

So was his sickness.

Jaycee shut him out of her head. Like the survivor experts she'd been forced to see in their high-rise mental health offices had taught her, she imagined a steel door separating her from Ben. With purpose and resolve, she slammed the door shut and brought herself back to Cushing Hall.

"Tell me about her, Ramona," she said softly. Jaycee settled onto a corner of Eve's bed, pulling one of her purple pillows into her chest. She inhaled. Bath and Body's Cherry Blossom. It was a bubbly, happy, and youthful scent, exactly what a teenage girl should smell like.

"Who is Eve?"

Ramona nodded. If she found it odd how little Jaycee knew about Eve, she didn't show it. She rose off her bed and plucked a picture from the mirror above her bureau. "Well, she's definitely pretty," she started, handing Jaycee the snapshot of her with Eve, both of them smiling into the lens as they clinked glass beer bottles together. "But that's not what she focuses on. She is like, naturally wicked smart, but still studies all the time." Ramona pulled her long black hair from the folded neck of her bathrobe and twisted it into a loose knot. "She took one sip of that beer and then gave it to me. That was our first weekend here and I'd smuggled in a six-pack. I've never seen her drink since then, even on weekends when Sammy's brother visits from college and brings bottles of Grey Goose. Those are the good times," Ramona said, smiling. "When we all forget our parents don't want us and our nannies are now vacationing together at some Sandals resort."

"Sammy is a girl?" Jaycee asked, thinking that beneath the trappings of privilege most of these kids just wanted to feel like they belonged to a family.

"Yes, she lives on our floor. Her dad is the CEO of some big pharmaceutical company. Ton of dough right there."

"She's close to Eve?"

"Not really," Ramona shook her head. "But that's kind of how Eve rolls. She's not really close with anyone."

Jaycee lowered her chin into the soft edge of Eve's pillow, her eyes squinting in concentration. Eve was a loner. A smart, pretty, sober loner. There had to be more.

"Does she have a boyfriend?" Jaycee probed.

Ramona shook her head. "No," she told Jaycee. "No boyfriend. But she could snap her fingers and have five. She's like nerdy librarian with a Carly Lloyd soccer body. She's pretty jacked but not dyke-ish, you know?"

Jaycee nodded. "She's a good player?"

"Oh yeah, really good. Even though she's a freshman she starts on Varsity."

"Do you think upper classmen were resentful of that?" It was a possibility, Jaycee thought. Maybe some rich, far less talented soccer player had done a fast broil and asked Daddy to have his people take care of that annoyingly masterful newcomer.

"Maybe," Ramona conceded. "But I don't know about that." Her nose crinkled. "They all sit together for dinner, and constantly disappear for team bonding events. Like, they walk through the woods blindfolded and holding hands and some shit like that. I don't see the team as a *thing* like that and Eve has never mentioned anyone having a problem with her being a good player."

"So the soccer team eats together, and bonds a lot?"

"Yeah," Ramona nodded. "I have Metaphysical Poetry class in Ward Hall every Wednesday at six o'clock and the soccer team has double session practice. It's really late by the time I walk past the cafeteria on my way back here and I can see them eating together. It's pretty empty by then— no one eats that late except for the athletes."

"Then she comes back here to study?" Jaycee asked.

"Sometimes she comes back here, or she goes to the library. It's open until midnight and she likes the quiet. Eve can get a little bitchy if the floor gets too loud."

Jaycee remembered those rowdy dorm nights. She'd joined in occasionally, whooping it up with swear-ridden rap music, and youthful carelessness. Bags of Doritos were passed around and then cheerfully pummeled into a cloud of orange dust that stuck to the edges of cheap Ocean State Job Lot carpet like dandruff.   It was all in good fun. How women stitched together the fabric of an environment until it was mutually appealing and, at least temporarily, heartfelt. Loud music, stupid fits of laughter, impromptu dance parties, and secrets divulged in Truths or Dares. Granted these were high schoolers here, but a certain camaraderie typically developed in these sorts of shared spaces.

"Don't you think her coach, at least, would worry if she missed practice? Or a teacher noticing she's not in class?"

"Sure," Ramona agreed. "Anywhere else that would probably be a concern. Here at Holy United Atrocity we are encouraged to 'self-nurture.'" She clawed her fingers into air quotes. Jaycee gave her a puzzled expression.

"In other words," Ramona told her, "we take a day off if we feel like our brains are about to explode. I've known some kids to pack up and head home for a week. The curriculum here can be intense."

"So no one would be alarmed when Eve doesn't show up."

"Not at first, no. Not the teachers, not the coaches, no one. It's not unheard of for kids to 'self-nurture' off campus. They come back when they're ready and clear it with their teachers and whoever else. But I called your aunt because Eve would never, like *ever*, take a day off. Her idea of 'self-nurturing' is hitting the snooze button. You know what I mean?"

"Umm ummm," Jaycee mumbled. Eve spurned ordinary in favor of superhuman. Her spotless side of the room told Jaycee she was orderly, careful, and deliberate. She attacked her day. Her schedule demanded tenacity from her mind and her body, yet Eve was just a kid. Distractions were unacceptable and she grew irritated and lashed out when there was too much noise. Her life was on an upward trajectory and there was no time for silliness.

It was sad more than admirable, really. Jaycee was writing up Eve's story as she would tell it on TV. A dedicated teenager chasing excellence in the classroom and on the soccer field. A girl determined to outshine, outperform, and outlast the competition. Everything in her life was a contest that she must win.

"… you need to find her," Ramona had been speaking, interrupting the report Jaycee had been putting together in her head. "If Eve really is missing or something has happened to her, she would know."

"I'm sorry, who do I need to find?" she shook her head. She spaced out when she was locked into her story.

"Cecilia!" Ramona snapped with a touch of juvenile irritation. "Didn't you hear me?"

"No, I was thinking," Jaycee explained, but suddenly Ramona was looking at her fixedly. The room was brightening with the rising sun and Jaycee's features became more obvious. She cocked her head, brushed the bangs from her eyes, and took a few steps toward Jaycee. In the tiny space, they were nearly nose-to-nose. "Does Eve have a phone?" she asked Ramona, moving away.

"Not a decent one," Ramona belched on a huff. It confirmed what Marcy had told her. "It's not here. I already looked. It doesn't let you call it. I didn't know they made those anymore. Or maybe it's just broken. I can't find her laptop either."

"Do you have a picture of Cecilia?" Jaycee pivoted. "Can you show me who she is?"

"I can pull her up on Instagram." Ramona reached for her own cell connected to a charger in the wall, and punched up the app. About thirty seconds later she ripped the cord out and thrust it toward Jaycee. "Here," she said, offering a view of the screen. A series of snapshots revealed a taut, tan body sprawled on an exotic beach, on horseback, or mugging a duck face selfie. Cecilia was pure youthful perfection and wanted everyone to know it.

"Classy girl," Jaycee murmured. "Is Eve on here?"

"No," Ramona told her. "She's too smart for social media." As Jaycee had been looking at Ramona's phone, Ramona had been studying her again … intently.

"Holy balls!" she yawped, "I should've known. How many tall, blonde Jaycees can there be in this world?" Ramona had both hands on her hips as she broke into high-pitched giggles. "Mother-frigger!" she exclaimed. "You, Jaycee Wilder, are a beast! I am a huge fan of your badass survival skills."

Jaycee sighed, her shoulders rolled down and then forward. She had hoped New Hampshire had been free of media coverage of the ordeal she had survived. Even her own family didn't seem aware, or maybe they were just oblivious. Not one former friend from her early years had made the connection and attempted to contact her. She had declined interview requests from every outlet except the one that employed her. Even though she was depicted as a hero, it felt like a scarlet letter. Jaycee had an almost anaphylactic reaction to being the story, she couldn't bear the attention. She took a step back from Ramona's adulation.

"Dude," Ramona continued, sensing the shift. "I'm from California. I know all about your shit but hey …" she put her palms up and retreated. "…I can totally respect your vibe."

Jaycee grinned. The petite Asian gymnast had morphed into intuitive west coast surfer girl. Californians shared the same air that fed superstardom and scandal all at the same time. They marked a moment and then moved on. They always respected the vibe. Jaycee's moment had been duly noted. Now, they moved on.

"So, back to Cecilia," Ramona repeated. "She is the only quasi-friend Eve has here on campus. When she's not with her team, studying, or playing the piano in the lounge—she's super good at that, too—the only person I've ever seen her with is Cecilia."

"Does she live in your dorm?" Jaycee was asking. "Is she in Eve's classes? Do they hang out?"

"Eve doesn't *hang out*," Ramona told her. "She doesn't talk about her family, her pets, or her friends. I live with her but I barely know her. The Cecilia thing is, like, cray." Ramona pulled a lock of hair across her mouth. "I don't get it, unless opposites really do attract and all that."

"But you've seen them together," Jaycee pushed.

"Yes. Cecilia is a senior and *way* hot. Freshman boys get one look at her and almost forgive their absentee parents for locking them up in this prison."

Jaycee nodded. "Seems weird someone like Eve would spend time with a girl like that," Jaycee noted, a point only further supported by Cecilia's Sports Illustrated Swimsuit Edition Instagram spread.

"I agree," Ramona nodded. "At first I thought maybe they both liked to swim in the lady pond but Cecilia is a notorious campus gamer."

"A gamer?" Jaycee narrowed her eyes. "What exactly do you mean?"

Ramona seemed surprised. Surely Jaycee was hip enough to get it, wasn't she? "A gamer, Jaycee. A female version of a player. She likes boys, a lot. Cecilia is basically a glorified skank, she gives it up to cute guys. Or, so I've heard."

Jaycee's lips pursed on Barton's proclamation.
Boarding schools are like sewers, Jaycee. I can smell the
stank from here.

He was right. This stunk. What the hell was a freshman
book dork doing hanging around with a posh high school
whore bag? Jaycee shifted Eve's puzzle in her head. She
moved Holy United Academy slightly to the right. She
pulled Cecilia closer to the middle. Was she just a gamer
with boys her own age, or did Cecilia pursue the Chesters?
Was she sniffing around the middle-aged molesters Barton
was convinced were lurking here? Like the subculture of
fetish nightclubs where Ben slaughtered his Throw Away
Girls, was this all about sex? Christ, was everything in this
world about sex?

If Cecilia was caught in the vortex, who else on
campus knew it even existed? Jaycee considered the odd
student-teacher touch in the classroom she had also seen
with her own eyes. A bit too familiar, a touch too low, and
a teenager a smidge too bold.

"When you say she gives it up a lot," Jaycee started,
"does that mean Cecilia is …"

"A pretty little teacher's pet?" Ramona suggested.

Jaycee nodded. Transformative education. Maybe the
subculture didn't lie so far below the surface.

"I can't say for sure," she explained. "But there has
been some talk …" she hit Jaycee with a glance that was
about as telling as she could make it.

"Tell me where to find her."

"That's easy," Ramona scoffed. "Lunch. 12:45 sharp. She is the only girl at the boy's lacrosse table. She sits next to Kurt, the hottest guy at school, and they pretend not to touch each other's legs under the table. You can't miss her."

Ramona thrust her chin down. Her wrist rolled backwards as she considered what she was looking at.

"In fact, she kinda looks just like you."

CHAPTER SEVEN

If you were to look at it from above, The Chapel at Holy United Academy was constructed in the shape of a cross. In its present capacity, it was meant to be more than simply a building. It was a call to arms. Students were encouraged to engage in Chapel-like activities including community outreach projects on the campus and in surrounding towns. They raked leaves, or painted houses, sang Christmas carols at nursing homes and walked dogs at an animal shelter. Four days a week, they gathered at seven a.m. for a celebration of prayer and to renew their commitment to the spiritual world order of selflessness. Before she went in search of the exquisite Cecilia, Jaycee wanted to see the entire student body together at once. She needed to watch how the students, especially the girls, interacted with their superiors. Were all the adults here peculiarly touchy-feely, or was it an invitation-only ritual?

Jaycee stood back behind the trunk of a sugar maple tree with ropy branches that hid her from view. The early morning sky was crystal blue and cloudless, and the air icy. She watched students wrapped in their school-issued parkas scurry along the path leading to a long row of granite steps that carried them through the wooden doors of The Chapel. They reminded her of ants marching toward a picnic basket—one ambled along looking just like the others. A man dressed in khaki skinny pants, ankle-high Chippewa boots, and a blue down jacket stood just inside the entrance to welcome them. Jaycee squinted. Pastor something-or-other. She recognized him from his picture on the school's website but had forgotten his name. Jaycee had closely scanned the faculty page, trying to identify potential predators from their headshots. Did the bushy eyebrows on the Art Director correlate to those of a sex offender? Was the skinny English Department Head a closet porn freak? Was Eve stowing away with the muscle-bound Dean of Student Affairs who liked James Taylor music and competed in triathlons?

She watched Pastor Whoever smile at the students, and then greet a couple of the boys with a friendly hand on their shoulders. She estimated him to be in his mid-thirties, definitely on the lean side with long legs and light brown hair stylishly cut tight over his ears and brushed up in the front. He showed much better in person. His bio pic didn't do him justice. She kept her eyes downward as she moved out onto the path toward the building. She was two steps behind a group of girls discussing the physics homework none of them could figure out. In deference to the rules of The Chapel, they hushed once they reached the stairs.

"Mornin' girls," the man said warmly as they passed in front of him and entered the foyer. Jaycee moved with them. She glanced at him as he turned to greet the group behind her. He smiled, showing off even, white teeth and a freshly shaven face. Up close, he was handsome in a young Harrison Ford kind of way, with a docile yet self-assured presence. He shepherded the stragglers through the doors and then brought them back together with a thud. Chapel was about to begin.

Jaycee sat on the end of the fourth row from the back. She smiled at the students seated around her but no one spoke, and none seemed interested in her. A good early sign her costumed adult body was fitting in well enough. Once they had settled into the sloped backs of the pews, the shuffling stopped and all was quiet. Jaycee inadvertently winced as gothic sounding madrigals abruptly reverberated through the air. She could feel the chords vibrate right through her legs. She looked around her. Sunlight arched like a rainbow through multicolored panes of stained glass over polished wood floors and dark cherry pews. The air was scented with the hint of leftover incense and aged timber. Ground-level radiators hissed and bucked as hot wind was pushed through aging pipes connected to a boiler in the basement. Older men and women Jaycee assumed to be faculty members joined together at the front of the Chapel and stood facing the student body. The man in the khakis had shed his heavy down jacket and joined them, taking his spot in the middle. In an elevated, practiced voice, he welcomed them.

"We come together this morning in prayer," he began. The youthful faces in the pews dipped their chins on cue. Would he pray for the safe return of Eve Levesque? Were any of these campus elders aware of a panicked mother anxiously awaiting word of her daughter's fate?

As if responding to Jaycee's silent questions, he began with a more innocuous lesson of the day, certainly nothing that would have indicated a campus wide Amber Alert was about to go out.

"Let us meet the challenge of our existence with open hearts and minds. May this day bring reflection and purpose for us as teachers, as students, and as members of our human experience."

Blah, blah, blah, Jaycee could already tell that Chapel was little more than a tart lecture for the entitled few. *Come, oh glorious ones, as we repeat our sacred oath to inspire the unfortunate souls who buy their produce at Market Basket or sling fries at Burger King. Lord, give us the strength to make them better. It is the challenge of our generation.*

The half-preacher, half-cult leader blabbed a bit more about walking paths together while seeking answers in individuality, but overall the morning blessing was brief and more spiritual than religious. They riffed through a folksy school anthem set to a surprisingly modern backbeat and then rose to allow the faculty to lead the procession out.

A few students stayed back to speak privately with the pastor. Jaycee watched them circle like juvenile tiger cubs testing out their new hunting skills.

"What's his name again," she asked a lanky, brown-haired girl standing behind her. Jaycee adopted the miffed inflection of a bothered teenager. She bobbed a lazy shoulder toward the pastor and his fan girls. "Like, I always forget …" she threw in.

The girl seemed detached and half-asleep. Morning Chapel probably galvanized unbridled disdain among its campus attendants.

"Pastor Anthony," the girl whispered with a lisp. Jaycee noticed two metal retainers on her upper and bottom teeth. Just a baby, she thought. All alone, far from home, and fresh out of braces. What were these families thinking?

"Oh yeah, thank you." Pastor Anthony, got it.

Jaycee watched him. Unlike the scene she'd witnessed through the fogged window, this was different. He stood a respectable distance from the four girls who had approached him. He was engaged yet kept both hands locked behind his back as he rocked on his heels. The tallest of the tender stalkers tried to hold court. She was dark-haired and lovely, but too obvious, with sharp features that needed the proper makeup to soften into bewitching angles and edges.

If she pushed, Pastor Anthony pulled. He was attentive yet coolly sequestered into his own territory. The pronounced seesawing was much more like what Jaycee had expected from a high-ranking official in an educational or religious environment. He enforced respect in a way that had all the trappings of being normal.

That made the bizarre group hug in front of the doors seem all the more hair-raising. Three girls and two boys were wrapped around one bulky man in the middle. Jaycee hadn't seen him as she entered The Chapel. Headmaster Buford P. Bowman must have just arrived. Jaycee frowned as she watched him. Either Buford had indulged in some serious photo-shopping or he was clearly enjoying the cafeteria food this semester. He bulged in all kinds of places not visible from his computer image on the

70

Welcome to Holy United Academy: Message from the Headmaster page. Jaycee sidestepped around his group and moved to the far right of the steps where she could inconspicuously position herself to watch. The arms disentangled but the students stood together laughing loudly and discussing something with Bowman that must be absolutely hysterical. Jaycee scowled at them. No one was that happy at 7:25 in the morning on a school day.

An attractive woman with strands of straight blonde hair escaping from a North Face hat appeared next to Jaycee. She laid a gloved hand on her elbow and peered out from the scarf covering her mouth. It muffled her words as she asked Jaycee if she was okay. She didn't resemble anyone on the faculty page.

"Oh, I'm fine," Jaycee moved away from her touch, and didn't look directly at her. She lowered her chin into her coat and explained she was just taking her time before heading to class.

"You sure?" the woman asked. "Is there anything I can help you with?" Even though Jaycee didn't recognize her, she had that teacher quality about her. A need to assist.

This was not Jaycee's idea of slipping in and out unnoticed. She needed to keep this exchange brief. "No, thank you."

Another boisterous round of cackling drew their attention back to the group near the door. The woman chuckled. "He has such a way with our student body, don't you think? A special connection to the young adults."

Jaycee mumbled an agreeable sound but immediately got the creeps. A special connection was just the thing she was suspicious of here at Holy United Academy. Who was this barrel-chested man with the boyishly full face and giddy Irishman bluster?

"Headmasters are usually so stuffy and reserved," she continued, giving Jaycee unsolicited information that might prove worthwhile. "But Biff is … well … he's just Biff," she crowed happily.

What the …? Jaycee dug her teeth into her lip to stop the chortle of shock from tearing up her throat. Buford was … *Biff?* They called him Biff? Jesus Christ! Biffs were cast as bullies in movies, or they became famous WWE wrestlers, maybe even hick HVAC mechanics with plumber butt, but they were *not* headmasters at one of the nation's finest private schools. What the hell? She couldn't react. Jaycee knew she had to keep this real. An authentic Holy United student would have already gotten that out of her system by now. Headmaster Biff jokes weren't funny past orientation.

The teacher-woman bid Jaycee farewell and moved along. Most of the students had disappeared into other buildings on campus, including the cafeteria where warm smells promised homemade breads, toasty bagels, scrambled eggs, and thick-cut slices of bacon. Jaycee's stomach roared and she desperately needed some coffee. The east coast time change and the hectic odyssey to find Eve needed fuel. She couldn't afford being tired or hungry;

time was crunching away the opportunity to flush her out. Jaycee needed to be sharp.

Finally, the group splintered and Headmaster Biff watched his young charges go about their mornings with a satisfied smile. It could be pride, or longing … and Jaycee wasn't sure yet if it was paternal or deviant. Of course Biff had likely been air-dropped into a jungle quite used to following its own rules, but he certainly maintained the healthy veil of vegetation. His role beyond the intellectual growth of children was to preserve the experience for the next generation. Students and teachers lived and learned together, each side devoted to a caring twenty-four-hour-a-day availability policy. Holy United Academy was a family that took care of itself. Biff was the quarterback calling the plays that would guarantee they kept putting up solid numbers on the scoreboard.

Well, Jaycee had another family to worry about. Hers. And one of its members was not where she should be. Jaycee felt her legs move before she had hatched a plan, just as they did on the scene of a breaking story. She focused first on physically getting there—the questions and storytelling stood by in development—they always waited their turn in her process. She skipped down the stairs and closed in on Biff.

"Good morning," she chirped, going with the informal greeting. Do students call him Biff? Headmaster Biff? Fat Ass?

"Good morning," he turned, all ruddy cheeks and husky jawline. "How are we today?"

Jaycee tightened her scarf around the collar of the borrowed Academy parka she'd taken from Eve's room. She covered as much of her face as possible. If Biff prided himself on knowing every member of his little tribe, she didn't want to stick out. Just her eyes were visible beneath Eve's black hat with white snowflakes printed on a pointy pompom. Students were allowed to wear hats and gloves of their choosing.

Barton would call this reckless. Van would remind her she wasn't a police interrogator, and Clare would demand she conduct a productive interview. Jaycee needed information but this time she couldn't hide behind being a reporter. She also couldn't be a concerned relative, that avenue had yielded nothing so far but a sinkhole. The only option she had was to be as she appeared: a concerned member of the Holy United Academy student body. After all, wasn't that part of the school creed? To take care of one another?

"I'm good, thanks," she began. Biff had brown eyes and feminine lashes that curled upward toward wide brows. "On my way to Brewster for trig class," she threw in. Jaycee had studied the campus map just in case she needed to pretend to know where she was going. Brewster Hall housed the math department.

Biff smiled and nodded. There really wasn't much to add to that.

Jaycee knew she was on the edge of the diving board. She had to just jump.

"It's a tough class. Sometimes I study with a friend of mine," she started. It was a total ad lib; she was making it up as she went.

"As you should," Biff replied. "Shared information makes us all better."

"I agree," Jaycee continued. "But I haven't seen my friend in a few days. She hasn't been around."

"Hmmm," he drew his mouth into a line. "Perhaps she isn't feeling well. I know the infirmary staff has been quite busy lately, it's flu season." He was merely placating her. It was hardly a show of concern.

"Maybe," Jaycee replied, pretending to consider that. "But she always has a tube of anti-bacterial gel and never gets sick."

Biff cocked his head. It was obvious he was becoming perplexed by Jaycee's circular inquiry. Students rarely challenged his statements. "Did you call her?" he ventured. "Text? Email?"

"Not answering," Jaycee told him. *Take that, Biff!* His expression turned thoughtful. When students unplugged at Holy United it usually meant they took themselves off the grid on purpose.

"Is it possible she needed some mental health time?" he asked, but more in a knowing way. "She could be indulging in a bit of 'self-nurturing.'" Just as Ramona had explained, it appeared that mental health days were built into the school calendar.

So weird. It sounded more like a Los Angeles new age spa lingo menu item. *The self-nurture rain shower with*

ginger honey-infused water and essence of water lily...
$425.

Jaycee shook her head. "She's not really the mental health type." She was watching Biff, waiting for any sign that he was connecting the call from a concerned mother to Jaycee's bogus report of a friend who didn't show up for trig. Had he personally spoken to Marcy or had some underling blown her off without even telling him?

Our students are very independent, Mrs. Levesque.
They come and go at will.

Was Biff even aware that Eve was missing or was his obscurity a bit more nefarious? Was he hiding something? Jaycee felt her back straighten and she exhaled a long trail of steam through the fibers of her scarf and into the brittle air. His silence was vociferous in its emptiness. She felt that ire bustle in her gut whenever victims in her stories were disrespected either by the thug witnesses who clammed up when she harassed them for information, or law enforcement who avoided interviews in favor of cold press releases devoid of empathy for all that had been stolen or destroyed. Jaycee worked with facts, but always sided with compassion whenever possible. She kept her victims warm when their own beating hearts were no longer able to. She told their stories with care.

This was different. These weren't Throw Away Girls in fetish nightclubs, or strangers met with horrific fates. This was her cousin, here, her blood! And this bloated buffoon didn't seem to have a damn clue that Eve was missing!

While empathy was a welcomed partner for a reporter, raw emotion could quash the other half's steadfast logic. Jaycee drew another long breath, but she could feel the energy between them begin to bend. Jaycee knew she was teetering between a breakthrough and a reprimand. While she was tall, Biff was mountain-sized, and glowered over her. The campus was empty. No one would see this. He moved his chest into her personal space and studied her. Two of his puffy fingers stroked the scruff on his chin. Gone was the benevolent mug. Replacing it was a menacing glare Jaycee knew too well from her days spent thrusting a microphone into the faces of people who had zero intent on talking to the media. Biff was suddenly looking more like a "no comment" kind of guy, rather than the chatty cutup she'd first noticed on the steps of The Chapel.

"Are you suggesting there is some emergency situation unfolding here?" he continued his advance toward her.

Jaycee shrugged and stepped back. She couldn't come off as an adversary. Not yet. She wasn't sure yet if pulling the alarm on Eve's disappearance was the right way to go about finding her.

"I'm not sure," she said dismissively, wrapping her arms around her stomach in withdrawal. She didn't want to cower to his increasingly aggressive tone but it was time to take this down a notch. Normally, this would be when she pushed for a breakthrough with an interviewee; she would release her sexy smile and try to use the sunlight to further accentuate her aqua-colored eyes. *Come on,* she'd tease. *I*

promise, no trick questions. It rarely failed but Biff
wouldn't respond to a reporter's maneuver when he thought
he was talking to an underaged minion. She had no
authority here. Jaycee recalculated. She shuffled her feet
and rocked her weight to one hip, figuring that most
teenagers would become outwardly fidgety whenever
challenged by an adult superior. "You could be right.
Maybe she just needs a break."

Immediately, Biff's stony headmaster act evaporated
back into jovial townie bartender, clearly the role he
preferred to play. "We all do," he replied condescendingly,
his teeth disappearing behind a tight-lipped sneer.

"No one …" he started, inching his snow-tipped
Timberland Chukka boot back toward Jaycee. Her nose
twitched as she picked up his scent: a pine-tree, vanilla
spice concoction that whorled like a dirt devil through her
sinuses. Nasty! She'd never let Van wear something that
stunk like dessert in the forest. His barrel chest broadened
like a linebacker taking on another goliath in football pads.
Biff was the enforcer, the messenger, and most importantly,
the peacekeeper. Holy United Academy couldn't afford a
soldier to fall out of order.

"… ever really leaves, you know. We may step back
every once in a while, but no one ever leaves Holy United.
We are a family here. We respect each other's space, and
foster responsibility in our young adults. But dear,
everyone always comes home. Your friend will be back
soon. I just know it."

Jaycee suspected most of his pliable pups melted under such a precise prediction. We don't worry here at Holy United Academy, oh no! That would render us demonstrably lesser-minded creatures who rose and fell with the whims of the universe. Here, we design our own outcomes because we are smarter, our techniques are better, and goddamn it, we deserve it. The universe answers to us!

No one walks away from the fortress, I mean, *the family*.

So if Eve didn't walk away, who took her?

Biff reallocated his Timberlands in the direction of the cafeteria. Jaycee wondered how much of his immaculate oration he actually believed.

CHAPTER EIGHT

She couldn't really go to Brewster Hall for trig class, or any class, so Jaycee headed back toward The Chapel to gather her thoughts. It was still early but she needed an ally. If she was about to dangle herself into shark-filled waters, she'd better arm herself with a sharp weapon.

Barton was the best shark repellant she had.

The Chapel door was closed but not locked. Students were never sealed out of their primary place of worship. Jaycee stepped back inside and could hear faint musical notes strummed out on a distant guitar. She looked around. The pews were empty.

It was ludicrous to think anyone on west coast time would be up and functioning at this hour, but Jaycee knew Barton was powered by adrenaline and fearsome memories. He rarely slept because that was when they were the most active, like mosquitoes at dusk. She slid into a pew, deposited her bag next to her, and yanked out her cell phone. She pointedly examined the four sides of the long room for any sign of Pastor Anthony or other students. The music in the background played on. Coast was clear.

Barton yipped at her before the second ring.

"You okay?" he demanded. He had survived this long only by knowing the wolf was always at the back door.

"Yeah, good." Jaycee kept her voice at a low pitch.

"Tell me where you're at."

"At this point, still trying to figure out if my cousin is missing or 'self-nurturing.'" She purposely punched the sarcasm.

Barton pounced. "Christ, you sound like the fucking psychiatrists who debrief us after a bloodbath. 'Scuse my language. All those 'get in touch with your feelings' fuckers who roll up in BMWs with vanity plates. No friggin' clue of the real world, Jay Jay. You are at ground zero of No Friggin' Clue Land."

"Oh, they have a clue, Barton. It's just highly subjective to those of us who don't fit in here at No Friggin' Clue Land." She rubbed her hand down her thigh. Even with the black leggings, she was freezing. "And it's ridiculously cold here. So much more brutal than I remember."

"It's New Hampshire in the dead of winter. What were you expecting it to be like? Sweater weather on the pier of the Hotel del Coronado? California has spoiled your ass."

Jaycee smiled into her phone. "Maybe," she conceded.

"Where are you right now?" He got back to business.

"Sitting in a church pew," she replied. "Plotting my next move."

"They allow visitors to just drop in and go to church?"

"No," she told him. "They don't. I am, shall we say, one of them."

Barton quickly deciphered what that meant; after all, they had met at the funeral of a murder victim neither of them knew in life. Jaycee went to great lengths to root out the information she was seeking.

"I won't even ask 'cause I don't want to know," he snickered. "What does your early evidence tell you? And what is it not telling you?" Barton had taught Jaycee to use evidence like training wheels. They may keep your butt on the seat but had the tendency to pull you in the wrong direction. "Evidence is like Play-Doh," he'd told her. "You can use it to make your round balls fit around square pegs if you push hard enough so don't let it define your investigation. Let it support it."

"Well, this is a bit different given there are no gory leftovers for me to comb through." She thought back to bloody messages and Throw Away Girls hacked to shreds.

"Doesn't matter," he reminded her. "The best investigators dig a hole beneath the most beautiful flowers. It takes finding the fertilizer in the soil rather than the beetle on the shrubs. The beetle flies away but the fertilizer is what makes that shit grow."

Jaycee sighed. "No beetles around here, they're all frozen into fossils." The amateurish guitar-plucking serenaded her mood. "No crime scene," she went on, thinking out loud. "No disheveled living quarters, her room is spotless, and her roommate confirmed she's an academic rock star, a social geek, and an exceptional soccer player. She doesn't have a cell phone loaded with zippy texts from possible accomplices, her family loves her but gives her space, and she not only appreciates being at this snooty training camp for spoiled brats, she works her ass off to earn her keep."

That sparked a hard, fast, and sudden realization. Jaycee sucked in her breath. What if she was approaching this from the wrong end? Could it be that Eve was using Holy United Academy? Was she the one controlling the balance of power?

"... you there?" Barton interrupted a possible new awareness of who her cousin really was.

"I'm here, just thinking. What if Eve is less of a victim than we thought?"

"In what way?"

Jaycee thought of Ramona's assessment of the odd relationship with Cecilia. Two polar opposites that had found something in common. What was it?

"Well, what if she's staying away for a reason. What if she had something to accomplish and knew she could take the time to get it done. No one would be looking for her. Not yet anyway."

"What tells you she has anything to work on that would take her beyond the fences of that place?"

Jaycee shook her head. As far as she could tell so far, Eve's entire world was separated into two spheres: a home life that had inspired nothing beyond a desperate desire to escape it, and a school schedule that barely allowed time to go to the bathroom.

And one friend. A notoriously loose campus vamp.

"Nothing," she replied. Jaycee rubbed her temple. "Just a thought."

Barton cleared his throat. "What are you not telling me?" He knew what she sounded like when she was marinating a thought.

"I'm just starting to wonder if Eve is too smart to let something happen to her."

"That maybe she is following a scent of her own making," Barton was following.

"Yeah, and I need to find the perfume factory," Jaycee told him. "I have been made aware of a lovely girl here who reeks to high heaven. Maybe that's the sewer you've been telling me about."

Cecilia. She needed to find the only girl at the boys' lacrosse table.

"Goes without saying," Barton began. "The sewer can hold poison both sweet and sour."

"You should've seen me just now with the headmaster. His name is Biff, by the way, what the hell, right? So, *Biff* wants to be one of them, one of the kids. He likes to jibe with them on their level. They think he's cool. But he didn't like me asking questions."

"He doesn't know you as you, though," Barton reminded her. "Even a guy named Biff would expect a student to know her place. I'm guessing you pushed him a little?"

"Yes, but then I backed off. You'd be proud. I'm learning to feel out my situation and think rather than act. Normally, as my TV self, I act because I can. Here, I need to think because acting makes me stick out."

"Is he hiding something?"

"Maybe," Jaycee confirmed. But Biff may also have reacted to her intrusive approach. He expected reverent youngster, not pugnacious newsperson. "And there's that hottie I just mentioned. I'm starting to think she's key in figuring out if little Evie is communing with nature during a 'self-nurturing' session in the mountains, or … worse …"

"Remember, Jay Jay, she's just a kid herself. You may already dislike or distrust her, but you can't let that show. You have to be an innocuous presence. Don't get her feathers all ruffled, especially if she's boarding school royalty. She won't like you right out of the gate. Be prepared to handle all that 'cause she's going to try to handle all of you."

Like two female lionesses circling each other, Jaycee anticipated a formidable counter-challenge.

"I'll keep that in mind," she quipped.

"Have you gone in search of your 'me' yet?" Barton asked.

Jaycee laughed softly. "You mean my loose-lipped law enforcement tag team partner for the east coast games?"

"No, wiseass, I mean your highly trained angel that sits on your left shoulder and yells at you when you do dumb shit."

"No, but that's next. Once I figure out if this girl is of any value I am headed to the Podunk Police Department that is doing zilch as we speak to find Eve."

Barton paused on the other end of the call. Jaycee wondered what she had said to make him go quiet.

"What?" she asked. "What did I say?"

"Sewers," he began. "Sewers can breed a lot of mean little spiders. Small towns can hide lots of spiders that come from the same web."

Jaycee listened. The same web. Barton was warning her of the dangers of blended priorities. One web can feed many offspring. Full bellies meant loyal eaters who wanted to make sure they were around for the next meal.

"On second thought," he told her. "Be careful about finding another me out there. Your sources may not be nearly as pure."

Jaycee promised to keep in touch and then ended the call. The web was widening. Was one little spider trying to weave her way out or were the rest of them trying to pull her back in? Was Eve entangled in the meshing or was she spinning it?

Jaycee was so caught up in her blossoming hypothesis she didn't notice the guitar had stopped strumming and the air had turned thicker as it flowed around another entity. She was no longer alone. She whipped her head around as her eyes locked onto his.

Oh shit, Jaycee scrambled for a cover story. A fib. Would the holiness of her surroundings give him the power to see right through her lie?

Pastor Anthony was waiting for it to begin.

CHAPTER NINE

His eyebrows had turned toward each other in deep concentration. Jaycee blabbed on, fully immersed in her fictitious story of poor grades and too much homework.

"If you are that worried you're falling behind, you need to speak to your counselor, that's what they're here for," Pastor Anthony told her, his lips pulled into a taut line.

"It's just so har … *d*," she wailed, taking extra time to hold onto the brisk taste of the letter "d." She wanted to be the opposite of Eve: needy, whiny, and desperate to be coddled. She needed him to feel sorry for her, not be suspicious of her. She also couldn't be a trespasser of his personal space. He hadn't responded well to the girls doing just that.

"I don't know how everyone else does it," she sniffed, further selling her anguish. "I know this one girl, Eve, she's like ridic smart and on the soccer team, too. She probably doesn't even need to 'self-nurture.'" Jaycee looked at her folded hands in her lap. She rounded her shoulders to appear even smaller and ashamed. It was how she could safely work her cousin into their fake conversation.

"Don't be so sure," Pastor Anthony told her. "Our finest student athletes feel the same pressure as the rest of us. It's how they work through it. How you'll work through it. And it's not *ridic.*"

He beamed at his own joke. See how cool I am? Cheeks puffed outward as he lauded his progressive willingness to use urban dictionary jargon. He was chock full of rational, spiritually sound excuses and examples. The pitch in his voice held the leftovers of a tired southern accent trying to ride the rough frontier of the northeast. There were too many auditory peaks and valleys here to keep a smooth flow, eventually everyone ended up sounding like a Yankee. Pastor Anthony kept a comfortable distance between himself and the broken little bird he was attending to in the pew.

"Do you know her?" Jaycee held her breath as she asked. "Eve Levesque, do you know Eve? She's just so calm and cool and I'm just a … *sniff sniff* … mess."

Pastor Anthony considered the name. He nodded slightly. "I have seen Eve when the soccer team plays on the weekends and I can attend a game, but no, I don't know her personally." So, he at least knew who Eve was.

"She's always at the library," Jaycee further lied, working from Ramona's information. "Like, every night. I always see her by herself on a computer and, like, surrounded by a gazillion books. I don't know how she does it all, it's like she's superhuman! But lately, I haven't seen her at all." She risked a glance upward at Pastor Anthony. Without the scarf to hide beneath, too much of her adult face was visible. Even though she had yet to pop a line or wrinkle, up close Jaycee was seriously straining the pimply, rounded-cheek boundaries of adolescence.

Pastor Anthony settled on that for a few seconds, his eyes narrowed and he took his time in looking Jaycee up, down, and sideways. She felt her stomach flutter. Had she pushed it too far? What was he looking for?

Instead, the gentle pastor smiled. He leaned against the ornate wooden seat, his body relaxed into the molding. He showed no sign of throwing the same shade Biff had. She was a troubled student and he was there to lead her out of the darkness. That's how they took care of business at Holy United Academy and exactly what he preached to his congregation whenever it became mired in the fretful angst induced by growing pains. He was masterful, really, almost seductive in applying a salve to coat Jaycee's distress. It was different from the grabby teacher she'd seen through the window, and not at all like Biff's snappy reproach on campus. Maybe being in Pastor Anthony's presence truly was the sanctuary Holy United intended it to be.

"Maybe you've answered your own questions," he began. Jaycee shook her head in confusion. "You are asking how Eve manages all the pressures of her life, right? The grades, the sports, all of it. And yet, you assume she does this perfectly. That there are no cracks in her sidewalk," he suggested jubilantly. Pastor Anthony was perceptibly getting off on leading her to the precipice of self-discovery.

Open your mind, my dear girl. Let me show you the way.

"She seems perfect to me," Jaycee responded dryly, applying some heat she hoped he took as jealousy.

"Really now." He looked amused. "Don't you think Eve recognizes within herself when things become too heavy? That's why we encourage time for yourselves. We understand how difficult it can be. You're all young adults, but most of you have never been away from home."

Jaycee grudgingly nodded. He needed to see progress. She glanced back at him with hooded eyes. Playing the clueless youth card, her expression told him she was willing to follow the leader with the best argument.

"Probably," she grinned shyly. "She probably recognizes that. I see your point."

"It's not an easy lesson to learn," he said, throwing her a bone. "Before you condemn yourself or start comparing your shortcomings to another's success, consider that Eve has felt exactly what you're feeling right now. She just uses her 'self-nurturing' skills to fix it. Don't worry, you'll get there."

Jaycee nearly laughed at the simplistic atta-girl suggestion that an imaginary toolbox would solve her problems. Instead, she clapped her hands together with glee. Pastor Anthony had swooped in and made it all better.

"Okay, if you say so." She grinned at him and he beamed back in a beautiful brochure picture moment, an idealistic life lesson learned in the most sacred of places. Jaycee questioned how many of these recitations Pastor Anthony had notched into his J.Crew knotted leather belt.

"Why don't you take some more time here to contemplate your thoughts," he suggested. "It's important to sit with yourself in the quiet to reflect."

"Umm," Jaycee rolled her mouth in agreement. "That sounds like a good idea. Thank you so much for helping me work this out." She turned to him wearing the sweetest grin she could muster.

"That's what we're here for," he told her, with full patronizing guilelessness capable of setting off even a toddler's internal bullshit sensor.

Jaycee watched Pastor Anthony walk back toward the doorway that led to his offices. She was pretty sure there was some sort of scent wafting off him, too. Was it the pure essence of holy water?

Or was it sulfur?

CHAPTER TEN

The cafeteria smelled like freshly baked cookies and Windex. Jaycee sat in a long-backed booth near the terminal set up for students to swipe their dining hall cards. The heat was blasting so she had adjusted her look. She removed the winter hat and pulled her hair into a high bun. She wore the thick black glasses she opted for when her contacts burned her eyes. The frames were large and took up enough space over her cheeks to distort her features. She wanted to avoid another astute California kid recognizing her as Ramona had. She listened in to snippets of distant conversations but had purposely positioned herself closest to the large oval table near the side exit that held members of the lacrosse team.

And one exceptionally beautiful young woman.

Cecilia.

She was exactly what Jaycee thought she'd be: beguiling, flirty, and extremely confident in her killer looks. She had long, shiny blonde hair captured in a simple low ponytail, just like all the other girls around her—yet her head sparkled in the bright noontime light like it carried a tiara. She was slender yet stacked beneath her uniform shirt, obviously ordered in extra small to showcase the goods. It would be difficult to tell which was more spectacular, her face or her body. Cecilia had it going on, and she absolutely owned the boy sitting to her right. He had medium brown hair, trimmed neatly, defined traps and biceps, and a strong face with pronounced full lips. He smiled broadly as he ate with one hand. Jaycee could imagine what he was doing with the other one hidden beneath the table. It wasn't a delicate courtship; there were no secret whispers or glancing touches. No, this was combustible and red-hot, like the spicy buffalo wings they picked at from the same plate. Cecilia worked a celery stick like a seasoned professional, dipping it in blue cheese dressing and then delicately licking the creamy tip with a languid flick of her tongue.

"Oh, you naughty little girl," Jaycee muttered to herself as she bit off one corner of her toasted everything bagel topped with a swirl of warm butter. She'd paid cash, hoping the woman sitting at the cash register wouldn't make too much of her lacking a student dining card. That concern was quickly bypassed when the portly woman sitting on the swivel chair hadn't even bothered to make eye contact.

The other boys at the table talked around the couple. They munched on sandwiches piled high with layers of deli meat and cheese. At least a dozen flattened Lay's potato chips bags collected in the middle. Low conversations buzzed around the area with intermittent spikes of laughter and a couple of coughs. A few teachers mingled with the students as they ate, but lunch was orderly and neat. Everyone cleaned up after themselves, deposited their trays through a half-window partition near the trash cans, and went about their days.

Finally, the lacrosse boys rose and left the cafeteria as a group. Cecilia walked alongside her favorite player as he tossed their trash and dumped the tray. She sidled up next to him and—despite it being against recommended campus etiquette—kissed him hard on the mouth. He looked around and then patted her bare skin just below the pleat of her skirt. Cecilia didn't bother with the black leggings.

With backpacks positioned across their shoulders they moved out in opposite directions but with the same satisfied smile and the heady knowledge that more was to come.

The lacrosse player glanced at Jaycee as he passed by her booth but Cecilia had stopped and was staring right at her. Her girl senses must have picked up on a potential challenger to her throne. Cecilia was like the sexy Los Angeles girls at the clubs in West Hollywood. They came all tricked out and ready to party, but spent most of the night sizing up the competition. Jaycee knew she had to appeal to this girl on the same level Eve somehow had. She'd analyzed the peculiar alliance the two reportedly shared. What was the glue that held them together? The only string Jaycee could follow was a financial one. Eve was a scholarship kid. Did that make her similar to Cecilia, or vulnerable to her?

Jaycee offered the first gesture of good will with a smile and a peppy wave. Cecilia's mouth turned down before it went up. She would've ignored her outright in this beauty-trumps-all ecosystem she ruled over but Jaycee waved again. Cecilia squinted at her, but gave her a limp wave back as her shirt slid open slightly near her wrist. Jaycee's eyes were drawn to a thin metal line suddenly visible below the fabric. A bracelet. She recognized it instantly because she'd just ordered one for herself less than a week ago. The Tiffany Infinity cuff was 18k white gold with a delicate splash of diamonds in the shape of a bow. Van had told her she was crazy to drop almost five grand on it, but Jaycee worked hard so she could do just that. Cecilia had the exact same one; Jaycee knew that was no cheap Pandora imitation. Did scholarship kids wear Tiffany bracelets?

She had to use this. This could be her way in. Jaycee rose from her seat.

"O ... M ... G," she sputtered, "is that the new Infinity cuff?"

"Yes," Cecilia preened, her voice rising with priggish pretentiousness. "But don't tell anyone."

"Oh, I won't," Jaycee assured her. Students weren't allowed to wear any jewelry except a watch or stud earrings. Cecilia refused to let those silly regulations tone down her sparkle. "I saw that in last summer's It List section of *InStyle* magazine," Jaycee crooned. "It was one of the top fifty must-haves," she sighed heavily. "It is like, *way* expensive, I can't even imagine how much that costs."

Forty-nine hundred dollars, to be exact.

"I'm Lexy," Jaycee fibbed. "I just transferred here from upstate New York."

She and Cecilia faced each other, almost the exact same height and build. Jaycee was slightly taller, her features more delicately defined, but the two women could pass as biologically linked.

"Hello," Cecilia purred. Her voice was deep, like an authoritative female boss in an office full of men. She put you on notice before you'd even done anything to piss her off. Jaycee felt some protection beneath her glasses and upswept hair. A less refined look was necessary to help her pull off the non-threatening, plucky wannabe bestie persona she needed to break through Cecilia's glass heart.

"It took a while for my scholarship to come through," Jaycee told her, adding a dorky snort. If Cecilia considered herself penthouse nobility, Jaycee had to put herself in the basement. Girls like Cecilia were too narcissistic to pursue a relationship with an equal. Eve was the intellectual superior, so that clearly wasn't what Cecilia saw in her. It had to be about money. Jaycee doubled down.

"I was supposed to be here last fall, but you know, paperwork..." she smiled broadly. Cecilia watched her. "I guess it can be complicated when all the financials have to come through."

"Yeah, I guess ..." Cecilia started. Her full lips puckered on a pout. She swept a gaze down Jaycee's torso and slowly back up to the crooked grin she was holding. Cecilia blinked twice rapidly as her mouth spread into the faintest of smiles. It was more pained than genuine, but Jaycee had to advance. Even if it was merely a miniscule crack in the door, Cecilia had allowed her to slip a toe over the threshold and reporters were trained to capitalize whenever possible.

"I was worried about fitting in here," she said softly, like she was sharing a big secret. She needed Cecilia to feel as though she were important enough to know a piece of information no one else did. It gave her the leverage she would need to take the upper hand in this exchange. Cecilia must feel unrivaled.

"Like, would everyone know I was a scholarship kid? Would they hate me because I'm not super rich?"

Cecilia shrugged. "Some of them will, for sure." She wasn't in the least concerned about hurting this stranger's feelings.

Jaycee hunched her shoulders like that had stung. "Oh, well...thanks for being honest." She smiled meekly. Jaycee was injured on the battlefield and like the dishonorable soldier she was, Cecilia smelled the blood. She circled her prey.

"Not everyone is like that though," she said, eyes widening. Her mascara-tipped lashes fluttered below her artistically etched brows. She wasn't supposed to be wearing makeup, and yet somehow Cecilia pulled it off under the guise of a natural glow. The brows were professionally waxed for sure, about two shades darker than her hair, perfectly symmetrical and ideally set to accentuate the deep, dark specs of blue within her light gray eyes. They reminded Jaycee of the Pacific just before the Santa Ana winds whipped it into frothy foam. Cecilia was like the sea, roiling just below the surface, waiting to crash the shore.

"You just have to meet the right people here."

"The right people?" Jaycee probed. "You mean like friends or teachers?"

Cecilia sighed in annoyance. "The teachers are lame as shit," she pronounced defiantly. "The women are bitches, and most of the guys only work here to stare at our boobs, I swear."

Jaycee laughed uncomfortably. "That's kind of gross," she said innocently. "They're like, my dad's age."

"Oh, at least! But just ignore all that." Cecilia waved that off as she rolled her lips together. Jaycee saw a tiny dimple snap next to her right cheek. Many years from now she'd probably have that Botox'd into an obediently smoother line. Her rigid back slacked as she shifted her backpack to the other shoulder. Cecilia was still scrutinizing the newcomer but had determined she was more of a gullible stray who had stumbled into her barbed wire, rather than an intrepid adversary plotting a coup.

Suddenly, the more sophisticated student was on her side, her mystical aura of coolness widening to accept a visitor. Jaycee felt the walls coming down in that defining moment kind of way, the nearly imperceptible flashpoint she had sharpened her senses to recognize when a reluctant witness became storytelling magic. She used these tactics to enhance her TV reports until they were more engrossing, engaging, and memorable than the competition's. Cecilia was almost fully on her side now but she needed to close strong. All of this was useless unless Jaycee could pull out critical information about how and why she had latched on to Eve.

"Okay, I'll try," Jaycee began. "It's nerve-racking to start over, you know? I don't know anyone here. You're, like, the second person I've even talked to so far."

"Well, trust me," Cecilia told her. "I'm much more important to get to know. Most of the losers here will tell you to work hard and get good grades. I know scholarship kids like you have to in order to stay."

It was beyond gratuitous and cruel but Jaycee ignored the slam. *Scholarship kids like you.* It implied Cecilia was neither poor nor on scholarship. So why pursue Eve? Cecilia's body was toned and lithe, but was she the athletic type? Had she met Eve while sweating it out on side-by-side treadmills at the gym? Jaycee had to know.

"Yeah, and if my grades slack I get booted from the volleyball team," Jaycee sputtered in exasperation. "I mean, isn't one separate from the other?" She went with volleyball, assuming if Cecilia knew Eve through sports, it would have to be soccer. She prayed volleyball wasn't this girl's primary activity here.

"Ugh," Cecilia groaned. Jaycee's shoulders slacked in relief. "That's just stupid. All the swamp asses on the football team are undeniably stupid and totally annoying. I know for a fact the teachers only pass them so college scouts think they're eligible to get recruited. It's like, so disgusting."

Jaycee gasped in spurious shock. Boarding school athletes did get first looks by the best national programs all the time, Cecilia was right. And obviously miffed. Jaycee considered that maybe she suffered from status anxiety over anyone she perceived as having more than they deserved, or more than she had. Athletes had an advantage she didn't approve of. So wouldn't that make Eve more foe than friend?

What was she missing here? Jaycee stepped back into her intricate dance of lies.

"It is disgusting!" she pronounced tightly. "Boys always get a pass."

"Totally," Cecilia agreed. She crooked her fingers on her right hand around to inspect the French manicure on her index finger.

"Not like us," Jaycee blasted out air in pulmonary defiance of all that was ruthlessly chauvinistic in the world. "Like, when I told you I'd only met one other person here, it was a soccer player who told me she took all honors classes and still worried about staying on the team."

Cecilia's pinky twitched. Yes! It was exactly the subtle sign Jaycee was waiting for. Less benign than rankled, it was nearly undetectable, yet Jaycee pursued the truth with a stealthy enthusiasm.

"She told me she's either practicing or studying," Jaycee watched Cecilia closely. Her mouth had tightened and her face was moving back toward that bitchy scowl she'd first thrown Jaycee's way. She had to bring the thunder, just let the deluge get underway and soak this kid.

"Her name is Eve," Jaycee told her. "Eve Levesque. Do you know her?" Jaycee's calves pulsed, her heels rocked inside the boots that now felt like miniature Easy Bake Ovens. Her body tensed and tightened. Was this hot-to-trot little number crafty enough to outrun her, or was this race heading for a photo-finish conclusion?

People who told lies came in all variations. Some were delicate, protective, believing the truth was too sharp-edged to ever surface in their manicured yard. Someone they loved would suffer so they kept it buried deep into the soil where it eventually rotted into the organic matter that fed the maggots and grubs. It was never spoken of again.

The best investigators look beneath the prettiest flowers, Barton said. He wanted her to burrow. If Cecilia was the exquisite bloom she had to snip off in order to extract the nutrients from the roots, was the hole still too shallow? Had she dug at her enough?

Or, was Cecilia so filled with rage her lies were fueled by a fire that rendered the dirt beneath her barren? Perhaps there were no flowers durable enough to survive in her garden. Her truth too searing to bury, so she carried it with her, on ground level, nipping at her conscience with its closeness. Liars like that were volatile enough to slip, especially when love of another failed to trump love for oneself.

Was she about to come clean? Jaycee willed her to show some points for righteousness over style. Do it, Cecilia! Let's turn this into an allied effort and find Eve before something terrible happens.

And if it already had, help us begin to heal the heartbreak. Jaycee pictured Aunt Marcy, diligently putting in her weekly order for cartons of Marlboros and cans of

Hormel chili at the gas station food market while her gut agitated with anguish.

Help me bring this poor woman some peace.

Jaycee waited. Cecilia's neck veins throbbed. She was either openly confounded or in the process of constructing a misrepresentation. Her proverbial flower bobbed in the wind but did not bend or droop. Jaycee inwardly sighed. She started to see which sort of liar Cecilia would be.

Unfortunately, the youthful seductress was no amateur landscaper. No, she was the fertilizer stoking the toxicity of her own venomous bulbs. She was what Jaycee would label an unproductive witness. If this were an on-camera interview, the video of this exchange would never see the light of day.

And neither would the truth behind the eccentric affiliation she had pursued with Eve. Cecilia was a vault. She stepped around Jaycee and headed toward the red exit sign above the door leading back out to campus.

"Nah," she uttered, employing a new brand of snobbery that was even nastier than before.

"Never heard of her."

CHAPTER ELEVEN

"For a minute, I thought I had her," Jaycee told Van, who was groggy on the phone from just waking. She was describing Cecilia in images, as Van's therapist had instructed. Some of our strongest memories were cemented in pictures, smells, or emotional reactions, so introducing one to induce another helped to reset the connections. If Van allowed his brain to focus on a picture first, it would help support the mental link he made with words. That would, in turn, encourage it to stay put rather than disappear. Slow, steady progress.

Memory restoration is like finding a new path in a crowded mailroom, the occupational therapist had told Jaycee back when Van had first shown signs of damage. *Consider the track each envelope follows to arrive at its final destination. The chutes are open and ready to receive the package, right? In Van's case, the chutes have been misaligned with the mailbox. The delivery is being interrupted.*

Jaycee focused on simplifying the delivery. "She's stunning, Van," she continued. "Picture all those loops and swirls of my cursive writing, the way the g's dip low, and the f's swing back up. You seeing it?" She gently drew imaginary letters with her finger in the air just below her chin.

"Uh hum," Van grunted. He made fun of Jaycee's elementary school-style cursive that was on the verge of being eliminated from the modern youngster's curriculum.

103

No one wanted to teach it anymore, but Jaycee always defaulted to the sweeping elegance of the beautiful script.

"So, she's like the long, arching lines of a letter 'm.'" Jaycee heard him breathing. He was working for it. She waited for him to acknowledge her description.

"Fancy," he finally stated. It was a dry response, not surprising. Van went along with the lesson but at times resented that he had to.

"Exactly," Jaycee replied with a forced lilt. So much of a person's successful recovery was based in patience and positivity. "Think back to when we were kids, how we loved to trace the curves of an 's' or the sharp lines of the letter 't.' Right?" she asked.

"Oh, yes, Jay Jay, we sure did. This conversation brought to you by the letters 's' and 't,'" he said. "We put 'em together and get … *shit.*"

"Don't joke, Van," she chided. "She is like all those pretty letters that fit perfectly into lovely words. Are you seeing it? She reminds me of that girl you shot the Calvin Klein underwear spread with last year." It was a stretch Van would remember anything about that shoot. Jaycee wanted to challenge his memory. Van gave it a few seconds and took a stab.

"Mandy?" he ventured.

Jaycee winced. It still ripped her heart to pieces when Van struggled with the simple facts of his life. Goddamn you, Ben! Her eyes stung but Jaycee was quick to slam the door shut again. Ben wasn't allowed into this conversation.

"Amelia," she corrected. "But really good try."

"Anyway, enough Sesame Street, please. Now that I know she's cute like the letter 's' tell me if she helped you in any way?"

"Only in the slightest," Jaycee told him. "And not because she meant to."

"But you definitely think she knows something," he asked.

"Yes," Jaycee snapped back firmly. She was back in her rental car and filling Van in on what she'd learned so far about her aunt Marcy, her cousin Eve, and her odd and only friend, Cecilia.

"I could absolutely tell she was lying. Eve's roommate told me they were together a lot. So why would Cecilia deny even knowing who Eve was?"

"Makes no sense, Jay Jay," he confirmed wearily. Van was never an early riser, and his injuries had further sapped his morning lucidity.

"No sense," he said again. Van had taken to repeating a phrase. Jaycee didn't know if it was to reinforce his point, or because he had forgotten he'd spoken it once already. She sighed again. First a giant crash and burn with Cecilia, and now a guilty reminder that she'd left Van all alone three thousand miles away. Sometimes Jaycee made decisions based on impulse. Half of the time, that served her well. She would hate to come up empty here in New Hampshire, while her boyfriend struggled with being home alone with a mending head injury.

"Are you eating?" she rotated.

Van laughed on the other end. "More than ever," he told her. "Deb has loaded me up with color-coded Tupperware. I have little post-it notes telling me what meal goes with what day and how to cook it. She'd probably give fewer instructions to Mason."

Jaycee smiled. She and Barton had arranged for the care of Van before she left. Deb would make enough to feed Van for several days, and would drop by with Mason when Barton was at work, depending on how long Jaycee stayed away. She didn't want Van to know that right now— they *did* give the six-year-old fewer instructions to follow.

She felt another tug of guilt. "Are you taking your pills?"

"That depends," he quipped. "You mean the pills the doctors gave me or the little orange ones I just got from the guy down the street?"

"Hysterical, Van," she trilled. "You're slaying me right now."

"I try," he said. "So tell me more about this school."

The school. Holy United Academy. Jaycee considered what she'd seen so far. Aesthetically, it was iconic yet charming. Vintage architecture nestled in between stately mountains to the north, glistening cold lake waters to the east, and the general population of the state kept to the south. It cultivated a religion of its own making, a gimmick based more on a spiritual development of self rather than a holy service to others. Sure, the kids worked. But at their core, students at Holy United were being taught to uphold their own brand once they were set free from captivity.

"It's not a place where I would ever send a child of mine," she began. "There are kids from all over the world, most of them come from wealthy families, but a few of them don't. Like Eve. The campus is pretty but there's a real coldness here, you know? And I don't mean the Alaskan temperatures. It's like, everyone's trying too hard to warm it up from the inside out." She thought of Biff and his over-the-top coziness with the other students. Not with her, though. He surely hadn't brought the heat with her.

"Is there tight security? These kids are pretty young to be so far away from home, right?"

"Yes, they are young but the culture here is very distinct." She tried to figure out a vivid way to describe the practice of "self-nurturing." "Do you remember when we went to the Haight-Ashbury Street Fair last year? Those weird families that floated around with their little kids?"

She could tell Van was searching for the illustrations inside his head. *Remember, Van!* The people dressed in long skirts and loose pants that wandered happily yet aimlessly through the San Francisco neighborhood, artistically drawn to the freedom and openness of the district. There were bright colors, loud noises, and erotic smells. Jaycee and Van had watched tiny children dart away from their parents with nary a whisper of a promise that they'd ever return. The hippie mentality was that they would.

"It's okay," she interrupted his process. "It reminded me of that. The parents we saw let their children wander around even though the streets were packed with strangers. I would worry someone would snatch my kid. They don't give it a second thought."

"So, the school is like a hippie commune?" he asked.

"No," she replied. "Not like hippies. More like …" she searched for a comparison. The students wore uniforms and reeked of money, yet they were growing into connoisseurs of self, allowed to express frustration, sadness, or stress by disappearing into thin air for as long as necessary. It was like a hippie had mated with a yuppie and the offspring was a freakish hybrid of the two extremes.

"…They're more like mini ambassadors of their own territories. And I'm strongly concerned there could be some inappropriate touching going on here and there. I can't say for sure but I've seen girls coming on too strong, and men giving them too much room to grow, if you know what I mean. They're so young and yet they all live together in sweet harmony. It stinks."

Like a sewer.

Van chuckled. "I get it. So none of the sugar daddies or sister wives seem at all worried about your cousin?"

"No," Jaycee shook her head in the car and closed her eyes. She breathed deeply. It was astounding, really. "Not at all. There's no alarm, no alert, no nothing. They think Eve is probably just taking a little break and, *poof*, she'll just come back when she's ready. And, you know what, Van? Maybe she will."

She squeezed the bridge of her nose with irritation. She followed clues for a living, extracting information from sources so dry no one else could tap them. She earned glossy awards and golden statues that pronounced professional accolades celebrating her zealous doggedness in uncovering scandal, deceit, and treachery. She had helped snuff out a nightclub killer! Sure, he'd fled like the coward he was, but the murders in her city had stopped. Jaycee Wilder never failed to stick the landing on her investigative reports, so why was she feeling like her ankles were about to buckle. Yes, she was fast-tracking this junket in case Eve's life depended on it, but the loose ends were wearisome when every moment counted.

Van went quiet, too, as he took everything in. Inexplicably, she felt her throat tighten with emotion. What made her think she had any clue how to find Eve? Why had she left Van? Why didn't anyone try to stop her?

They had tried. She'd resisted their advice and sought out on her own, like she always did. Even though her family had all but abandoned her, she had rushed back to her bloodline without hesitation.

"What's next?" he asked finally.

"Next, I find her soccer coach. Then, I plan to pay a friendly visit to the local police department."

"Good luck with all that, Jay Jay. Be careful. I love you."

She hugged him through the phone. "You too," she said softly and ended the call.

Jaycee unwrapped a stick of Juicy Fruit and chewed hard. As saliva built near her molars she imagined herself by Van's side, on the beach towel, oily with sweat and contentment. Her mouth drew in. She blinked deeper into his face, the groove of Van's chiseled chin, that tiny freckle that gave him a faint pinch of authority. "Pretty soon you'll be eligible for all those poor, grieving father roles," she'd kid. "The suddenly single, ridiculously handsome family men, you know? Nicholas Sparks has been waiting for you, Van, time to take your rightful place inside the minivan, once and for all!" Van would wince. "Minivan?" he'd shirk back in horror. "The only big daddy I want to be is yours," he'd nuzzle into her neck, sprinkling light kisses up into the back of her head.

Big daddy. Jaycee nearly choked on the gum. Van had come through for her again. Sugar daddies and sister wives, he'd wisecracked. Was this campus crawling with them both?

Sugar daddy.

She took a last look at the shiny black lines of fencing holding the occupants of Holy United Academy safely within its wardship. She didn't want to come back unless it was to return Eve. Even then, she had fresh sprouts of doubts this place would do right by her at all.

Jaycee twisted the defrost knob, inviting the superficial exercise to chase away the rush of doubt that was cold like death. She drove in the direction of the new athletic complex still under construction. The facility was described as a top priority in the campus' master plan, a modernization to further enhance the optics.

Was the state-of-the-art compound with all the bells and whistles also holding a coach with his own ideas of what a competitive marketplace really was?

Do sugar daddies play sports?

CHAPTER TWELVE

Schroeder Benedict Field was named after *the* Schroeder Benedict, a graduate of Holy United Academy who had gone on to a storied career in the NFL. His foundation had put up grotesque donations to secure funding for the new stadium, complete with improved seating and WiFi capabilities. It would fully modernize the football experience for … basically … kids still growing into the game.

Jaycee bumped along the yet-to-be paved road. Students entered through the locker rooms in the back. Yellow tape prevented them from walking where stacks of construction materials were covered by black tarps and snow. The extra space gave each coach a private workout area for the teams, upgraded rooms to view game tapes with huge whiteboards and audio visual equipment, and roomy offices that held L-shaped desks and computers. The complex stretched on like The Pentagon, with internal practice fields and social spaces where students could gather before or after events. It was grand and excessive and completely fitting for the future athletes of Holy United Academy. Jaycee suspected not a dime of external borrowing had been necessary in the construction of the new facility. Alumni took care of whatever good ole Schroeder Benedict had missed.

Jaycee hurried to the makeshift entrance that led her to the girl's locker room. It still smelled of fresh concrete and rubber flooring. The lockers were painted a cheery yellow and the wooden benches were shiny with a recent coat of polyurethane. Shower stalls and toilets took up one long wall, while a large whirlpool tub sat in the middle of the tiled floor. Jaycee wandered through the empty locker room and then passed through a set of two doors that took her to a row of dark classrooms. She passed by four windows before she saw a light on inside the fifth. She walked in that direction, paused by a half-open office door, and knocked three times.

"Hello," she called out.

"Hi there," she heard a man's voice in response. "Can I help you?"

Jaycee entered the office. A younger man wearing a Holy United Academy sweatshirt was seated at a desk, his hands paused above the keyboard of the computer.

"Do you know if Coach Whalen is in?" she asked. William Whalen was the girls soccer coach. His office was among several dedicated to each sport's coaches, trainers, and the Athletic Director. Jaycee knew him to be in his mid-fifties, balding, and, from his pictures on the website, a man who rarely smiled. He screamed serious.

"If he is, he's probably watching tape." The man went back to typing. "It's all he does." She noticed the snarky sarcasm. Jaycee thanked him anyway and wandered back down the hallway. Where the hell do they watch tape? She poked her head into every room she passed. Nothing there, empty over here. She kept moving deeper into the chasmal space until eventually she came across another partially closed door with soft light leaking out. She crept quietly through the opening and stood in the back. A balding head was supported on one hand with the elbow planted on the table holding several open notebooks, a few Sharpies, and two Styrofoam coffee cups. Coach Whalen was entrenched in the video of soccer games from his past. He watched the girls fly around the field in short sleeves and shorts, the trees still held the vibrancy of early fall, and the grass was a well-watered deep green. He stopped the tape occasionally to scribble something in his notebook. No one was around to bother him. He lived in his own world of endless fields aerated by soccer cleats and filled with young, ponytailed female athletes.

Jaycee watched him. At times, he went into full conversation mode yet he was alone. She overheard him mumbling soccer lingo, discussing with himself things like corner kick success ratio, developing left foot shots on net, and switching up the formation of his defense. She felt his passion but suspected he could have a narrow view of his team. Did he know his players as people? As young women?

"Knock knock," she tapped cordially on the door. "Coach Whalen?"

"Yes," he answered, hitting the pause button on his remote control. He squinted in the dark. Jaycee stepped into the room and waved at him.

"I was hoping I could have a moment of your time."

"Sure," he said. "Just doing what I always do," he laughed. "I could use a break." He was friendlier than she'd expected. Maybe she was wrong about his coaching depth.

"My name is Lexy, I'm a transfer student," she started. Again, lying wasn't her favorite way to glean information but she had no choice. "I wanted to ask you about trying out for next season." It seemed the most sensible way to shake him down. Stay right there in his lane.

Coach Whalen lowered his gaze. He had his finger on the pulse of every potential soccer player who came through Holy United long before they even filed their admission papers. He'd recruited most of them himself, although he couldn't officially call it that. More like, recommended, or encouraged. He had to follow the rules, but had learned how to bend them to stack his roster. This girl was certainly lovely and looked strong, but the best players didn't just drop out of the sky.

"Really," he began. "I usually have the chance to meet with soccer players before they arrive here at our school."

Use that, she told herself. Make that work. Jaycee nodded like she'd known that all along.

"Sure, it's been a complicated process," she explained. "I think my paperwork got hung up."

Was he buying it? He placed his pen aside one of his notebooks and folded his fingers together. He smiled at her so Jaycee took that as a sign that he would at least hear her out.

"I've heard from some of the girls that winter workouts are underway."

"They are," Coach Whalen confirmed. "Mandatory weight training and conditioning sessions run through winter break, then we try to get out onto the field as early as March, weather permitting. Some years we've had to wait until May for all the snow to clear."

"That's also what I've heard," she said enthusiastically. "I've been talking to Eve Levesque; she's been filling me in on how the off-season works."

She watched him closely. You know, Coach, *that* Eve Levesque. Your exceptional student athlete whose current whereabouts are unknown. *Tell me*, she willed him. Tell me what you know. She waited for a sign that Coach Whalen was about to shut down as Cecilia had. Was he aware of Eve's absence? Worse, was he in on it? Did he dwell in the sewer? Was he glued to his videos for all the wrong reasons? He gave a cursory bow through the neck that was impossible to read.

"Eve," he spoke her name on vibrato. "Highly skilled young player." He reached for his pen again. He tapped the plunger at the tip several times. It made that spastic sound that drove so many people batty. "I'm sure Eve was honest about my expectations then."

Hmmm. Jaycee squinted. What did he mean? Expectations on the field? Or was that code for expectations of a different kind. Were they still talking about soccer?

"Oh, she was honest all right." Jaycee played it right down the middle. She'd passed the ball straight back.

"It's not a program designed for the casual player," he told her, still maddeningly imprecise. Again, was this about his soccer program?

"I'm very serious about what I do," she replied with a stony tilt of her chin.

"Okay then," he said firmly. The bald section of his head reflected the still video frame on the wall behind him. A cleated foot balanced in the air in a perfect arc right near his temple.

"I'd recommend you spend some time with Eve off the field. Pick up a feel for how the athletes approach their schedules."

Jaycee noted the opportunity. She struck. "I have been, Coach. Until recently. I can't find her."

Tap, tap, tap. The pen tapped out again in an aggravating rhythm. If he was suddenly uptight with worry, that was the only reaction he mobilized.

Tap, tap, tap.

"Like, she's not here. She's kinda, like, gone," Jaycee laced in the fashionable teenaged stutter words. "Do you think she may have taken some time off to 'self—'"

Coach Whalen pushed back his chair. One by one, he closed his notebooks and stacked them into a small pile. He put the pen into a shirt pocket and stood up. He walked by Jaycee and over to the light panel on the wall. He flicked the switch and lit the room.

"Most … ridiculous … I've … heard," he griped to himself under his breath.

Jaycee watched him. His muscular back had tensed, he carried his head too high, like a rooster that had just sensed the presence of a stalking predator. His entire body seemed to be resisting the introspective Holy United Academy approach to handling stress. He was the personification of an old-school coach. Jaycee had known a few of them herself. The win, work, and zip your mouth playbook.

"I know," she started. *Go ahead, Coach, tell me more*, she thought. This is a safe place to let the hate out. "I don't really understand why it's okay to just leave. We're just kids. It's kind of weird. Did you know Eve hasn't been around?" She threw it out there, just to see what stuck.

"Nope," he stormed. "And that's the funny thing. They don't have to tell us, not until they come back all enlightened like *dude*, life is good." He shook his head in pure bitter exasperation. "This is what happens when a group of overpaid …" he abruptly stopped himself. He knew better than to let his anger control his words. He straightened himself again but Jaycee could see the sinewy muscles along his forearm flex and strain.

"Talk to Eve," he told her finally. "Whenever the hell she comes back from wherever the hell she had to go." Coach Whalen looked almost hurt. Was it disappointment that his toughest player may have succumbed to what he considered just another weak-minded practice of her generation? Like Ramona, it seemed clear Coach Whalen hadn't considered Eve the type of kid who would take a day off for any reason. Was that it?

Jaycee could tell that Coach Whalen lived in a box with four walls. It probably had served him well. He maximized a player's potential by running drills and perfecting technique, *certainly not* by talking about feelings and self-discovery. Hard work delivered good results. He angrily defied the philosophies that called for him to expand his box, open his mind, and visualize a new path. What the fuck for? His own path had been leading to state championships, college scholarships for his athletes, and trophies for the glassed shelves in the lobby—how was that wrong? All this searching for knowledge and acceptance bullshit had even his toughest athletes believing they could just step away and go meditate on top of a mountain.

It pissed him off and he had a difficult time walking the line.

"You'll figure it out soon enough, Lexy," he told her sharply. "Good luck."

With that, Coach Whalen strode past her and down the hall.

"What the …" she mumbled, trying not to scream for him to come back. Jaycee watched his back until it disappeared.

Coach Whalen had gone from friendly enough to riled up. Mad, even. But if he knew any more about where Eve was, he certainly wasn't going to talk about it. He had a job to keep.

He'd wished her good luck. What the hell did he mean by that? Good luck finding Eve? Or, good luck trying to make his soccer team? He'd had the final word. Like Cecilia. He'd said just enough to manifest the notion of a conspiracy and then left her hanging.

Jaycee wasn't sure where, if at all, Coach Whalen fit into her mental puzzle. He may be angry with Eve, but would he harm her? Or would he lie about where she was? She just wasn't sure.

Jaycee blew out her cheeks in annoyance. She scurried back to her rental car and put the resplendent Schroeder Benedict Field and the frenetic soccer coach in her rearview mirror.

CHAPTER THIRTEEN

The road and Jaycee's mood were marred by ribbons of ice. She was white-knuckled, her winter driving skills had long expired, and her fingers wrapped around the steering wheel as if they held the power to keep the four tires connected to the compromised pavement. These were the streets and avenues of her childhood and yet she felt like she didn't belong there. She was just a stranger passing through.

Her reporter tricks were freeze-dried and useless here. Holy United Academy was throwing up a force field that was keeping her locked out. First by Cecilia, then Biff, and now the coach who should've dropped that irritating pen and everything else to help her find his superstar striker.

Jaycee kept the radio low, her thoughts spinning as she made her way from plowed interstate tar to rimy country lane left to melt mostly on its own. It was early afternoon and tiny wisps of white had begun to swirl around her windshield wipers. Her shoulders rose up near her ears to absorb the chill racing through her skin beneath the thick cable knit sweater. The uniform had been exchanged for her usual civilian garb, but the jeans wrapped around her thighs felt stiff and unforgiving.

When was the last time she'd seen snow fall? Before she'd been able to buy alcohol legally.

Jaycee never climbed the trees of her childhood for very long. She sometimes looked up at their foliage, but preferred not to search for things buried in the growth. She

121

stayed rooted in her present, opting to apply all her energy to the relationships she could control, rather than the ones that had already collapsed. Her early life in New Hampshire was a collection of events, nothing more. The gentle hush of snowflakes was merely what happened when meteorological conditions collided, and certainly not an invitation to go marching through the cobwebbed attic of her heart to stir what was better off staying numb. She had raced here without a single consideration of how she might *feel* once she'd stopped to look around a little. To remember where she had come from. And from whom.

That one time her dad had helped her roll a snowman to life.

Stop it!

That other time her mom had zipped them both into her Snoopy sleeping bag, spread out in front of the wood stove because a ferocious nor'easter had clipped the transformer down the road. They'd lost power for ten days. Jaycee had loved every minute of it. Both her parents had been forced to stay inside. With her. Something neither of them would have chosen to do without Mother Nature's intervention.

Okay now, seriously, knock it off.

You couldn't pick your family. No one could control how the universe saw fit to divvy up the pollinators and their resulting lineage. You got what you got and you either became just like them, or you broke the shitty, malformed mold they threw you in. Jaycee had gotten out, but was part of her still here? Was that why she had dropped everything, including the boyfriend who needed her, and raced back?

Maybe she should have been a better cousin to little Evie. She should have known where she went to school, who was coaching her, how many goals she'd scored. When she cut ties and scrambled off to college, far, far away, and then bounced around from one TV market to the next chasing her dreams and a larger audience, perhaps she should have checked on the branches of her snow-covered family tree. Was the smallest one drooping under the weight? Was it really her responsibility to care?

Well, she cared now. Late, sure, but better than never. When all of this was over, and if she had the chance to, Jaycee would tell this young girl that she wasn't all alone in this big, scary world.

Not anymore.

Her right boot pumped the brake as she approached a dark maroon building with a square sign above its front door. She had completed the series of turns and straightaways Google Maps had instructed her to. Her destination was ahead.

Police Department was spelled out in large block lettering, with one "t" tipped awkwardly sideways.

Jaycee pulled into the empty front parking lot. She scanned the side lot, noticing two cruisers parked side by side near a large rectangular trash bin encased by a chain link fence. Bitterly cold air stole her breath as she left the warm front seat of the car and hustled toward the glass door marked Entrance. She stepped onto a salty black mat that promptly got stuck beneath the door. Jaycee gave it a kick to shake it free, discharging granules of ice melt from their resting place. They scattered across a dingy tile floor. A metallic-sounding male voice shot through air grates in the window separating the receiving area from the work space.

"Help you?" the voice wanted to know.

Jaycee craned her neck to see into the room. "Hi," she began, as her eyes scanned the compact space. Four computer stations, with papers strewn across keyboards, and bulletin boards loaded with mugshot pictures, announcements, and official police notifications that included several papers with bold black lettering at the top stating: FBI Notice.

The face behind the voice wasn't friendly or rude, just matter-of-fact and efficient. The officer had streaks of gray dispersed through longish russet-colored hair. A few feathery wisps covered the thin gold lines that hooked his reading glasses across each ear. They appeared to float on his face.

"I'm hoping you can help me with some information about my cousin," Jaycee began. She couldn't lie to police. Barton had warned her not to perjure herself to law enforcement.

"The fucking liars," he'd told her. "Drive us nuts, 'scuse my language. No one will talk to you if they think you're a fucking liar. I know I wouldn't."

So Jaycee was going with the truth. She hoped they would, too.

"She's a student at Holy United Academy," she continued. "May I speak with a detective, please?"

"Are you reporting an emergency?" he inquired dryly. His chin fell into his neck as he looked over the rounded edges of the glasses. He gawked his way down the entire length of her as she cocked her head sideways. Jaycee threw him an elongated smile that was neither cheery nor authentic. More of a *yeah-I-just-caught-you-looking-at-me* sort of acknowledgment.

Eyes up here, asshole.

"Well, I'm not sure. Maybe."

A door clanked behind him. Airy bursts of high-pitched whistling filled the small room, the unmistakable yet wildly distorted chorus of the folksy summer drinking tune "American Pie."

Drove my Chevy to the levee but the levee was dry.

The whistling stopped but the presence was noted. Both the officer behind the glass and Jaycee felt it.

"Got you Dunks, Stan," the growly voice shot through the foyer like a gunshot. When Stan didn't immediately gush out a thank you, the voice roared again.

"Stan!"

"Yeah, Chief, I got you. Just workin' out here."

Jaycee imagined the chief was big and broad, with burly arms aside bulging buttons on a shirt that was years past its ability to restrain his advancing girth. She narrowed her eyes. Where are you? Come on, show yourself.

Chief George Solomon rolled around the corner as if on cue. His feet pointed out diagonally in a lifelong attempt to lead him in two different directions. By default, he walked like his stomach was in charge. Jaycee watched him waddle toward Stan with an extra-large white Styrofoam cup festooned with dark red snowflakes. A jolly leftover from the holiday season.

The chief grumbled a greeting and handed off the coffee. Jaycee got a strong whiff of hazelnut. She imagined the Dunkin Donuts employee down the road knew the order by heart and greeted the chief like the homespun hero she thought him to be. "You tell Stan I said hello, now," she'd tell him as she bid him farewell until the next morning. It was a routine built upon physical closeness and mutual habit. The polar opposite of Los Angeles, where elaborate recipes had reduced the clerk-customer relationship to names scribbled on paper cups. In L.A., no one got to know each other because it didn't matter. Back here, coffee was sharp and simple, and orders were memorized and then made with care.

Suddenly, he seemed to notice they weren't alone. His beady eyes followed the same route Stan's had just completed before he swallowed a cough and asked if everything was okay.

"Sure, Chief," Stan confirmed. Chief Solomon would only delegate to his staff once he was fully apprised of what was going on. While he knew Stan was totally okay, this was his way of inserting himself into the situation. Jaycee wasn't about to let herself be dismissed. It was lucky she had happened upon the head of the department. No better place to start than at the top.

"Chief?" she leaned into the glass. "May I have a word, please?"

He and Stan exchanged a glance. He took a loud sip from his own extra-large container and motioned with his head. Stan recognized that as permission for the visitor to enter the belly of their department. He pushed a button beneath the counter holding his phone, computer, and coffee, and a door built into the wall buzzed open.

Jaycee moved swiftly through the entrance. The room smelled of Lysol, Old Spice, and ancient wood.

"Chief Solomon," he informed her, thrusting one giant paw toward her hips. Jaycee met his grip and introduced herself.

"What can I help you with, Ms. Wilder," he continued.

"Please call me Jaycee," she corrected him. She wanted him to relate to her on a more personal level. She always went by her first name whenever possible.

"All right. Jaycee."

"Well, Chief, I'm not certain if you took a call recently from a woman who was concerned about her daughter."

Jaycee was careful in her presentation. Barton's spiders were climbing around her head. Did any of them live here?

"You'd have to be more specific. We take calls all the time from parents worried about kids. Especially now given the heroin epidemic we're caught up in around here. Is this woman in need of information about treatment? We have quite a few resources now that the state is finally stepping in with some ..."

"Actually," she cut him off. "This isn't about drugs. The woman was my aunt and she's been worried about her daughter. She hasn't heard from her and doesn't know where she is."

"Oh, I see," Chief Solomon tilted his face. He wandered around a desk toward the keyboard of a computer. "Is this a parental custody situation?" His chunky fingers waited to transport information into the network.

"Not exactly," Jaycee explained. She had already decided she wouldn't come in guns blazing about them not returning her phone call, or dismissing her aunt's concerns. She'd handle this more delicately. Jaycee wasn't sure yet if the department, or its occupants, were inclined to sniff around a private school that might be heartily contributing to its police fund.

"My aunt called because her daughter hasn't been seen for a few days," she nursed the story slowly.

"How old is the child?" he asked.

"She's a minor, a teenager," Jaycee said. "Barely sixteen. Both parents have custody, it's not a family crisis type of situation."

Chief Solomon nodded and tapped away at his keyboard. "Okay," he prompted.

Jaycee had little room to dance so she had to get to it.

"Her name is Eve Levesque. She's a student at Holy United Academy," she stated, feeling her spine tingle as she watched for a response. Just like Cecilia's pinky finger, a small furrow appeared on Chief Solomon's generous

128

forehead. His hands retracted as he leaned back into the cracked leather of his high-backed chair. He glanced at her with a prudency he hadn't yet had to utilize.

"In my experience, Holy United doesn't just *lose* its students." It was almost a defensive response. Jaycee didn't want to incite him. Not yet.

"Of course," she began. "But she's still not where she should be."

Chief Solomon rubbed his eyes. "Have you talked to Biff?"

Ah, good old Biff was on a first-name basis with the Chief of Police. Great. Of course, he was.

"I have," she confirmed, even though it was purely one-sided, she thought. Biff had no idea the conversation he'd had with her on campus was anything more than a student-headmaster interaction. "But I wanted your help on this." She blinked rapidly.

This would be about the time Jaycee plied a disinclined witness with a slinky smile or a smooth line about how an interview would make her story *pop!* Persistence was so much more effective when the pain-in-the-ass was good-looking. How far could she push George?

"Honestly, Chief ..." she continued, pausing to encourage a flush to spread across her cheeks, and her eyes to moisten. Van had taught her how to fake cry on cue. She didn't go all the way to full sob but her fragile-girl vulnerability was on point. "I just don't trust them. They're teachers ..." she sniffed gently, "...not highly trained law enforcement professionals. Like you."

George Solomon had been married for nearly four decades, two of them happily. His wife granted him the occasional conjugal visit but he'd stopped looking for more long ago. At his age, a warm body next to him at night was all he needed. And yet, the heat radiating off this golden-hued outlander in tight jeans and a molded sweater was scorching him in all the wrong places. He felt off-balance as his blood flowed along a searing trail to his groin. He was grateful he'd remembered to take his heart meds this morning. On the days when he wanted to feel like a much younger man, he purposely forgot about the prescription bottle tucked behind the glass tumblers in the kitchen cabinet.

"When was the last time she was seen?" he asked, not recognizing his own voice.

"Last week," Jaycee supplied. "It's been several days since my aunt has been able to reach her."

"Does she have a history of running away?"

"No, never."

"Boyfriend?"

"Not that we know of."

"Is there a family property she may have gone to? Another home? Older step siblings or parents?"

"No, and no."

They were the questions Jaycee would ask herself, not overly probing and certainly nothing groundbreaking. The chief ran through a few more standard inquiries and then circled back to Holy United.

"This doesn't sound like an Amber Alert situation, she's not in imminent danger from a family member, and as far as you can tell, hasn't been abducted." He was watching her hands, her legs, waiting for movement elsewhere in her body. Jaycee could sense he was imagining what she'd taste like with some steak sauce.

"I can't say that for sure," Jaycee reminded him. "It's suspicious enough that her family (well, just her mother) is concerned. They're also lifelong New Hampshire residents." She was hoping to inspire him to have a "take care of our own" reaction to that, but his face didn't change. His expression remained flat. She preferred not to mention Ramona at all, she was just a minor and Jaycee didn't like the idea of bringing any attention upon her until she absolutely had to.

"But the school isn't," he started icily, flat out ignoring a neighbor's crisis. *So much for that angle.* "Isn't suspicious, I mean." he repeated. Again, it was a quizzically defiant statement.

"I don't think they're acting in her best interest," she told him carefully.

"What makes you say that?" he pushed.

"Because there's no sense of urgency. She's just a kid, Chief." Jaycee blinked, her lashes sloshing through fresh moisture. "Please."

He sighed heavily and dragged his eyes off her. He loudly took a quick slog of his coffee. Jaycee held her breath like she had just before Cecilia had revealed herself to be a deceitful wretch. Would this grown man in a position of power and authority do the right thing and help her find Eve?

Remember the spiders, Jaycee, Barton had said. Mean little spiders in small towns. Do they feed from the same web?

He's wrong, she thought. Barton is wrong here. Chief George Solomon will rise from the chair with permanently embedded imprints of his swollen ass, and move swiftly to find a girl who should be in biology class at this very moment. He would become Jaycee's east coast Barton, a mighty warrior and stealthy partner in the pursuit of all that was just and right.

She waited. He sat. Seconds ticked by.

"Here's what I can do," he said finally. Jaycee jumped to attention.

"Oh, thank you!" she told him with relief. Finally, she'd have some real assistance. Maybe they were just hours from bringing Eve home!

He turned back to the keyboard and began typing. "I can enter her name into the NCIC, see what it kicks back. Now, it could take some time to process and I can never guarantee the right department in the right location is looking at the right time … but … at least it's a start."

Jaycee grimaced. Her lips twitched as anger slid dangerously close to rage. What the fuck? He was blowing her off, too!

"That's not a start!" she sneered. "That's an end and you know it."

"Excuse me?" he was rapidly rankled. It was a disgraceful about-face. She stepped backwards.

"That will take days, maybe weeks, for God's sake! A teenager is missing and this is the best you can do?"

Chief Solomon circled around to the front of the desk. He squared his chunky backside against its flat back.

"I don't know you, Jaycee," he declared with a salty indignation. "You come in here all demanding of my time and assistance, and I think I may have a crazy woman on my hands. Happens all the time." His eyes were watery and tight, they shot arrows at her like hot coals kicked up from a campfire.

Jaycee folded her arms across her chest. She glared at him right back.

"Here's what I *do* know," he continued, loudly clearing his coffee phlegm throat. "I know that my town here hasn't had a person, let alone a teenager, go missing in over a hundred years." He was starting to sweat. It was an atrocious overreaction.

"Doesn't mean it can't happen, Chief," she said hotly. "The world is much different than it was, say, a hundred years ago."

You ass, she bit back.

He ignored her entirely. "Thing is … I also know the fine folks at Holy United Academy care deeply about the safety and well-being of their students. In my experience, anyone who suggests otherwise might be suffering from some type of delusion."

Oh, great, she thought. Now, he's back on the PR team. Jaycee was alone again. There was no database she could access, no team-building with the local cops, and zero chance new information about Eve would be shared with anyone but useless George. Well, maybe Stan. Together they would clink their Dunks cups and laugh at the naïve out-of-towner who had dared impugn the integrity of the mighty Academy.

Stupid girl, they'd gloat. Everybody knows no one goes missing from Holy United. Just like Biff had told her, no one ever leaves. They always come home.

She had to get out of there. Jaycee knew when it was time to cut her losses and move on. She grunted on the realization that yet again, Barton, in his jaded yet excruciatingly intuitive way, had nailed it.

Well-fed spiders became greedy. They always stuck around for their next meal. Not entirely conclusive, but his theory was holding more water than it was leaking away.

"Thank you for your time, Chief," she said curtly. He nodded to confirm their meeting was ending and swept a glance toward the door she had entered through. Jaycee was being dismissed. She just knew he'd watch her ass as she walked away.

Stan refused to even look at her as she swept back through the door and into the foyer. He sat behind his glass, intently focused on something that required him to look down. Jaycee stopped and breathed in and out through her nose, building a time pad. Let him have a moment to consider doing the right thing. She never gave up on a potential source until she was absolutely certain it was officially closed for business.

First Cecilia. *Closed.*

Then Chief George. *Closed.*

Maybe Stan would surprise her.

One … two … three.

She held her feet still. The lobby was silent.

"Everything okay out there, Stan?" The question was hurled at him like it was wrapped in fire.

"Just fine, Chief," he replied calmly. "She's gone." Stan looked up from his immensely important work. They locked eyes and she knew he'd just shut down, too.

Stan. *Closed.*

Jaycee groaned quietly in her throat. This was ending just as it had begun.

Sure, everything was okay, if okay had suddenly become code for something else.

Bullshit. She could smell it like she was standing in it.

There was no code that could cover the stench of that.

CHAPTER FOURTEEN

Jaycee's hot foot punched the accelerator as she fishtailed out of the department parking lot. Back on the main road, she had no idea what to do next. She tried to put a call into Barton but it wouldn't go through. She decided against informing Marcy of the unproductive nature of her day thus far, and besides, the poor woman had told her she couldn't accept personal calls during her shift anyway. Ramona had promised to text or call if Eve suddenly reappeared at school. Her phone revealed no texts, no calls, and no good news.

She headed west only because it was in the direction of her hotel. Her neck hurt. The coarse scar was irritated by being wrapped up in scarves and winter gear. Her stomach turned. It was protesting her failure to coat it with high octane coffee and regular sugar breaks. She usually carried at least three miniature Twix bars at all times. Her body was used to the grueling pace she set chasing her stories every day, but this was a deeper lethargy. Her limbs felt heavy and her heart was taxed by this emotional burden. They were the physical sensations of failure.

She twisted the volume dial. A Mount Washington Valley Top Hits radio station was the only option besides static. In zippy fashion, Taylor Swift shook it off, over and over again.

Jaycee didn't hear the siren until it sounded like she had swallowed it.

"Jesus Christ," she said to herself, shaky from the noise. The cruiser was so close behind her she could make out the facial features of the young uniformed officer behind the wheel. She squinted. The driver was slim; she could tell just from the rearview mirror that it wasn't Chief George. Too young to be Stan. No, this was someone new altogether. And he wanted her off the road immediately.

Jaycee slowed and turned onto the shoulder, which was difficult given the substantial space filled by super-sized snowbanks. She remembered those. They were so thick and fortified from the inside out, many of them remained stubbornly in place long after the first spring crocus had sprung free from the earth. She held the wheel firmly as she tried to maneuver her car off the road into minimal space, the cruiser on her rear bumper.

The officer was, in fact, young. So youthful Jaycee noticed his chin sported downy hairs instead of whiskers. He walked briskly to her window and knocked twice.

"Roll it down," he told her firmly.

She did as he instructed and was promptly shushed when she tried to speak.

"Follow me," he said looking left, and then right. "There's something I need to tell you." It was cryptic and weird but Jaycee had received some of her biggest news tips in similarly irregular ways. She nodded and he jogged back to his cruiser, pulled around her car, and took the lead on the road. About two miles later he signaled he was taking a right. Jaycee followed onto a thin rock driveway that had been plowed down to dirt. It wove around an enormous boulder and then widened into a yard that held a child's red and orange plastic playhouse, a rusted Monte Carlo stripped of all four tires, and a double-wide trailer with a puke-green washer and dryer on its front porch. The shitty dwelling had once been yellow, but currently it was bathed in the motley hue of graffiti.

She swallowed hard. Giant trees cast shadows on the perimeter. It was isolated and eerily empty. She wondered why anyone had bothered to plow a path. If someone lived here, well, that was a story unto itself. Jaycee had a spooky feeling that if this went sideways, no one would hear her scream.

Reluctantly she parked next to his cruiser and waited for him to instruct her further.

He got out and again had her roll down the window. A broad spectrum of freckles disrupted the youthful slope of his nose. His hair was a dusky ginger. A pronounced Adam's apple bobbed in his skinny neck. Jaycee estimated he was probably in his early twenties.

"I have, like, two minutes," he started. "So listen carefully."

Jaycee nodded. She pointed at the broken-down hovel.

"It's abandoned. No one's here."

"Okay," she said. Winter air poured through her open window but the dainty flakes of white had dried up. Stripes of sunlight broke through a low overcast. The young officer's eyes blinked. They were a bold green. Jaycee assumed they had yet to behold the true horror of a grisly crime scene. She hoped they stayed that way.

"I overheard your conversation with the chief," he began. Jaycee shirked back in surprise. She knew for sure he wasn't present when that had gone down.

"Trust me, I was there. There's a back door where we park our personal vehicles," he explained. "It's down a hallway. I heard talking. I stayed out of sight."

"Oh," she replied, thinking at least he didn't seem to hold the same animosity toward her the others had. At least not yet. She wisely remained quiet and let him do most of the talking. Her pointer fingers tapped her thighs in anxious anticipation.

"There's more to it," he went on. "There's always more to it when it involves Holy United Academy."

Jaycee's heart punched out a hammered beat against her ribs. She could feel it pulsing blood straight through to her temples. She was right! The murky undercurrent she'd felt was real. She nodded at the officer, prompting him to continue. He gnawed on a fingertip, clearly wired and fidgety about betraying the confidence of his brotherhood. He was still innocent enough to feel compelled to do the right thing. Thank Christ for that.

Jaycee wasn't much older but felt motherly as she coaxed him to reveal more. "It's okay," she prompted. "I will never reveal you as a source," she generously supplied. Depending on what he told her, she may have no choice. Especially if Eve was in serious trouble here.

He reasoned that and determined he trusted her enough. "I have a feeling Chief Solomon looks the other way from time to time. Not on regular stuff like break-ins, or robberies around town. But anything involving that friggin' school is untouchable."

"He's being bought off," she advanced tentatively.

The callow face was saddened. He hated the entanglement of knowing more than he should. It violated his duty to the people of his hometown. He'd wanted them to feel safe in knowing he was there protecting them, but the chief was failing a kid and it wore on him like a painful blister on his heel, jammed against the back of new sneakers.

"I can't say for sure," he cautioned. "But I was the officer who spoke on the phone to a woman about her daughter. I remember her name, Eve. I nearly pissed— *ugh—sorry*, peed myself when you said you were concerned about a missing girl named Eve. That was an intense phone call. The first one I've ever done regarding a potentially missing kid." The Adam's apple rose and fell as he took a gulp of air and ingested it. He was still professionally tactless enough to be honest, and it tugged at Jaycee to see him bared wide open. Life experience would harden him one day, but for now, it was a gift she would eagerly unwrap.

"I can imagine it was. Eve's mom needs to know she's okay. I need to know she's okay."

He nodded briskly. "I took the call straight to the chief. At first he was equally concerned. I thought I had my very first big case …" he trailed off wistfully.

"But," she turned toward him, her shoulder twisted and then rested atop the steering wheel.

"Yeah, but," he answered. "He showed me how to enter the information into the computer and was really complimentary of the interview I'd conducted with the mother. He told me I had asked all the right questions."

"So what changed?" she nudged.

He looked away. He seemed to be debating his next move. Disclose potentially critical information involving the safety and well-being of a teenager, or expose his one-time mentor as the selfish, soulless prick he really was.

His eyes found hers. "Sorry, this is … it's just … starting to get real."

"She *is* real," Jaycee told him firmly, but her voice fell to a whisper. "She's a real girl with a real life. If something has happened to her, we need to find out."

Please, please, please. Jaycee pleaded with him as his face darkened into a shade resembling mottled blood. Poor kid was in the midst of a moral crisis and unsure he could still preserve the righteousness of the only job he'd ever dreamt of holding. Her throat itched with empathy. Yes, she desperately needed his information, but Jaycee also wanted this once altruistic and enthusiastic crime fighter to realize his honor would remain intact. Yes, you can make a difference, young man, she wanted to blurt out. But this is the only way to do it.

He jerked his chin upward, as his lips came together in tight alertness. It was as if his internal drill sergeant had just told him to snap to it.

Come on, soldier!

"There are rumors," he started. Jaycee's head reeled. The most despicable rumors always began with a shred of truth.

"About what?"

"About young girls."

"Holy United girls?" Here we go …

He nodded. "Young girls and older men."

Bam! And there it was. Every nerve in her body that had been dulled by setbacks snapped alert. Jaycee's mouth fell open on its own. She began to move the pieces of her puzzle once again. While Holy United Academy stayed in the middle, she placed horny older men in a line just outside of the border.

"Tell me." She folded her jumpy hands back into her lap. "Tell me how it works."

"That I'm not entirely sure of," he said, frowning. "But the rumor is that it's some long-standing tradition. There's money involved. A lot of money. The men are important and really stinkin' rich. I've heard that girls are hand-selected to … *ummm* …" he searched for the right word. "… to participate."

He gripped the warped rubber edging of her lowered window. He scuffed his right boot back and forth in the snowy, rocky ground. Pebbles jounced in tinny succession as they rebounded off the tires.

Jaycee watched him fumble with the red-hot secret he cursed himself for knowing. The weightless twine of a spider's web wrapped around her. How wide did it go? She remained quiet as he worked out the pressure building up within him.

"I can't say for sure that Eve is involved in all of this. I can't even say if I believe it. All I can tell you is what I've heard and how he acted."

"The chief?"

"Yeah," he nodded. "As soon as I told him Eve was a student at Holy United he shut me down. Hard." The young officer shook his head, remembering the strange dissolution of what should have been an important investigation. "He told me he had contacts at the school and he'd take it from there."

"His exact words?" she asked.

"More or less," he confirmed. "I tried to get more but he was done. Like, all done talking about Eve, and Holy United. He asked for the woman's name and number and told me he'd follow up with her. I can't really defy his instructions on this. You know? He's the chief."

She nodded. "So, basically he was shutting you out of whatever happened next."

"Well, that's the thing," he continued. "It was almost like he knew nothing would happen next."

He was vacillating between being royally pissed off and genuinely stumped. He really couldn't say for sure that Eve was in trouble. But he couldn't rule it out either.

"I have to believe that if the chief honest-to-God knew a teenage girl was in serious trouble, he'd help. Not just because he'd taken an oath to, but because he felt compelled to … as a man."

"You feel that way because you can't imagine doing something like that yourself, and that's admirable," Jaycee told him. "But we can't risk it. You see that, right?"

The green eyes constricted with reflection. Clouds built in the sky above them, pulsing channels of shadows onto his uniform. His badge, poking out from behind the zipped panels of his overcoat, glistened.

"If I had to guess, I'd say he knows where Eve is. And that she's probably going to come back. Eventually."

No one ever leaves Holy United Academy. Biff gave her the same premonition. They always come home. Eventually.

Jaycee's sixth sense was cooking up a much different scene. Even if her exceptionally brilliant, fireball of a cousin had somehow gotten herself mixed up in the dark world of men and money, she may need help finding her way out.

"What's your name?" She veered off. She had to elicit one more feverous clue, that final breadcrumb that would lead her to the next leg of this outlandish expedition. She wanted him to know he was important to her. She cared about the simplest thing in the world: who he was. "That's only for me to know. No one else."

I will never divulge my source, she told him silently. "I promise."

He peered down at her. His face looked suddenly older than it was. Worn out already.

"John Wheeler," he told her softly.

"Okay, Officer Wheeler," she started. "I'm going to ask you for a favor now."

He nodded.

"Tell me everything else you know, or have heard. I need a name, or a place. And, I need it right now."

They locked eyes.

"I have never heard any names," he told her softly, but Jaycee knew there was more and he was being honest.

"But ..." she coaxed.

"But, I have heard of a place."

"A place where they go?"

"Yup," he confirmed gruffly.

"Here? In New Hampshire?"

He nodded. Officer Wheeler told her of an old hunting lodge enfolded into the upper wilderness of the northern reaches of the state.

"That's all I know, I swear."

Jaycee believed him.

"... and Jaycee ..." he told her evenly. "If you get into trouble, I'm not sure ... *ummm* ..."

Jaycee put her hand over his left. She understood. She was on her own from here on out.

"It's okay," she said meaningfully.

He looked behind him and lifted his hands from her car. The connection was broken.

"Wait about a minute after I pull out. Then get on your way. Good luck," he trailed off. His narrow back swiveled and he trotted over to his cruiser. He never looked back.

CHAPTER FIFTEEN

New Hampshire shared a border with Canada that stretched for miles. Jaycee, and a hastily thrown together pack of liquor-fueled cohorts, had once had the dim idea to stuff their gym bags full of extra beer and drive to Montreal for the night. It sounded spontaneous and fun at the time, but they ended up sleeping on the side of the road when they realized the Canadian border crossing facility shut down at midnight. By breakfast time the next morning, they all had a vicious hangover and a sense of relief that a uniformed port of entry officer was spared the delight of throwing their underaged asses into the clink.

She remembered that drive so many years ago. It was similar to the trek she was taking once again. The conditions, the same. Long, lonely road, intermittent radio stations, and weak, undependable cell service. The clouds hung low in wispy, ghost-like tangles of air as Jaycee accelerated onto the highway that climbed along the ridge of the White Mountains. The blacktop echoed a peaceful hum through the cabin of the car, as if content to be free of the potholes and sandy craters marring the winding avenues she'd been traveling upon. The views around her were stunning, an ascending tree-lined winter wonderland taken straight from inside a Christmas tree ornament and brought to life. New Hampshire's grandeur was iconic and celebrated, but its frozen gorges and rocky mountainside gallows sure could make a person feel mighty small.

Jaycee appreciated the rugged grace of where she'd grown up, but it left her cold and empty. It would never feel like home. Too much choppy water had run beneath the bridge of her childhood; its relentless waves had worn away the footing until it became impossible to pass. Jaycee longed for beach sand, blazing sunshine, and the hurried cadence of her fulfilling work life. She wanted to leave home, in order to get home.

She never apologized for being complicated; it was often the personality trait that helped her mind open in order to consider all possibilities. Barton worked like that, too. He knew it could be bad so he braced for bad. That way, when good showed up it was a joyful and totally unexpected surprise. Some would call that a blunt and shitty way to live. Jaycee didn't believe she ever had a choice. Her circuitry was more elegant than functional, it had a tendency to lead her in precarious directions, rather than away from them. Truth be told, she wouldn't want it any other way.

It would be getting dark by the time she navigated her way into the region slightly to the west of Pittsburg, New Hampshire. Officer Wheeler had told her to go as far north as she could. *Just keep driving,* he'd said. They referred to it as the Great North Woods, the snowmobiling capital of New England, where people and wildlife lived in reserved appreciation of one another. Residents of these far-removed municipalities stayed in them because they preferred the simple benefits of a common-good existence. No one tugging or forcing, life just happened. Sure, they relied on their communities for the resources they provided—who didn't want someone on the other end of a 9-1-1 call—but they found true peace and purpose in the independence achieved through living in wide open space. If gossip tried to travel out here, it got swallowed up and silenced in the sweeping airflow. Only the darkest and dirtiest of stories survived, and even then, neighbors tucked them away from prying outsiders. People helped when they had to, and listened when a neighbor needed to talk, but otherwise barricaded themselves behind the serenity of homemade patchwork quilts on their beds, clean food on their tables, and wholesome daily itineraries that put a man's hands to soil and his wife's to family.

It was livin' life like the good Lord had intended.

Jaycee flipped her headlights on and radio off. She was fatigued yet propelled to see this through, no matter what it revealed about her cousin and the illustrious boarding school she attended. Either she brought Eve home unscathed, or she instructed her already overburdened aunt to examine her insurance policy to see if it covered mental health evaluations. Eve was going to need one if she had, in fact, entered willingly into some type of kinky, time-honored, members-only sex association.

What the *hell* made people commit the unthinkable? She'd always wondered that whenever she took up space in courtrooms watching justice being delivered to the wronged. Killers, rapists, thieves, con artists, all getting more than their share of television notoriety, their faces and lousy acts leading newscasts while their victims remained silent and anonymous. What made a person inflict pain and suffering just because he could?

Ben had been driven by hurt. An abused, neglected, tortured child had grown into a twisted, injudicious vigilante boldly driven to rid the world of the scourge of smutty women. He sought power over money. That control was the ignition switch on his psychosis. But what happened when the delusion was supported by dueling purposes? The first, using it to seek an unnatural fulfillment, while the second needing the fundamental end result. Was it *then* evil? Unlawful? Who was the victim when both sides took from it what they wanted?

Eve was a child. She wasn't even old enough yet to vote.

Children were victimized every day. Jaycee reported on it too often. A trusted relative, a revered member of a church, even a peer, could warp a relationship in the most shocking of ways. Babies, even, stripped of their virtue before they even knew what it felt like to have it. Many of them spent the rest of their lives fighting off the monsters under their beds who brought endless nightmares and one undeniable message: you are bad and should be punished.

Surely, Eve was too shrewd to believe that. Wasn't she?

Eve was brilliant. She was strong. She wasn't one to "self-nuture," and she would never befriend an auspicious tyrant who hissed and snapped like an irritable turtle.

Right?

Cecilia and Eve. Eve and Cecilia. Jaycee moved them as a unit into her puzzle. They were attached, two pieces that didn't look as though they would fit together, yet oddly, did. It had happened to her. She had also been one half of a lopsided equation, the sane half. Had she been strong enough to see beneath Ben's folds of duplicity?

No. She had fallen for it entirely, swept up in a charade that had almost killed her. Despite seeing the absolute worst of what humanity could accomplish, she had not been brilliant, strong, or cunning enough to notice what was right in front of her.

Why would she expect more from Eve?

Jaycee's cheeks reddened. Her chin lifted a notch as she activated the tug of a family tie she never realized she had. No one else would come. Aunt Marcy was incapable, and no one else cared. Not Holy United Academy, not Chief George Solomon, not her headmaster, not her coach, and certainly not Cecilia.

If Eve had been seduced into believing life could offer an easier path, Jaycee was the only one trying to determine which fork in the road she'd taken.

And how far off course she really was.

About a quarter mile off the highway, just to her right, a single bright gleam broke through the dim tinge of twilight. A snowmobile. It was difficult to get out of a stint in New Hampshire without having had at least one excursion on a snowmobile. They were everywhere: under tarps in backyards, lined up for sale at dealerships, and hitched to oversized trucks hauling them to some snowy getaway destination where the heavy din of work, wives, and kids evaporated into that peaceful feeling long lost to responsibility and adulthood. Jaycee's father had spent one winter working the trails with a volunteer group that maintained the snow pack and groomed the runs for the machines to pass safely. She'd gone with him once when school was canceled due to snow. The exhilaration she felt zipping around for hours on what was basically a snow-covered superhighway almost overrode the panic that came later when her father forgot about her in one of the warming huts. He'd stopped to let her defrost, promising to return after he got gas. She'd settled by the wood stove and thought happily of what a fine day it had been. Her mood darkened after hours slipped by and darkness crept closer to the small, triangular chalet in the middle of nowhere. Finally, she heard the distant *zing-zing-zing* of a throttling snowmobile. She ran outside, having already forgiven her father simply because he'd come back for her. But it hadn't been her father at all. A stranger named Goose swung his gloved hand at her, and motioned for her to climb on the back of his machine. She remembered feeling grossly close to his rear end as she clung to his back, clenching her thighs to stay on the single seat. By the time they returned to the dingy motel, her father was passed out on the only bed in the room, snoring away, his fingers loosely gripping a bottle of Jack Daniel's. Jaycee curled herself into an uncomfortably angled chair, and using her forearms as a pillow, fell asleep with tears stinging her wind-chapped cheeks.

No one but Goose had come for her.
She had to do better by Eve.

CHAPTER SIXTEEN

New Hampshire had a hands-free law restricting use of devices while driving. But when Barton's name lit up her phone, Jaycee took the call anyway. Maybe she had summoned him in her mind at just that moment.

"Tried to call you earlier," she didn't bother with a greeting. They had business to discuss. "It's not like LA out here, calls drop out. I may lose you."

"It's okay. Tell me what you have."

"Well, the news of the moment is that I am currently traveling at seventy-two miles an hour, and headed due north."

"North ..." he repeated.

"Yah, north. There may be a house up here. Some nasty shit may go down at this house and even though it still astounds me to say it, I am getting some strong hints that my little cousin may have her own key to the front door."

Barton mumbled. "How'd you find this information?"

"You had a point with the boarding school culture, and I picked up on that. I even saw some of it."

"It's real," he said. "But only a problem if one side becomes disenchanted. Otherwise, it's just built into the tradition."

"Right," Jaycee agreed. "If no one complains then nothing changes. I mean, Jesus Christ, you even need opposing sides to play tic-tac-toe." Absolutely nothing was illegal if it never got reported. The pursuit of justice was wholly dependent on one side blowing the whistle to start the race.

"But there's more …" he urged.

"Oh yeah," Jaycee said. "Much more. I think you're right about the spiders, too. Let me ask you this, if you took a call from a mother whose kid may be missing, what would you do?"

"I'd bust down doors 'til I found her kid. That may violate department protocol a bit, but if it involves a child I go balls-to-the-wall until I can tell her mother she's safe. It's what I'd hope someone would do for me if Mason, Christ fucking forbid, ever gets his ass in a tight spot. 'Course I'd kill the little fucker myself, 'scuse my language, but it's just what you friggin' do."

"Exactly," Jaycee knew he would light himself on fire if that meant saving an innocent life. "You would, but I just left the department that took a call just like that from my aunt. Then I show up and I'm yet another worried relative. Sure, the chief humored me right up until I told him where Eve goes to school."

"Then he shut down," Barton finished.

"Shut down faster than a gypsy paving crew with no tar in their truck."

"Probably on the take," he said. "A missing teenager is suspicious enough that it would at least get the due diligence of a lengthy interview with a concerned relative, or two. Adults are a little different, but a student at a nearby school should inspire more concern."

"Gave me some spiel about entering her into the NCIC, yadda yadda. He wanted to like me, I think, but then I asked him stuff he refused to talk about. It went bad. We didn't part on good terms."

"Shocking," Barton huffed. "He didn't like you once you became more brains than boobs."

"Sure, there's that. But if his pocket is being lined, I'm not sure he's sharing."

"You mean you found a talker?" he asked.

"More like he found me. Chased me down as I was leaving. He confirmed some of what we thought was happening. Said the chief will go after your run-of-the-mill thug or thief, but it's a do-not-touch policy for anything related to Holy United. He told him he'd personally handle the case and then basically dropped it."

"What else?"

"Then there's the rumor mill," she told him. "I'm the first one to admit I didn't see this coming like you did. Apparently, the sewer lines are longer than we thought." Jaycee called up her puzzle—the lustful men lurking on the periphery. "Imagine a sex ring that starts at Holy United, extends to some house in the boonies, and then circles back again. The girls flow out, then up, and then back again. But not all the girls. Only the specially selected ones."

Barton exhaled. He hated this as much as Officer Wheeler did, except he'd already seen it. Too often.

"It's unfortunate that this may involve someone you care about, Jay Jay, but it's hardly an outrageously original phenomenon. Horny guys will find it whether it's at a brothel in Amsterdam, that shithole in Nevada where Lamar Odom nearly off'd himself, or, and this is the sick part, at a boarding school full of babies."

Jaycee nodded to herself. A talented Los Angeles-based documentarian she'd gotten to know during her medical hiatus had told her about the scathing undercover investigation he'd embarked upon to expose the international sex trade operation. It was booming. She'd seen the video evidence when he'd invited her to his office to discuss her doing a larger story once the project released and she returned to work.

"Jesus Christ, Jaycee," he'd said, his eyes huge and forever altered by the unseemly lifestyle he'd just witnessed. He had a daughter of his own. "The girls take on a couple of guys every night and make enough to get their nails done and watch soap operas all day. It's pure mint!"

He'd shared the rough draft of what will no doubt be an award-winning feature. His journey took him inside smoky lounges where juvenile bar girls flirted and tickled men with fat bellies and low expectations, and to hovels where underaged Thai children were paid by Westerners to fondle and canoodle, and to karaoke bars that featured more than just open mic night. He'd seen the exploitation, the carnal services, the no-money, no-honey relationships that often became lengthy and lucrative for both customer and laborer. Many of the women considered that the most coveted prize of all: a profitable, long-term alliance with someone they grew to trust. A man who may be twisted and perverted enough to travel across the world for sex but didn't beat her, burn her with their American cigarettes, or report her to her father.

Or her mother. Which brought her back to Eve.

"Still doesn't explain where Eve is. Why she hasn't been at school or in touch with her family."

"You think she's at this house?"

"Well, it's becoming a possibility I can't ignore. Honestly, I'm not sure how I feel about that. She's my … my …" Jaycee attempted to finish but was bungling it.

"She's your family, Jay Jay."

It was simple and yet interlaced with another truth: Eve may be family but she was also just a visitor in Jaycee's life. She had come in unexpectedly and without notice, and she didn't yet know if Eve would be sticking around for the long haul. None of that mattered if she couldn't accomplish the most important part of her cross-country mission.

Finding Eve.

"You there?" Barton broke back in.

"Yup," she said. "I'm here. I'll let you know how it goes."

"I'll be waiting. Something else to consider. Rumors have a way of gettin' around. Maybe the closer you get to this house, there are rumblings. If I were an investigative reporter, I'd be poking around gas stations, convenience stores, you know the drill."

"I do the drill every day, I know it well." She smiled into the phone.

"Goes without sayin' …" He dawdled, it was difficult to disconnect knowing he was so far away. He couldn't save her. Barton despised that feeling. It ate him whole.

"You take care of you first."

"I'll be careful. Promise. And maybe once this is all over, there's a law enforcement friend of yours who might be willing to have coffee with a nice young officer from New Hampshire. Someone who does his job with integrity. Think you might be willing to put in a call on his behalf? Get him somewhere where honesty still matters."

Barton was quiet for a few seconds.

"For you? I'd hire him myself."

"Barton?"

"Ya?"

"Thank you. For picking up whenever I call, for giving me information I can't always get on my own … and for taking care of Van."

"You got it, kiddo. Talk soon."

She felt an odd thickness in her voice. Family. It wasn't always a lineage that connected people. Her family may be here in New Hampshire, and she was willing to chase them until she could bring them all back to the same nest.

But her heart was in Los Angeles.

CHAPTER SEVENTEEN

Jaycee gassed up at the first station she came across. The Sunoco name sat boldly atop a rusted out sign with a Green Mountain Coffee plaque and a blinking red light advertising a food mart. She walked the food aisle slowly, stepping over lazy pools of grimy water where boots had left behind pieces of the icy parking lot. She rummaged through the Sun Chips, Doritos, and Smartfood bags but watched the door for customers. Would anyone be willing to talk? The clerk was an elderly man wearing a Red Sox sweatshirt that looked as though it had been produced back when the slumping team was still embroiled in the Curse of the Bambino. It cuffed around each wrist in frayed, tattered strips of faded red fabric. That sweatshirt was definitely not official championship gear.

She ended up with a medium-sized bag of BBQ flavored Fritos and a diet Coke. At the counter she made small talk that was met with silence. Either the old guy couldn't hear her or didn't feel compelled to chat. No other customers entered the store.

She moved along, driving northwest another five or so miles. Finally, she came across another sign attached to the front window of a one-story, ranch-style restaurant. A narrow line of white smoke trailed upward from a rooftop chimney. The Dine In Take Out. Three SUVs sat in the parking lot. She pulled her car into the open space next to a handicapped ramp.

Stickers along the door announced yearly membership status in the New Hampshire Lodging and Restaurant Association in bright blue medallions that dated back to 1996. The wooden door required work from both her arms to open. The tangy aroma of freshly brewed coffee hit Jaycee like a snowball to the face. She folded her body onto a stool at the counter. Although she had to find this house soon, she needed more information about what might be inside. What did the locals really know? How much could she confirm?

"Hi, sweetie," the waitress dropped an empty mug onto the placemat without even asking. Everyone wanted hot coffee here, why bother? She did a loop over to a burner with two warm pots, grabbed one, and was pouring Jaycee's coffee before she'd taken off her coat. A hand-painted sign announced that breakfast was served twenty-four hours a day. That worked perfectly. Jaycee could use the caffeine. She needed to approach the house in the darkness, without warning, and under as much cover as she could find. If Eve was stowed away inside, she may have to sneak her way in.

She kept her Patriots hat on, glasses in place, and her scar all covered up. She smiled back at the friendly waitress as she tended to her coffee, and requested a menu. She hadn't eaten since her lunchroom shakedown with Cecilia, and her stomach didn't appreciate that. She ordered a couple of eggs over easy, toast, and home fries with onions. The waitress took the order in her head, and then disappeared through saloon doors that led to a stainless steel table holding plastic-wrapped loaves of bread and boxes of aluminum foil. She breathed in. Christmas morning. The place held that delightful buttery, baconesque scent that made you feel like you were taken care of. The homey essence of New Hampshire. It was a good smell.

Jaycee scanned the row of red-topped stools anchored into peeling linoleum, the red picnic table pattern of the curtains, and the light oak tone of the fake wooden table tops. Steaming coffee pots sat on-the-ready atop burners with only two options: high or off. Characters ate here. People with stories. But would they share them?

She looked to her right, near a glass-doored fridge that hummed out its age in those guttural electrical gulps emitted by kitchen equipment. It featured shelves packed with frothy pies, and individually wrapped plates of chocolate cake layered with buttercream frosting. A teenage girl and a boy loaded with swollen mounds of acne were boisterously discussing the health benefits of watching cat videos. The girl was failing to convince him that studies had shown it was almost as good as therapy. They chortled with the carelessness of having nowhere to be, and nothing to do. Two booths over, a group of heavyset men peeled off layers of snowmobile gear, having just parked their machines in the designated spot near the dumpster. They were scarlet-cheeked. Their hair mussed from helmets and sweat, a sour scent wafted off them as glistening skin emerged from the layers. Jaycee wrinkled her nose. They had that musty, cloying spice that reminded her of oily rags shoved away in the back of a garage. Her head swiveled to the left. An older couple sat near the wall that held a giant dormant air conditioner. Both sported plaid jackets and feasted upon giant pancakes that spilled over their oval plates. Jaycee watched them pass a carafe of syrup back and forth without having to say a word. The years, and the habits, now carried out ordinary activities in quiet conciliation.

They could be a treasure trove, Jaycee knew. She would wait until they were done eating, and then give it a go. She considered it good fortune to stumble across the old-timers who knew where everyone was buried. In fact, once they started gabbing, many of them admitted they had done some of the digging. Jaycee filled as many of her reports as she could with the authenticity and rawness of people just like that. The woman had her back to Jaycee, but the man had indeed noticed the mysterious young woman who didn't look like she came from around there, and he was interested. He lowered his fork and held onto the syrup even though his partner had signaled it was her turn. That break in custom forced conversation.

"Norm," she directed. "Please …"

Norm wasn't listening. He wasn't sure if he wanted to greet Jaycee or just stare at her. She could feel him watching as she took a long sip from the mug. The coffee was hardy and immediately gave her a jolt as it spread like heated epoxy through her empty stomach. By the time she reached for the mug to take another taste, Norm was behind her shoulder. He had jumped first.

"Young lady," he began, his middle finger hooked around his coffee mug. His approach was part ruse, part calculated attempt to find out what had brought this bewitching stranger to his neck of the woods.

"Not sure I've seen you here before," he continued. "Take some more, Kendra." He placed the mug on the counter and tapped his finger on the rim.

"Sure thing, Norm," the waitress hurried over and topped him off. He sipped loudly without ever taking his eyes off Jaycee.

"Hello," she responded warmly. Norm's skin slacked over a thin mouth hidden in a thicket of grayish white whiskers. He had enormous ears that sat aside thinning sideburns. Jaycee couldn't tell if his eyes were green, blue, or some variation of both. He wore faded Wrangler jeans belted below a swollen belly, and boots with muck caked along their heels. Norm had done some serious living in his time. Jaycee could use that. She needed Norm on her side.

"I'm Jaycee," she smiled brightly and offered her right hand. Norm's wrapped around her fingers, rough like a nail file, yet somehow gentle. They shook up and down but Norm was still tentative and on notice. He had yet to return a smile.

"Norm Grandell," he stated. He was like the chaperone at a high school dance whose sharp eyes had detected a squatter from another town who may be trying to steal all the girls. Oh, no you don't. Not in my school.

"Well, Norm, it's very nice to meet you." Stay cool, she told herself. Norm rules this land, not you.

"Passing through?" he asked.

"Sort of," she replied, purposely imprecise.

Norm cleared his throat. He had plowed fields and roads his entire life, he didn't stand for the rocky layer of bullshit. "That's not an answer, young lady," he told her. Sure, Norm treated people like equals but only after they came out of hiding.

Jaycee believed in the power of energy. It was all in how you held yourself. If you presented like a snarling spectator at a cockfighting tourney, people backed off. She considered her next move. Buying time, she pressed her lips together, and sharply tilted her chin down. She maintained eye contact. Blue. In that moment, Norm's eyes were a tepid blue.

"Let me ask you this, Norm." Jaycee was trusting her perception that Norm was more bark than bite, and preferred to be a gentleman if possible.

"Arr—umph." It was a growl, but Norm's boots stayed put.

"Say I was looking for some information," she began. It was important to respect this space. People became deeply entrenched in their hometowns. They lived similar experiences, ate at the same diners, and at night, stared out at the same starlit mountaintops that sent those swirly gusts of cool wind through their window screens. Many of them also shared the same intimate feeling that the air up there often took shape as feather-soft kisses from above. Hallowed territory. Tread carefully, she told herself, this ground was well-guarded.

Norm was cautious yet intrigued. "'Bout what exactly?" By now, his wife had craned her neck and was twisted over the back of her chair. Norm liked to think otherwise, but he didn't have the freedom to just go sniffing around.

"About a big house," she started, tripping her heart into a quickened pattern. "And some little girls."

In all his years, Norm hadn't yet mastered the art of disassociation. If he knew something, he knew it. It was foolish for his face to try and trick his mind into thinking he didn't. He was, however, a guardian of his circles.

"Not sure I know what you're talkin' 'bout," he said, watching her closely. He ignored the tap on his shoulder until it became a moderate thump.

"Norm!"

"Good God, woman," he snarled to his wife. "I'm talking here …"

"Young lady," she ignored him and leaned forward to grasp Jaycee's hand from her lap. "He's old and rude. You come on over and join us now. No one here eats alone." She tugged gently but firmly until Jaycee was forced to rise onto stiff legs before she toppled over sideways. "Kendra, she's with us now."

"Got it, Mol!" the voice yelled from behind the swinging door. Kendra rolled with whatever came up.

"Molly Grandell," she smiled with pronounced pride. It was a statement. Molly's face had taken on that rounded look supported by a few extra pounds on her frame. She had sharp eyes but her cheekbones were long and

165

pronounced. Jaycee would bet she had been an astounding beauty back in her prime. "I'm sixty-seven years old for only two more months so time's a wastin' and I don't tinker around."

"Fair enough," Jaycee grinned back. She had been wrong. Norm didn't rule this land, his wife did. "I'm Jaycee, I'll be thirty soon enough and I don't live around here anymore, but I used to a long time ago."

Norm watched them zip back and forth like he was following a tense tennis match. An ornery frown developed below his long nose. Wouldn't be the first time Molly had swept in like a gale force chinook. Damn woman drove him nuts but he still folded her underwear into neat triangles and drew her a lavender bath every Friday night.

"That makes you one of us then," Molly confirmed with a firm nod. "A Granite Stater. Your people are still here?"

Jaycee shrugged. It was a loaded question. That word again. Her people … her *family*. It was a yes, but she had to qualify it.

"My family is still here," she started. "But my people … are not. Does that make sense?"

Molly considered that. "Enough of it, I suppose," she said, attending to the browned edges of the pancake lolling off the side of her plate. She stabbed through it, twisted the fork upward, and nibbled from the bottom. "Best to take that hat off, you'll overheat in here. So why'd you come back then?"

Jaycee looked over at Norm. He had shifted in his seat to place both elbows on either side of his own pancakes. She got the feeling no one disobeyed a direct order from Molly, so she slid her hat off and tucked her hair behind her ears. Molly didn't watch her; she was still hungry and had her pancakes to look at, but Norm wanted to listen more than eat. He looked at her expectantly. The bell atop the front door rang as more patrons entered. A blast of frigid air slammed Jaycee's back. She shuddered. "Overheat? I don't think so."

Molly chuckled. "You've gone soft, Jaycee." Molly didn't miss much. "New Hampshire's new to you again."

"Somewhat," she replied. "From what I hear, childbirth is so excruciating a woman's brain is programmed to forget it right after it happens. For me, that's winter." She chuckled to herself as Molly and Norm exchanged a glance. They both grinned tightly but Jaycee could sense something else. What was it?

"And maybe there's this feeling that I had no choice," Jaycee offered. "Historically, I have a difficult time saying no if I think there's even the slightest chance that I might be able to help."

Norm inhaled loudly through his mouth. "Classic," he choked out. "Sounds familiar, huh Mol?"

The two exchanged another long look until Molly methodically tended to the dissection of a fat blueberry. So much could be said without uttering a single word.

"Don't pay him any mind," she instructed Jaycee. "He wants you to think I'm just an old busybody nosing around everyone's laundry room." She tilted her mouth to lick away the syrup runoff from her fork. "If someone puts their business up on the clothesline, I'd be a fool if I didn't notice their unmentionables flapping in the breeze, wouldn't I?"

Jaycee laughed. "It would be hard to miss, yes."

"So, of course I would notice someone like you," she told Jaycee. "And he's not dead yet either." Molly didn't blame her husband for his curiosity. It was more of a trait she rather enjoyed exploiting.

Norm huffed.

"I'm not trying to hide," Jaycee told them. "It goes back to that annoying need to jump in and take over."

Molly knowingly nodded. "That can get a girl into trouble, you know."

"I've been made aware of that more than once," Jaycee said. She stared into her lap. "And yet I keep coming back for more."

"Understood," Molly told her. "Now tell me what exactly brings you home." Molly had crinkles around her brown eyes, lines that had settled in long ago and made themselves at home. She kept her hands moving, the utensils making slicing noises against the glass plate. She would patiently wait but Norm was jumping out of his skin. It was the mystery of the stranger at the diner, and he was just getting to the good part.

"My cousin may be missing," Jaycee told her. "Or may not be missing," she amended.

"How old?" Molly asked.

"Sixteen," Jaycee told her. "She's in high school." It was a dramatic declaration, yet it didn't inspire any panic. Norm and Molly had a more thoughtful rebound.

"Makes me think of that girl, Mol," Norm interrupted. "Remember?" He snapped his fingers together in that common way people use to spark a recollection of events.

Molly nodded. She picked up the story. "Lovely young girl, nursing student I think down at UMass Amherst." She pinched at her own cheeks. "Dimples," she said. "She had the most adorable dimples."

"Mary ..." Norm added.

"Maura," Molly corrected. "Her name was Maura."

"Yeah, Maura." Norm bobbed his head up, and then down.

Jaycee watched them. "What happened?"

"She left school, called a few people, told a few lies, had a car accident, and was never seen again."

Jaycee's heart beat faster. She could now remember this story, too. *Dateline*, *20/20*, and *60 Minutes* had all done special reports on the inexplicable case. A pretty young girl, with a loving family, friends, and a bright future, promptly disappeared. Her car, found abandoned and damaged, but its driver never seen again. That was over a decade ago. Whatever had happened to Maura remained known only to whoever had hurt her. If she hadn't hurt herself.

"God, that's scary," Jaycee sighed, feeling herself heat up. She was grateful she'd decided to swipe her deodorant one extra time across her armpits early this morning. The

constant shift from blazing hot to icy cold made it difficult
for her body to acclimate. It was like a climatological roller
coaster. At least in Los Angeles, automated air conditioning
kept everything at a pleasantly consistent seventy-two
degrees.

"That doesn't mean your cousin is in trouble now,"
Molly told her, as she clanked her fork onto her plate. "Just
means we've seen it go bad before."

Norm nodded, he mashed his lips like they were sewn
together. "Damn tragedy," he groused. "No body to bury.
No one behind bars. No one even lookin' for her anymore,
that stopped long ago." Norm grew disturbed but Molly
remained more measured.

"I like to think she just went to sleep," she said softly.
"Simply got lost and settled down onto the leaves. Just
closed her eyes and faded away."

Norm looked at his wife. "Mol can't bear the thought
of someone hurtin' that girl," he explained, realizing that to
a stranger, Molly's version was equally tragic. "That's all."

Jaycee looked at him. She could understand that
feeling. She was starting to get the same uncomfortable
tingling sensation through her chest whenever she thought
of anyone harming Eve. She almost couldn't let herself
linger on that feeling, it was that calamitous.

"I have no reason to believe Eve has been in a car
accident," she started. "Nothing's been reported about that
at all. She just seems to have walked away from school."

"Didn't come home from school?" Molly asked her. She turned back to her husband. "Like that other girl, right Norm?"

He confirmed with a grunt. "North Conway high school kid. Kidnapped, tortured …" he shook his head. "Sorry, that was another tough case. We were all shooken up by that one."

Jaycee groaned. Shooken up, indeed! How were there so many? She took an unsteady sip of coffee.

"Well, this is a bit different. Eve lives away at school. She's a student at Holy United Academy." She watched them closely. Norm had already reacted once, let's see what she could get out of him this time. And his wife.

"I see." Molly was the first to speak and her voice was still steady, unchanged. If she knew something, she wasn't ready to reveal it yet.

"She's a good kid," Jaycee lowered her eyes. "Very smart—"

Molly coughed. Jaycee abruptly stopped talking as though she'd been ordered to. Molly slowly lowered her fork until it lay beside the uneaten bottom corner of her pancake. She and Norm exchanged another deliberate stare.

"Pretty? Like you?" Molly asked after several quiet moments had passed. She and Norm watched Jaycee fixedly.

"Yes, Eve doesn't really look like me at all, but she is pretty." Her picture. Jaycee remembered she had Eve's picture.

That feeling enfolded itself again around her throat as she reached inside her bag, rifling her fingers over her phone, wallet, and keys. Finally, she scooped up the picture Ramona had given to her from the bottom of the bag, near the side pocket where she kept her ChapStick, and bottle of Motrin. She pulled it out. She looked into her cousin's smiling face. She was very pretty, in fact, attractive in that beguiling way that revealed itself slowly, rather than hit you over the head at first glance.

"This is her," she told them, handing off the picture first to Molly. She reached for it with stubby fingers free of polish. Her hands were practical, not provocative. Nothing physical about Molly outweighed her simple functionality. Molly looked it over and then handed the picture to Norm. He did the same. Instead of giving it back to Jaycee, he placed it between them as if Eve had, in a weird sort of way, just joined their group.

"Holy United is a ways down the highway from here," Molly said, reaching for her mug again.

"I've already been there," Jaycee told her. "They don't seem alarmed. It's ummm …" she rolled her hands in thought as she worked on how to best describe the eccentric practice of "self-nurturing."

"Well, they do this thing there …" she hesitated again. Molly and Norm were old-school. The spiritual custom would sound ridiculously indulgent to people who followed doctrines based more on sacrifice than service to oneself. Molly and Norm had field hands: calloused, wrinkled, and bent at the joints. They wouldn't know a paraffin wax from a snake bite, both sounded hideous.

"Self-nuture," Norm whispered. Jaycee snapped her head around. Did she really just hear that?

"What did you say?" she asked, her voice rising.

Molly took over. "Jaycee," she began. With her middle finger she pushed back wiry wisps of pepper-colored hair that had sprung free from a loose elastic band. "How long has Eve been gone?"

"A few days," Jaycee raised her eyes. "But if you already know about how they 'self-nurture' there, then you understand why the school isn't alarmed. And talk about unhelpful? No one is doing squat to find her."

"Because there's no emergency situation," Molly confirmed. "At least not as far as they're concerned."

"Exactly!" Jaycee smacked her hand on the table. Eve's picture skipped to the right, near Jaycee's coffee mug. She twisted the paper with her finger until her cousin's eyes were lined up to beam straight into her own. Emotion got the better of her. Norm and Molly watched her as she brought herself back. She took a few deep breaths. "Sorry," Jaycee said softly. "But it's been very difficult to find someone who gives a sh—," she clipped the word. It was improper to swear in this setting. "Who gives a darn about finding Eve. It's maddening! She's just a kid."

They examined her face. Jaycee could feel them watching her and felt compelled to keep talking.

"I don't think the cops care either. Well, maybe just one but he's not in a position to help. At least he told me that if I really wanted to find Eve, I needed to head north. So that's how I ended up here. And I think I know where I'm going next."

In that moment, the couple made a decision. Jaycee's hunched shoulders rose as her vertebrae snapped to attention one by one. They began to tell their story.

CHAPTER EIGHTEEN

"To our west is a village so small it doesn't have a name," Norm told her. "It's the general area around Moose Alley, mostly full of woods, with a nice little stream running through it. Families sometimes picnic there. Otherwise, it's a hell of a lot of wide open land."

"No one builds anything out there," Molly added. "It's desolate, and that alone makes it undesirable for most folks, but it's more of an unspoken rule. You can come by and visit for a while but you can't stay there."

Jaycee instinctively knew that was exactly where she was heading. Where Eve may be.

"Every year, the town that borders Moose Alley throws a summer gala. Everybody in the county shows up. Free food, local bands play through the night, beer breweries put out their homemade lagers. You get it, it's a big deal."

"I get it," she told them. She could see it in her mind. A tall white party tent filled with vendors hocking handmade crystal jewelry, farm-harvested strawberries piled atop crumbly shortcakes with real whipped cream, and all-natural eucalyptus bug sprays. She closed her eyes and saw the crowd. The friendly greetings and cheerful laughter. She could almost smell the cinnamon sugar-coated funnel cake.

"After nightfall and just before the fireworks show begins, the town manager makes an announcement," Norm continued. Molly watched him. "He's very formal about it

…" he started to explain, but Molly had to make a correction.

"He's not formal, the man's an ass."

"Oh, don't you start now," he pointed a wagging finger at her. "Molly's never liked him, and she makes sure I know about it."

Jaycee had no concern for whether or not they liked the town manager.

"It's okay …" she put her hands up to end the bickering, but this was an important point they both wanted to make.

"He's Norm's older brother," Molly clarified. "He's stodgy and stuck-up, not to mention an angel's breath away from a heart event, I tell you. Any man who refuses to work some green vegetables into his diet and smokes like a chimney is … exactly what I just said … an ass."

Norm sighed. He would never win her over, and his brother had stopped trying long ago.

"Anyway, my brother Chet always makes sure every member of the town council is on the stage with him." Norm started assigning a finger on his right hand to the following list of guests. He counted people off. "Who else is there, Mol? The police and fire chiefs, the treasurer … who am I missing?"

"Sandy's always up there, too," she spat like she had to dislodge a fly from between her teeth. "Sandy is fifty but dresses like she's nineteen." Molly scowled but Norm grinned.

"… And Sandy," he pushed on his middle finger to add her in. "She dresses just fine," he threw in quietly. "The cheerleaders from the high school, too. I almost forgot the cheerleaders."

"O, *kaaaay*," Jaycee replied tentatively, impatient but not wanting to sound like it. She tried to picture Barton at such an event and quickly gave up. Not his scene and not really hers either. So what were they getting at with this folksy homestead festival?

"Once they're all ready, Chet announces that year's municipal project."

"In grand fanfare," Molly huffed. She waved her hands back and forth in feigned excitement.

Jaycee could give two shits about town projects, and old women wearing young clothes, she needed something good here! Something that either helped her find Eve, or brought forth someone who knew where she'd gone. She didn't want to be disrespectful, but her tolerance for useless banter was waning.

"I'm sorry, I am so enjoying our little talk here but I need—"

"More," Molly filled in. "We know. We're getting there."

Jaycee shifted her hips back against the arch of her chair. They would do it their way. She nodded. "All right," she told them.

"We've lived up here for a long time now. Our town shares a fire department with two others, most of the staff is volunteer, but we have three shiny, new red fire engines.

Count 'em, one, two, three. Most of the time, they're sittin'
on display down at the four corners near the
Congregational church, and boy, do they ride well in our
4th of July parade." Norm and Molly shook their heads.
Jaycee watched them. What did they have against good-
looking fire engines?

"We, our friends and our neighbors don't pay much of
a property tax." Molly looked intently into Jaycee's face. If
that was some luscious hint, it went right over her head.

"Is that good?" she asked. Her accountant took care of
whatever she owed each month on her condo in Los
Angeles. She knew she paid property taxes and assumed
they were in line with whatever everyone else paid. Which
was, probably, exorbitant. So, was it a good thing taxes
were low, or was Molly trying to tell her it was more like
fuzzy math had been done with a crooked calculator?

Jaycee crossed her arms. In her experience, sources
either blurted out information like chunky throw-up, or
they were more tactful, forcing her to flush out obscure
inferences on her own. The nightclub sex maven, Olive,
she'd sought out in the Throw Away Girls investigation
had been like that. Barton was somewhere in the middle.
Norm and Molly may be, too.

As she waited for them to answer, she thought of
several other stories in her career that involved businesses
or employees accused of cooking the books. Was that
where they were leading her?

"Well, hell yeah!" Norm exploded, confirming her
supposition. "Too damn good, girl. That's the point."

Ah, hah! Jaycee shifted her mental puzzle. Cecilia, Eve, sex, Holy United, randy men, and small-town money. She had firmed up the pieces enough to have a strong border. Now, she had to build her way through the next layer. She had to learn more about the house in the woods.

"Money," she said, squinting at them. "But if something is that obvious, wouldn't the state come looking for answers, too? Does the Attorney General or US Attorney get involved on something like that?"

"You'd think," Molly agreed. "I would suspect it might entice a few different agencies to come poking around. So if something didn't look right, they'd be on us like flies on … syrup." She stared pointedly at Norm and reached for the syrup as a convenient prop.

Jaycee followed her hands, thinking, moving pieces, asking herself how they all fit together. "So, then, it looks right …" she began. *Looking* right and *being* right were entirely different animals. Like the swordfish she'd eaten recently. It had been charred beautifully on the outside, but she'd gagged it up all night with whatever bacteria it was hiding on the inside. Its core was rotten, yet it could be gussied up and hidden away. No one would know. Okay, but what did that have to do with Eve?

"This spring, we're building a community center." Norm took a long sip of his coffee and raised his arm to signal to Kendra that more was needed. "That's the big municipal project. The landscaping committee is already selling off bricks for a hundred bucks a piece to have your name chiseled permanently into the new walkway. Never had something like that this far north, and honestly, given the tax stress that would put on families barely making forty k a year, how the hell can we afford it?"

"Well, you … can't?" she offered.

"Nope," Norm shook his head. "But the engineer's plans are already posted for everyone to see. Phase one is complete. Phase Two kicks in once the ground thaws."

Molly held her coffee mug with both hands. "Now, beyond Moose Alley, there's a grand estate a very wealthy family built up long ago. It's unlike anything else around here. No one lives there that we know of, yet we hear it's being used."

Jaycee's eyes widened. This was it! The nugget she was waiting for. The house Officer Wheeler told her about. *Go north, and stay north.* Take this right and that left. You'll see it. You can't miss it.

"A house in the woods," she confirmed.

"Yup. Like Mol said, it's a rather large house," Norm told her. "Big enough to hide all sorts of secrets."

"With guests who are willing to pay for their privacy," Jaycee noted. Even in the pristine wilderness of The Great North Woods, gluttonous corruption seeped in. Like a clock, bits and pieces started ticking, moving her slowly toward building a scene, and a motive.

"If Chet were a better man," Molly stated, "he would crack that nut wide open and let its dirty seed out for all to see." She had obviously struggled with her husband's loyalty to the town manager who happened to be the man he'd grown up sharing a bedroom with. If Chet was shady,

180

no one would hear it from Norm. And by association, from Molly. She respected family first, even if one of its members happened to be someone she'd never choose to associate with.

Jaycee felt the heat of realization. She could blow this wide open. Right here, right now, she could take this to an enterprising reporter, tell her to bring a backhoe and start moving the earth. All those righteous juices inside her began to flow, but only got as far as her chest before her heart hit the brakes. Eve. This was about Eve. Norm and Molly wanted her to know this because a girl's life was in play. She had to honor their forthrightness with her own.

"Somehow, we think money is passed out of that house. If there are red lines in the budget, whoever runs that place kicks in whatever it takes to make all the columns line up."

"Taxes are low, projects get expensive, and yet the books appear balanced," Jaycee stated.

Norm and Molly nodded in unison.

"Residents are happy, too." Molly told her. "You ain't goin' to hear no one complain when their bank accounts stay fat and their town looks pretty as a postcard, right?"

"Right," Jaycee agreed. "So in exchange, no one goes beyond Moose Alley. No one asks any questions, or answers them if someone does."

"No questions," Norm confirmed. "Now, we can't say for sure how many residents have a clue as to what's going on. It's not something widely discussed during church on Sunday mornings. But I can say for absolute rootin' tootin' sure that access to that house is invitation only." He dropped his gaze on a long sigh.

Jaycee felt sick. How many people here chose to deny, deflect, or dismiss what was happening around them? How much did they know? It seemed unimaginable because Eve was stuck in the middle, but pay-for-play was a common and often preferred method of operation. How was it ever justified as a legitimate option? Well, Jaycee had asked the question before. It had been explained to her in a variety of ways, including from a man who'd gone to prison for doling out state contracts to a third cousin he'd grown up with. Turns out, the cousin's wife had been sick and the family was underwater with medical bills. "Think about it, Jaycee," he'd told her during a tense interview that had her rethinking her perspective by the end. "If you have conscious knowledge about what you're doing, do you justify that by believing it's only to protect yourself and those you love? Once you lie, are you always a liar? Or, are you doing everything you can to ease someone's suffering? Shouldn't we help ease the pain they never did a damn thing to deserve?"

Exposing wrongdoing then became slippery and treacherous. Few wanted to climb that mountain because the risks far outweighed the gain. Young Officer Wheeler suspected something screwy was happening, yet the threat of revealing it tested even his most altruistic reflexes. He would help, but only to a point. Norm and Molly might be willing to direct her, but they'd never tried to make it stop themselves.

"Who's at the top?" Jaycee returned her focus to the table in the diner. "Who runs it?"

They shook their heads. "If you want fact," Molly told her. "No idea. But there are rumors …" she looked sideways at Jaycee with an unspoken question. Did she really want to know?

Eve's picture spun in the air wake of the teenager who was walking briskly toward the bathroom in the back. Jaycee steadied it, holding the paper with her left hand as she examined the depths of her cousin's eyes. Even though she was smiling for the camera, her eyes were dull. She was so young and yet, seemed internally defeated and empty. Had she resorted to what she thought was a quick fix to a temporary problem? Was Eve searching for a gateway to an easier life? Jaycee had to find her, fast.

"I want whatever you have," she told them firmly. "Tell me everything."

Molly gave a subtle nod to Norm. Permission granted to proceed.

"Helicopters are interesting machines," Norm began. "People who get around using helicopters are usually pretty wealthy individuals, wouldn't you say?" he asked her. Molly sat quiet.

"Yes," Jaycee said softly.

"Maybe big-time politicians, right Mol?"

Molly shrugged. "Or perhaps movie executives, renowned surgeons, and CEOs of the nation's most famous companies."

Jaycee's face reddened. She considered Barton's sewers and spiders, Chief Solomon's disgraceful ambivalence, and Holy United's odd "self-nurturing" policy that seemed to fit perfectly into unexplained absences for its students—particularly the girls. Was the web here? In the solitary calmness of this vast back country?

"When the helicopters arrive," Norm continued. "The passengers expect everything and everyone to be in place."

"They already know no one will bother them. No one ever has." Molly folded her hands into her lap.

"It's organized, and efficient," Jaycee was thinking out loud. "Like a business."

"Yes," Molly told her sharply. "And just like every other business, money exchanges hands, and contracts are signed."

Contracts. Non-disclosures. Jaycee worked under a contract at every television station she'd been employed with. Her agent dealt with the details, but Jaycee had never looked at them that closely. The world was full of contracts. No big deal, right? In fact, Jaycee's favorite hairdresser would often cancel at the last minute because of an impromptu booking with a top actress. She'd signed some lucrative yet lawyer-y deal that demanded she drop everything and dash off with her curling iron at a moment's notice. She'd told Jaycee she had no choice, it was "in her contract." Had her little cousin signed some erotic pact? Good Lord, Jaycee shuddered. Again, she wondered how in the hell this could happen. She wasn't of legal age to sign her name on anything but her homework!

"The helicopters come and go, and then poof, like magic, a community center gets built." Molly slid her arms by her side. She seemed suddenly smaller and decidedly elderly.

"And a brand new fire truck rolls down the road," Jaycee added. "Year after year, taxes stay low, budgets stay fat, and no one says a thing." It was unspeakable, and yet, supremely capitalistic. A windfall of good fortune, as long as everyone kept the helicopters safely in the air.

"It's easy to not have a stomach for what we're telling you, Jaycee." Molly said. "And I understand how horrible it sounds."

"But …" Jaycee swallowed the warm fluid trying to rise from her gut. There was always a "but" when someone was trying to explain away defective scruples. It was never really their fault.

"But, it keeps life simple." It was an oddly tangled way of whittling down a knotty situation. It was like trying to argue that a bathtub full of grain alcohol was the quality equivalent of a painstakingly fermented and lovingly distilled bourbon. It wasn't the same at all. One was swill and the other was liquid gold. What Molly was trying to explain was that, despite the process, both still got you wasted.

And wasn't that the only thing that really mattered?

CHAPTER NINETEEN

Norm helped Molly into an old stable coat that shed silver coils of horse hair.

"Gonna go warm up the truck," he told his wife. "You take care now, Jaycee."

She thanked him. Norm stopped at the counter and took out his wallet. He passed a bill to Kendra and motioned back to their table. Jaycee assumed he was covering her food, which she hadn't yet had a moment to touch. She had lost her appetite, yet knew she needed sustenance for what lay ahead. Molly swept a fabric pocketbook across her torso, and put a hand on Jaycee's shoulder.

"Be careful, Jaycee. You may not like what you find," she said gently. "But I give you credit for trying."

Jaycee exhaled. "I have to try. She's my family." That time it came out so fast she shocked even herself. It was an extraordinary admission and after letting it sink in, Jaycee then allowed it to feel good inside of herself.

Molly squeezed. "It's good to see you looking so well. You're very brave ..." Molly paused as Jaycee jerked her body against the chair. She felt the hard spindles against her bones. How long had they known exactly who they were talking to?

"I spent two years in the fashion industry before it burned me to toast," she explained with a hearty laugh. Jaycee had been right. She was a looker long ago. "I know, I know, shocker." She wasn't embarrassed, just honest. "I lived in New York for about six months, and Los Angeles for two. I still subscribe to the *LA Times*. After church on Sundays, I read it all, cover to cover, even the crime section."

"I tried to be incognito," Jaycee provided shyly.

They looked at each other for several seconds and in that, traded a look that filled in whatever blanks remained.

"I never really had a fondness for reporters," she continued. "I've always considered them rather obnoxious people. Until now."

Jaycee grinned.

"I used to know someone just like you," Molly said. "She was very beautiful and smart as a whip. Sure knew how to push all my buttons," she shrugged. Jaycee could sense a blanket of sorrow lowering upon her. What was that about?

She wouldn't know. Because Molly was ready to join Norm in the truck and head back to their ordinary lives in this deceivingly complicated place. As she was about to leave she left Jaycee with one more direction.

"I do believe Kendra may know a thing or two about that … that …" she snapped her fingers, "… that odd "self-nurturing" thing you were talking about."

Jaycee blinked rapidly. Kendra was still at the counter, attending to the new customers who were shrugging off their coats, but looking for the warmth of an immediate cup of coffee. She reached for clean mugs and put out a new bowl of chilled creamers.

"May help you a little," Molly hinted, "to, you know, figure out the rest of it."

"Thank you, Molly," Jaycee said sincerely. She almost gave in to a strong urge to wrap her arms around this woman and hold on tightly.

* * * *

Kendra was friendly yet efficient. Her dark hair swung between her shoulders in a low ponytail. She used one of those thin workout headbands to keep strays out of her face. She attended to not only the customers slouched on stools and eating from the counter, but also the diners who opted for tables in the tidy dining room. In spite of the cold outside, she wore thin, loose black pants and a green short-sleeved shirt with the slogan Breakfast On Your Time printed on the back. She used her forearms as trays, loading them up with several plates she then delivered to hungry patrons. Kendra had this place under control.

As Jaycee moved back to the stool she had been seated on before Norm and Molly moved her to their table, she watched Kendra drop off a plate of French toast with white powdered sugar sprinkled on top. As she placed it in front of a delighted woman ready to dig in, Jaycee noticed the shiny skin below her wrist. She winced. Something awful must have happened to leave a scar like that behind. She looked back up at Kendra's lively face … what had she been through?

Jaycee's eggs had gone lukewarm and had started to congeal, but she ate them with determined bites. She dipped the potatoes in a smear of ketchup and added some salt and pepper. It was predictably tasty and quickly filled her up. She left the toast untouched and finished her coffee. Kendra was delivering a grilled cheese to a little boy perched on a high chair and clutching a fork like it was a prize. She ruffled his hair and returned to the counter.

"Norm covered that," she told Jaycee, referencing her plate on the counter. Norm had paid the bill.

"Nice of him," Jaycee replied. "It was delicious." More like adequate.

Kendra sprayed some cleaning solution onto the counter left vacant by two men who'd left her three dollars crumpled into a pile. It smelled somewhat like lemon verbena, a pleasing aroma when mixed with the heavy scent of food. She carefully straightened the bills, folded them, and tucked them into the left pocket of her pants. Once that was done, Kendra reached for a large glass of ice water, took a long sip, and returned to Jaycee's section.

"Not sure what they've told you already," she began. "I overheard a little." Kendra had a small, sharp nose with a couple tiny beauty marks and a pin-sized hole through one nostril. The owner must force her to remove her nose ring while she works. She also had a pronounced line that zig-zagged above her right eyebrow. The skin had been roughly stitched at some point in her life, and hadn't healed evenly. Were all the injuries sustained at the same time?

Jaycee looked away. She didn't want to appear to be staring. "They've been helpful," she started. "But, yes, I have more questions."

Kendra nodded. "Okay, how can I help you?"

"I'm looking for a girl. She's my cousin." Jaycee thrust Eve's picture onto the counter. Kendra looked intently at her for several seconds. She shook her head.

"I haven't seen her," she told Jaycee. "I'm sure of it."

"She's a Holy United student. She hasn't been around for a few days and that's highly unlike her. She doesn't just disappear on her own. She's not that kind of kid."

"Well, aren't they all that kind of kid?" Kendra asked. She wasn't being unkind, just matter-of-fact. "I mean, that's what they do there. From what I've heard." Kendra was holding on to something she knew was useful. Jaycee could tell. She was silent for a moment as she considered the best way to approach this girl. As a reporter, she was usually the active ingredient that elicited a response. Add this, to that, and boom, you get smoke and fire. Someone had told Kendra something and Jaycee had to spark the flame.

But who? Eve had never been here before. So, who had?

Cecilia! Jaycee's eyes narrowed.

"Kendra, I promise I won't get you in any trouble. You have my word. But I need to know if there's a girl who comes here sometimes. A girl who looks sort of like me?" She took the brunt of the discovery, sparing Kendra from any guilt she may have felt over betraying someone's confidence.

Kendra's lips tightened. She wiped at her nose and sniffed.

"Please," Jaycee pleaded. "Even if she's your friend. My cousin may be in trouble. I need to know." She touched Eve's picture and slid it closer to Kendra. She stared at her face.

"I know a blonde girl," she admitted. Jaycee exhaled with relief. Thank God! Okay, proceed with care. "And she looks almost exactly like you."

"And this blonde girl is a Holy United student?" she furnished.

"Yes," Kendra concurred. "She is."

"She has … um … told you things?"

"Sort of …" Kendra explained. "She comes through here sometimes but she's always alone. I have never seen her with anyone." She considered that. "Maybe that's why I felt like I should be friendly to her. She seemed lonely for someone so young. And I know everyone who eats here. But she didn't fit in. Like, we get kids here all the time, the teenagers. There aren't any other places for them to go. She wasn't one of them. You know?"

Jaycee nodded. "What did she tell you?"

"That she lived at a boarding school. And that she hated it there."

Jaycee could see grouchy Cecilia, so narcissistic she couldn't tell how vile it was to whine about her privileges to a diner waitress. "Did she come right out and say Holy United Academy?" Jaycee asked.

"Eventually," Kendra told her. "Not at first, though. I kept it real chill. We'd talk about food; she was particular about what she ate."

Of course.

"Did she wear her school uniform?"

"Oh, no, she was always dressed in stuff most kids wear. Jeans, sweatshirts, backwards baseball hat. She did wear nice jewelry, though."

"Expensive-looking?"

"Very. One time I asked her if her earrings were real diamonds. That's sort of when she started to fill me in on why she comes through here so often."

Jaycee's fingers pulsed with energy. Helicopters. Community Centers. Money. Sex. Cecilia. All that was wrapped around a salty twinge of pretense. Cecilia felt safe here. For some reason, she may have revealed to Kendra what she had refused to tell Jaycee.

The truth must set Eve free.

"She goes to that big house in the woods," Jaycee felt herself whispering but no one was paying them any attention. "The house no one wants to talk about."

Kendra bowed her chin.

"I think so."

"You know so." Jaycee pushed.

Kendra's eyelids fluttered. "Yeah, I do. I know she goes there. I also know she gets paid a shitload of cash to do funky things with really rich men. She loves the money, and, I think … loves everything else, too …" Kendra paused. She had already incriminated herself so why not take it all the way home.

"She's a Legacy Girl," she said softly, her hands wrapped tensely around her side of the countertop.

"A wh … aaa … *ttt*?" Jaycee asked, her voice escalating.

"A Legacy Girl. She fuc—" she cleared her throat. "Sorry, she screws men for money. And she does it at that house. That's where it all goes down."

Jaycee's mind clicked. The sewer. The young police officer telling her of a place where he'd heard they go. Police turning a blind eye to it all. Money in exchange for an information blackout. Community centers for sexual profiteering. Young girls marched in like concubines encased in sin—and no one had the balls to make it stop!?

Why would they? A lot could be overlooked when the wheels of good fortune were properly greased. The gravy train gave a luxurious ride.

And her baby cousin—the girl with the resplendent brain and melancholy eyes—was right there in the thick of it. Jaycee frowned. Was Eve drowning in this noxious marshland, or was she laughing all the way to the bank? She questioned again if she was trying to rescue a girl who didn't think of herself as a victim.

But it was impossible to turn back now.

"How does Holy United fit into this?"

Kendra drew in a breath. "Someone there, I think, knows about all of it. Someone high up."

"So it's coordinated, someone's in master control?" Jaycee asked, the TV image locked in her head. The director, working the switches to pull off the seamless production.

"I guess so," Kendra told her. "From what I've been told, each girl is carefully selected. Someone at Holy United has to sign off on …"

"On what?"

"On who becomes a Legacy Girl. It's a process. A time-honored tradition. And once they're in, it's forever." Jaycee noted the distaste.

Jesus Christ! "So they're taken care of," she provided. "The girls don't want anyone to know about it because it's a good thing for everyone involved. They rake in the dough as long as they uphold the tradition."

An escort service offering up kids who don't know better yet. Charming.

But what came first? A culture of "self-nurturing" or a cleverly crafted excuse to give certain girls a well-paid pass to miss a few days of school?

"So, if the blonde girl missed classes for a couple of days …" Jaycee goaded.

Kendra hunched her shoulders. "I asked her if anyone is ever worried about that. You know, skipping classes or being off campus for days on end. She basically shrugged it off." Kendra's eyebrows went up. The movement tugged on her healed skin. "She told me everyone does it. For different reasons, of course, but that's their business. She said the students are encouraged to take a break if they need to. I'm sure most kids think that's something totally different than what she uses that for. But whatever, that's how it works for her."

"How many people around here have a clue this is happening?" Jaycee asked Kendra, who pondered that with a worried brow. It made her scar redden.

"I honestly don't know," she shook her head. "Some towns deal with dirty heroin needles in school yards, crackheads passed out on park benches, shootings, drive-bys. They may see it every day but that doesn't mean they talk about it at dinner. Right? So, we have … this." She shrugged. In other words, we may hold our noses to shut out the stink, but we go about our business because that's how we've been taught. Ignore this, don't talk about that, and enjoy that pretty red fire truck with the town emblem proudly displayed on the side.

Jaycee realized she had grasped Eve's picture again. It was bending between her fingers. Thank God she took a daily anti-heartburn pill; the eggs were almost unstoppable in their attempt to come back up.

"When was the last time you saw the blonde girl?" she asked.

Kendra looked into the air behind Jaycee's head. She thought about that. "Two days ago, maybe? Yesterday? Recently … hope that helps."

Jaycee pulled out her wallet and selected a crisp fifty-dollar bill. Although it felt somewhat unethical, she wanted to give worthwhile thanks for Kendra's data windfall. A tip for a tip.

She stared at the bill. "Oh, don't worry about that. I told you Norm took care—"

"No," Jaycee interrupted her. "That's for you."

Kendra half-smiled. "Thank you," she murmured.

Jaycee took a final sip of her now chilled and murky-looking coffee. If Cecilia had been here "recently," there was a good shot that Eve had been, too. She transitioned out of their intense discussion.

"They've been here a long time, yes? Norm and Molly." It was meant to be a casual question. It became so much more.

"Forever," Kendra told her. "Even when there was nothing left to stay here for."

"What do you mean?" Jaycee was puzzled. It was a random statement.

"They lost their only child a few years back," she told her. Kendra's anguish was distinctly palpable. "Katherine. With a K. We'd been together since that first day in kindergarten when we were next to each other by first names in alphabetical order."

"I'm so sorry …"

Kendra nodded. "It crushed them. Hard. Everything around here reminded them of her. People were surprised they stayed."

"It's their home," Jaycee offered. "Where else would they go?"

"Anywhere to get away from me," her voice quivered. Kendra had been tormented by the loss, too, but in a much deeper way.

"I don't understand."

"We'd stolen a bottle of whiskey from Norm's stash. Smoked some pot in Mikey Lappem's barn. It was snowing that night; the roads were slick. I was driving …"

Oh, God, no.

"I got hurt pretty badly, but Katherine …" she stopped. Jaycee's gaze returned to the taut, wounded skin that had regrown around a tear. The scars had all been delivered on that one terrible night. "Anyway, they didn't want me to go to jail. They asked the prosecutor to sentence me to rehab instead. I did six months in a treatment program that they paid for."

Jaycee had no words. She tried to offer comfort with her expression.

"They forgave me," she grinned sadly. "They told me everyone makes mistakes and it easily could've gone the other way. They wanted me to have a life, even though I'd pretty much destroyed theirs."

Jaycee merely dipped her chin.

"So, as much as you probably want to hate the blonde girl for doing this to your cousin, think about Norm and Molly."

Jaycee looked into her eyes. "She's nothing like them."

"Isn't she? She has her reasons for doing this. And maybe your cousin does, too. We all make mistakes but not everybody is lucky enough to get forgiven for them."

Another cold wind ruffled the hairs along Jaycee's neck.

The Dine In Take Out. She was definitely taking out much more than she'd brought in.

CHAPTER TWENTY

Darkness masked the highway like an onyx crayon had melted over it from above. Jaycee pulled off and followed a thin, winding road until she could see the glow of lights dancing in the distance. As she drove closer she slowed down. She felt herself tense with those tentative tugs of wonder. What the *hell* was this?

What she saw didn't resemble a humble hunting lodge in the least. It was no cozy, woodsy retreat either. Even all those exalted Beverly Hills compounds surrounded by glamour and exclusivity were real estate mutants compared to this country plantation. The closer she got, Jaycee could feel the behemoth humming with an energy all its own. She sensed its secrets, heard the echo of its murmurs. She squinted, deciding this place had that otherworldly crazy-shack feel that had turned Jack Nicholson into a dull boy. To this day, Jaycee's thumb hovered over the remote anytime *The Shining* showed up on some obscure cable channel. She was eerily possessed to keep watching, as if something other than her own mind was in control.

Jaycee didn't spook easily. This wasn't a movie scene, even though an artistic director would have clapped with joy as the shadowy blanket of late day garnished the roofline with long streaks that looked like pulsing fingers. She pretended not to notice that the house appeared almost demonic, with dozens of sinister eyes watching her approach. She breathed deeply.

Focus. Be smart. Eve may need you.

She blinked wide. The car bucked backwards slightly as she threw it into park and idled just outside the first granite post placed on one side of the entrance. Outdoor lights twinkled but hadn't yet warmed to full blast. The house was divided into three quadrants. To the right, a wing that was entirely dark. In the middle, a sparkly chandelier hung behind a Palladian window that arched almost to the rooftop. Four garage stalls flanked the estate on the left, with bright lantern lights hoisted into symmetrical design between each door. They were the house lights that attached to a timer when the residents wanted you to believe they were home. There was no warm glow of firelight through the windows, no table top lamps skittering animated shadows through the curtains, no sign of life. It looked cold, empty, and anemic. Just like Jack Nicholson by the time he came crashing through the bathroom door to fulfill a set of instructions delivered by a malignant spirit.

She killed the headlights. No need to announce her arrival. The element of surprise was a crucial utensil of her work. Rolling up on someone, microphone thrust forward, with questions already loaded on her tongue, Jaycee could usually scrape something together to round out her stories. She needed to approach with caution yet remain primed for opportunity. This may be the last place Eve was seen …

Alive?

Dead?

"Self-nurturing," as a Legacy Girl, for money?

Jaycee inched along the lengthy driveway, wondering if multiple security cameras were trained on her vehicle.

She prepared herself to be confronted by armed guards, Rottweilers, or the Abominable Snowman. Her neck craned over the steering wheel, inciting a ring of pain that wrapped around her upper ear. She ignored its pulsing objection to the position to stay alert. The wheels crunched over gravel and stubborn ice patches, lifting the tires and then haphazardly dropping them on the backside. Jaycee felt every roll, turn, and rise. She crept along.

The driveway opened into a rounded brick walkway abutting a portico supported by three Roman-looking columns. Jaycee's nose twitched. The building was such a mish-mash of styles. It was old, for sure, but well-kept, and isolated enough to avoid a closer look from the road. In order to really see the place, you had to be right up in front of it. Whatever esoteric events unfolded on the inside, the world at large wouldn't be able to watch.

Jaycee pulled the car around to the far side of the last garage stall. There was a patch of pavement large enough to hold a car. She stopped there. No other cars sat in the driveway. She was alone.

She counted to sixty. No dogs. No alarms blaring, no firing squad. Barton had once told her to consider carrying a gun. That had been when a maniacal killer knew she was looking for him but she wished she'd taken him up on that. With nothing but her wits and charm, she went looking for a way to get in.

She passed through a retaining wall entrance and climbed a set of steps. Instead of going to the door, Jaycee hid around a shutter and peered into the window. She could see polished floors and cherry wood molding so shiny it was almost crimson. She craned her neck to look up. The foyer ceiling made her dizzy. Dark rooms broke off to the right of the entryway and glass-paned French doors were closed shut to the left. A winding staircase hugged the wall and then straightened into a catwalk that connected both sides of the main house. She glided over a few steps and gingerly twisted the elegant knob on the front door. She hadn't worn gloves. The metal casting was freezing on her bare fingers. The knob resisted.

Locked.

Okay, recalculate. Jaycee had gotten into other places that had tried to keep her locked out. Be smart. Be creative. She talked to herself as she stepped around to the other set of windows. Same empty view as the one she'd just left.

The back. Surely this house had doors only the servants used. Utility entrances for deliveries, or perhaps ultra-secretive clients carrying out their pedophiliac fantasies while their pampered wives stayed at their *other* country estates. She hopped down the steps and walked deliberately around to the back, behind the garage, and then reversed course to slip through a fence that shielded an enormous swimming pool covered for the winter, a square hot tub with seating for at least a dozen built in like custom bleachers, and a fountain designed around a tall, naked female that was half-woman on the top, half-mermaid on the bottom. Her stone tail wound to the bottom, waiting for summer to return when it could once again deliver leaping cascades of decorative water art.

Jaycee envisioned nubile Legacy Girls lounging on chaise lounges, delicate glass stemware between their fingers, filled with the alcoholic liquid they couldn't yet legally sip. Did they have conversations with the men who paid for them? What exactly did they discuss? World peace? The ongoing tension between Israel and Palestine? Gun control?

The wind whistled like it was trying to talk to her. Jaycee drew the collar of her coat high against her ears and stuffed her chin near her chest for warmth. She looked out into the dark yard. Nothing stirred. A series of glass doors filled the back of the house. Above them, balconies jutted out from several rooms on the second floor. Jaycee assumed they were probably bedrooms, with gorgeous views of the spa-like yard, and the nothingness that stretched beyond it. She went one-by-one to the doors, twisting the black handles. The first one was like the front door; it failed to even budge an inch. The second one was more worn; it gave a little before it met resistance. The third however, was barely connected to its lock. Time had done its trick and worn the space. If she pulled and twisted, she may be able to convince it to finally let go.

Tiny needles assaulted her fingers. They turned bone white in the freezing air. It must be around fifteen degrees this far north. She shut the feeling off and kept twisting. Forward to the right and then backwards to the left. Over and over again. Like a wiggly tooth with a thick root, it had to be forced. She heard rustling and froze in place. Oh, crap! *What was that?* She knelt down, her chest flattened along the tops of her knees. She rounded her back to appear like one of the big flower pots that littered the patio area, listening, mentally connecting to the auditory pulse of the open space until her own rapid heartbeat was the only sound that filled her ears. Jaycee rose and promptly doubled back over. Ouch! The fibers in her muscles stung and ached. She resumed the twisting and turning. Harder this time, because it was so goddamn cold out there.

Click.

Jaycee gasped. It worked! There was now space between the door handle and the threshold. She could see a hardwood floor. She paused and listened again for any sounds inside, or the sudden angry bleat of an activated alarm system. Nothing. Thank you, Jesus. Carefully, inch by inch, she pushed the door open just enough to step fully inside the room. It was overcast inside but warm, and Jaycee stepped down two wooden planks into a sunken living room. Toe to heel, in a silent advance. In the middle was the largest sectional couch she'd ever seen. Several coffee tables were strategically placed over an Oriental rug with cream-colored, Persian-style swirls. Bookshelves were built against one wall, with hundreds of titles stacked between ornamental glass bowls and animal busts. She squinted to see a lion's head acting as a bookend. The room held durable leather recliners on all four sides, one of them left with the foot rest open. Someone had sat there. But how recently?

She moved toward the foyer. The house had been modernized with recessed lighting turned down low. It lit the hallways but didn't chase away the shade. She walked on softly, skipping along quiet steps that carried her to a set of swinging doors. They lamented her attempt to open them with a noisy creak. She halted. Again, her heartbeat was the only sound she heard. One beat, two, and then three. On the fourth, she tried again, but slower. She looked through the crack. Long marble counters filled the narrow room. Cookbooks sat open. A large industrial-looking refrigerator warbled with the current of electricity in the corner. Butler's pantry.

She continued to the next opening in the hallway. The main kitchen. It was straight out of *Architectural Digest*, designed for efficiency yet handsome and refined. And empty. Copper pendant lights hung from the ceiling in threes. Three over the island in the middle. Three over a table in the breakfast nook, and three above a peninsula that featured place settings for at least … Jaycee counted quickly … ten. The backsplash had been updated with white subway tiles and a Tuscan-looking scheme of vibrant colors behind the eight-burner Wolf gas range. A stainless steel toaster flanked the cooktop, along with a tall glass-domed blender, a red Cuisinart food processor, and a coffee station that held stacked piles of small yellow espresso mugs with something printed on them. Jaycee couldn't read it from where she was. She stepped closer and leaned from the waist. She could see the overstated calligraphy … a T, and below that, an H.

T … h … The. H … e … gh … Heights.

The Heights.

Was that someone's last name. Like, welcome to The Height's? Or, was the place … The Heights? It was magnificent enough to have a name? She silently rolled that around behind her teeth.

The Heights.

The Legacy Girls at The Heights. That sounded about right, she thought, like a fitting destination for a couple about to be married. Join us at The Heights for the marriage of Jack and Jill. All of this was an illusion. No one lived a real life inside a home that required a name. This wasn't real.

But that sound she heard on the floor above her sure was! Footsteps. Someone was here, all right, and moving steadily in her direction.

CHAPTER TWENTY-ONE

She flattened herself against the pantry wall. The steps had gotten louder and closer until she could hear the *tap-tap-tap* of purposeful heels gliding down the hallway outside the kitchen. She was hiding with the brooms and mops, in the narrow alcove between the shelves that held canned goods, bags of potatoes, and stacks of twenty-four packs of bottled water. Jaycee breathed through her nose in shallow gulps. First to prevent herself from hyperventilating, and second, to stop her teeth from chattering together. She was suddenly chilled to her marrow but could feel lines of sweat flow down her neck, over her bra, and disperse like tiny streams near her waistband. Like an insect's rangy legs skimming along the surface of her skin—formless and painless, yet disgustingly itchy. She was smack dab in the middle of the spider's web now.

Be smart, focus! She kept the words on a loop in her head. She played it when that paralyzing dread grew so hot it scorched her blood. She had to control it. She had to use it. She had breached the compound, now she had to storm the castle.

The fridge opened. Light poured out with a sallow, orange-tinged glow. Jaycee hunched her head around the corner. She squinted. It was hard to see and she'd taken off her glasses when she parked the car outside. A man had his hand on the fridge handle and his back to her. He was scanning the bins and racks for something that wasn't readily available. He used his other hand to move items out of the way. He was not a large person, more medium-sized, but narrow across his shoulders. He had short silver hair that fell neatly into place along the back of his neck. His pants were ironed, with a black belt marking the place where a white shirt was tucked into them.

Jaycee's calf muscles weren't having it. They started to cramp. She couldn't stay this still for much longer. What would he try to do to her? If she went after him with her fists, would he pull a knife? Could he kill? If he called the police, would they even listen to her side or would she immediately be arrested, or run out of town? How did they do it when they were being paid to *not* protect and serve?

The man turned from the fridge, his arms loaded with plastic bags full of leafy vegetables and cartons of robust-looking fruit. Green grapes strained against the wrapping of their container. They were fresh, for sure, just bought for someone staying here. Someone who was working up an appetite.

She swallowed hard. Was that for Eve? Was Eve making some man ravenously hungry? Was she in one of those balcony bedrooms upstairs, swept up in a world of faux romance and rapture? She flinched as the man turned on a faucet. The pinging water into a pan sounded like a waterfall in her head. He was making dinner. Jaycee inspected her mental puzzle. Rich, old men moved over the border and more into the middle. Rich old men did not *cook*. They had their people cook for them. That's it! This man was a servant. He was staff. How could she use that?

Whenever people in high positions got into trouble, their staff zipped up faster than a plastic baggie. Because they knew too much. They knew exactly what was on the email server, in the safe behind the portrait in the study, and in the bedroom on the second floor.

Somehow, Jaycee had to get this guy to talk.

CHAPTER TWENTY-TWO

Sauces with heavenly scents simmered on the stove. The man worked in a comfortable silence, only his chopping, dicing, and stirring cut through the serene noiselessness of his kitchen. He collected two plates from an upper cabinet and arranged upon them two portions of whatever he'd just made. Jaycee could see him pluck silverware from a soft-touch drawer, nudging it deftly with his hip to engage the tract that brought it back to closed. He used a towel to wipe away any smudge around the edges of the plates, and then lined them up side by side on a wooden tray with rounded handles. He went back to the fridge to extract two bottles of water, a single yellow rose, and two green apples. He was delivering dinner to two people shuttered away somewhere inside. He removed his apron and brushed off his shirt. Finding himself in proper shape to cart away his cuisine, he lifted the tray, adjusted the direction of his heels, and moved swiftly out of the kitchen.

This was her chance. Jaycee pounced. Her legs almost buckled, her quad muscles angrily tried to match the speed with which she had instructed them to move. She caught herself before she stumbled and spent a few seconds doing fast squats to wake them up. She rounded the corner into the hallway and could see the man's legs approaching the stairway. She flattened her back against the wall to keep out of sight. She followed at a safe distance behind. At the bottom of the stairs she stopped and tucked herself into the space between the banister and the bottom step. If he looked down, he wouldn't see her from the angle above. He didn't look behind himself once. He climbed across the top steps and turned left across the catwalk. Jaycee watched his back disappear and then scurried up the stairs.

The hallway upstairs almost exactly resembled the one below, only doorways were cut in where bedrooms existed behind them. Jaycee watched the man walk past two doors on the right, and then stop at the third. She leaned behind a plush chair with an ottoman and waited. He knocked twice. Jaycee begged her heart to stop pounding so she could hear what was said next.

"Dinner, sir," the man said. She couldn't actually see who was talking but assumed that was him. His voice sounded younger than he looked, and it held a British flare. It was practiced and precise, which made Jaycee shirk backwards when a Texas twang belted out a casual, "Thanks, man. Y'all go to much fuss here?"

"Not at all, sir," the man replied formally. "You enjoy now. Let me know if there's anything else I can do to be of assistance." Jaycee could hear the door click shut, but the booming accent rebounded out.

"Darlin' come on over here now 'fore it gets cold." She listened carefully for the sound of a young female. A giggle. A cough. Something that would confirm the youthfulness of the dinner companion.

Nothing.

The thought of some slick southern oil tycoon sharing his supper with a woman-child she might be related to choked out all hope of decency. Jaycee grimaced as the situation degraded from possibly shady to downright rotten.

No cars in the driveway, and no friendly wreath on the door to welcome them inside, but guests were obviously staying at the inn.

She thought the servant had taken a left when he exited the bedroom. She could've sworn she'd seen him start down the other end of the hallway.

She'd been wrong.

As she turned toward the doors, to try her luck at persuading another lock to open, she tripped. Not on a stair, or a cuff in the throw rug, but on a foot.

She went down hard on one knee. Blistering pain shot from front to back, but it was nothing compared to the glacial realization that she'd just been outed.

CHAPTER TWENTY-THREE

"For God's sake, let me help you up." The man reached for her arms and pulled her with strength he didn't look like he had. Jaycee rose up so fast it was as though she was controlled by marionette strings. She was caught between the pain in her knee and the shock of coming face to face with someone before she had a plan to handle it. Another black mark against her acting-before-thinking way of doing business.

"Uh," she stammered. "I'm … I'm … so sorry." She didn't have a clue what to say. She tried not to look at him. Her blonde hair hung in long sheets across her face, most of it having been pulled free from a ponytail when she stumbled.

"Shhhh," he reprimanded her. "Be bloody quiet. You'll disturb him!" he told her in a modified yell-whisper. "Come along, let's get some ice on this."

He tried to hook his arm around her waist but Jaycee flinched. "No," she said softly. "I'm okay. I can … try … to walk …"

The knee held but it wasn't happy about it. She kept her head down, resigned to the fact she'd have to follow him back down the hallway, down the stairs—gingerly, and one at a time—then into the kitchen where he pulled out a chair and motioned for her to sit. She saw him from the front for the first time. He had a nice face, everything fit well together, and nothing stuck out as distinct or disturbing. Barton would call that having *no discernible characteristic.* He reached into a lower cabinet, pulled out a dish towel, and went over to the ice dispenser on the outside door of the fridge. He pushed a lever and was rewarded with a rush of thick, blocky ice cubes. Depositing them inside the towel, he collected the ends together and twirled them around to lock everything in. He then handed it to Jaycee.

"Here," he told her. "Get this on your knee before it swells."

She knew she had to thank him but was having a hard time speaking. There was no way she was going to get out of this. The jig was up. She had no leverage to sweeten the deal she'd stumbled into. This was it. She was screwed, just like the rest of the girls who came here.

"What are you doing here, Number 13," he asked curtly. "You do not have another scheduled night. And you shouldn't have come back so soon after …" he paused.

Jaycee's brain scurried in concentration. She was in a vortex, being sucked into something thoroughly unexpected. Questions popped like fireworks in her head.

So soon after what? What was a scheduled night? And why the fuck had he just called her Number 13?

Oh my God. Jaycee's mind raced like an engine bolting through its gears. He thinks I'm someone else, she realized. But who? Who was Number 13?

"I, uh, I …" she needed time. Stall him! She risked a faint glance. His eyes reflected cordiality, but not quite camaraderie. *Watch it,* she told herself. They were clearly not equals.

"I think I need a glass of water."

He thought about that but then nodded and walked back over to the cabinet. Jaycee frantically worked the scene to reveal the culture. Reporters used their settings to mingle with the people inside them. She fast-tracked the discovery process. *Think!* Were there no names around here? Was everyone assigned a number? A nickname? This English bastard thought he knew her? Did they spend time together often?

Ever? Recently?

You look kinda like her. Ramona's face danced in Jaycee's head. *Find Cecilia. She looks just like you.* Kendra said it, too. She was Cecilia!

And Cecilia was Number 13!

Okay, okay, great! But what the Christ did that mean?

The man was back. He handed her the glass full of ice water. She gulped it down, not realizing how thirsty she really was. "Thank you," she told him.

Jaycee had always been excellent at memorizing parts of her stories before she told them during the evening newscast. Whether it was information from a press release, or elements of an interview she'd conducted, she had near flawless recall when she needed to add a line or adjust her tag. Her trip home to New Hampshire had been expedited because when someone was missing, time was your biggest enemy. She had exhausted herself in the pursuit of information, but had to remain astute and alert. She had to use all the instruments she'd learned to play.

Think! Focus. Remember what you've learned. Like the facts of a press release.

He was watching her. "You're a bloody mess," he said finally. "What happened to you tonight?"

Jaycee almost laughed. Well, gee, she thought. Should I start at the ass crack of dawn, when I went traipsing into my cousin's closet and came out a coed? Should I tell you my most trusted police source nailed this before I had even fully explained it to him? Do I tell you about Biff? What about Chief Solomon, and the poor kid stuck covering his boss's filthy tracks? Or maybe I should just spill the beans about the townspeople who know what's going on here, yet can't wait to have their own locker in the new community center you're funding.

What happened to you tonight, he wanted to know.

Really now, where should I start?

Jaycee rubbed her eyes to compute some quick math. Eve had been missing a few days. Did that mean Cecilia had been here at the same time? Did Cecilia stay, but Eve left? And what did he mean by suggesting she was back too soon. Either way, it didn't explain where Eve was now.

"I needed a break," she began tentatively, thinking how she could twist the "self-nurturing" theory to fit her setting. *Work the scene.* "I wanted to get away," she told him. "Be by myself for a while."

He shook his head. "That may be, Number 13, but you're not allowed to be here without your Messiah. Come on, now. You know better than this." He was disappointed in her. She was making one poor choice after the next. It was unacceptably reckless.

Jaycee kept her face intact but her insides took another hit. *Your Messiah.* Who would that be?

Think. Focus. She nodded. Okay, okay, Jaycee knew she needed to play. Fine. She put herself into a teenager's mindset, rolling the situation through that prism. Teenagers cajoled. They stroked. They used their innocence like a magic wand.

"I'm sorry," she told him, as she tried to look horrified and sweetly guilty. *Okay, I did it, but aren't I so darned cute?*

He sighed heavily and returned to the fridge. She moved the ice around her knee. It felt better. She might be able to run if she had to.

"You need to keep your nose clean," he told her, returning with a plate of cut cheese, celery sticks, and apple slices. "Here." He set it down next to her. Jaycee thought it wise to nibble on it even though her stomach was rolling. She bit into the apple. The cheese smelled grotesque.

"I'm in trouble then?" she asked. What had Cecilia done besides be a super bitch?

"I would say so," he scoffed. "It's been quite some time since we had two Messiahs on the warpath at the same time." He clucked his tongue. Obviously, it had not been amusing for anyone. "I mean, *two!*"

"I didn't mean to …" she sniffed, "… to do anything to upset anyone." It was appropriately obscure and kept her sounding rather dense. *Work the innocence.*

"Well, obviously you had an enormous lapse in judgment. Number 14 was a bloody horrific choice and her Messiah was deeply disappointed. As you know," he stared intently at her.

"Was it that bad?" she changed tactics. Force him to explain the ways she had failed.

"Uh," he looked sideways at her in pestered annoyance. "Yes, indeed, my silly girl, I'd say it was *bad*," he adopted a surly American tartness to make that word hurt. "Number 14 was an utter disaster. The worst we've seen in a very long time." He put his hands on his hips. "She was unprepared, which is totally your fault, and she was uncommitted, which … again … that's on you."

Damn! Jaycee reflexively pulled her chin back in a self-protective stance. Cecilia must have royally fucked this up.

"But … but … how was I to know she wasn't prepared? I thought she was ready? I mean, she told me she was ready for anything." Keep him talking.

"Your number one job as her Mother was to make absolutely certain that by the time she met her Messiah, she was one-hundred-percent ready for him."

Ewwww! Her mother? Cecilia couldn't raise a snail, and yet in Legacy Girl Land she was someone's mother? How could it get worse than that?

It could. Oh, God, it could. The puzzle pieces turned again. She put Eve *under* Cecilia. Like a parent would a child. It got worse because suddenly Jaycee understood it all.

217

Cecilia had recruited Eve. And Eve had failed them both.

And somewhere out there, two old Messiahs were very pissed at both of them.

CHAPTER TWENTY-FOUR

Two glasses of water later, Jaycee was able to fake-cry, just a little, as a means to further work that teenaged innocence. She desperately needed to find out what Cecilia and Number 14 had done that was so catastrophic.

"You'll have to go back to the beginning," the butler told her. "Both you and the Governor will need to sit down and figure out what part of the process failed."

Now we have a Governor? Jaycee nodded. She wiped at a tear. "I will, I'm just embarrassed. I have always worked very hard to be the perfect Legacy Girl." She held her breath. Using the title alone was speculative, maybe even hazardous. What if that was also some violation of code? She waited for a reaction.

"Your Messiah has noted that, Number 13. He is working on your behalf to smooth things over. But I can't say for certain if he'll punish you on his own."

Punish me? How?

"What, what … do you mean. Punish me?"

"You know he reserves that right. It's up to him, really. He may not call for you for some time. He may not pay the insurance on your car. I don't know. Messiahs have many options. He may do nothing at all. That depends on how valuable you are to him."

"But you don't think he'd …"

Kill me? Maim me? Make me disappear? Jaycee also wondered what Cecilia was driving. Did it match the Tiffany bracelet?

"… he'd hurt me … do you?"

The butler looked into her now tear-streaked, mascara-lined face and tried to reassure her that, no, that wasn't *likely* to happen. He smiled without showing his teeth.

"Number 13," he started. "I know your Messiah has been very pleased with you thus far." He sounded like a principal speaking to a straight-A student who had somehow just failed her Spanish final. You aren't stupid, honey … not all the time anyway.

"That's good, then. Right?" she tried to sound buoyantly hopeful.

"Very good," he confirmed. "And you have to think that after your years together, all the fulfilling experiences you've shared, this will all but be forgotten."

Jaycee gulped. How utterly vile! Fulfilling experiences? With a kid?! She drilled her upper teeth into her lower lip to prevent them from sneering in repugnance.

Years together. Messiahs and Legacy Girls spent *years* together?

Jaycee thought of Norm and Molly. How they described contracts getting signed.

"Has he spoken to the Governor yet?" She needed to figure out who that was. And was the real Number 13, aka, Cecilia, getting reamed by him?

"I don't know. I am not privy to the communication between Messiahs and the Governor. If he hasn't summoned you as of yet, perhaps not."

Jaycee drew in air through her nose. Cecilia wasn't her primary concern. If Eve was Number 14, what, if anything, had been done to chastise her? Was she plied with BBQ sauce and then thrown to the wolves and coyotes that roamed northern New Hampshire?

"Number 14 …" she said quietly. "Is she … is she … okay?" Her heart pounded again. Even if Number 14 wasn't Eve, what would she do if she was made aware of harm coming to some other innocent girl?

"We won't be seeing Number 14 around here anymore," he told her. "Her Messiah already took care of that."

Her airway narrowed. Jaycee rolled her knuckles against each other. "Was she returned to school?"

The butler shrugged his tapered shoulders. His torso went limp. He didn't appear to approve, but much like everyone else in Legacy-ville, it wasn't his place to have an opinion.

"Maybe," he replied. "Maybe not. Perhaps she will 'self-nurture' somewhere else permanently."

"I know she hasn't been at school lately." Jaycee stirred the stew to find the chunks of meat. What else did he know?

"I'm not certain she'd be in any shape to be at school right away. If, in fact, she was to return at all."

"How do they …" careful, she told herself. She can't act like a prosecutorial aggressor. She had to remain the forlorn, yet curious kid just a tad too nosy for her own good.

"They have their ways," he answered impatiently. "Number 13, remember your place now. Ours is not to

221

question. Ours is to accept the terms of our agreements and then act accordingly. You really need to get yourself together here. If your Messiah calls for you, you need to be in better condition than this."

Jaycee was trying to cover extra distance, but she realized she may not reach the finish line with him. The butler had decided this race was over.

"I realize it's getting late but you can't stay here tonight. This is an unscheduled visit and I won't have it." He looked at her pathetic state. "I'm sorry, but I can't."

Jaycee nodded. "Can I just ask you one more question?" she begged the gods of decency to pinch this butler until he felt his conscience kickstart.

He peered at her. His nod was almost indiscernible.

"Did you see Number 14 leave? Was she …"

Alive? Please, you English bastard, tell me Number 14 got out of here alive!

"… was she … well?"

The butler weighed her question. He had seen much more than he was willing to tell this ridiculous girl, but he felt her torment. He had three granddaughters back in the UK, and while he'd rather decapitate them himself if they ever engaged in what went on here, he still knew how deeply girls could hurt.

"She was well enough."

Jaycee huffed out relief. Thank you, Jesus.

"You need to be going now," he told her. This was it. Her borrowed time was up. Now get the hell out!

Jaycee rose. Her knee moved stiffly but the pain was greatly reduced. It would be fine. She placed the wet towel on the kitchen counter and then had to decide, quickly, how she would exit the house. Someone familiar with it would choose the front door. How did she get there? She'd entered improperly through the back. It was still dark in the main room. She couldn't fuck this up. She had to leave as Number 13.

But the gods of decency covered her again. The butler didn't just send his guests off on their own. Even the Legacy Girls were shown out. He led Jaycee back down the hallway and took a sharp right once they reached the living room. She followed. About thirty steps later they crossed the foyer she'd only seen through the windows and he reached for the door handle. He touched her back and sent her on her way. No more words were exchanged.

Jaycee hoped he didn't watch her walk toward her hidden car. Surely, he'd realize it wasn't the vehicle on loan from her Messiah? The one he may not pay for any longer. She couldn't look backwards so she limped over toward the garage and took her time climbing back into the rental.

The butler wasn't watching anyway. He had already returned to the kitchen to attend to the uneaten food and the dirty towel. He had neglected to inform Number 13 of what else had happened that doomful night.

What he should have told her was Number 14's Messiah had *attempted* to take care of her. The butler was under contract to never utter a word about any of it, even on the rarest of occasions when a Legacy Girl went rogue. That, especially, went to the grave when he did.

CHAPTER TWENTY-FIVE

Going rogue wasn't what she'd planned to do. It had just happened. Like when you walk across the wooden planks of a pier to board a fishing boat. The splinter that tears into your flesh just happens … it's never something you can plan for. But once that little fucker draws first blood, you have to deal with it.

Eve had reared back with a mixture of discomfort and apprehension. Her Messiah was too forceful. Just that alteration in his approach was more than enough to snap her senses back. This was not who she was! It struck her almost before it was too late that she absolutely could not allow this to happen. She had made a stupendous mistake. She had to salvage whatever she had left.

"I'm sorry …" she told him firmly, pushing her palms against his chest. She could feel each of his ribs. It was a hideous reminder of how close she'd allowed him to get. "I can't do this."

He pulled his head back, his lips disconnecting from where they'd been nestled near her carotid artery with an ugly sounding plunger-like discharge. His eyes constricted. He had, at least, figured he could get something out of this girl before he ended their relationship for good. It was an unfortunate development and the old man felt his inner rage rise like a hot whitecap, that notorious temper that worked flawlessly in the boardroom. The idiots would cower when he reminded them of who owned the controlling shares.

Who did this little slut think she was?

"Number 14, this is unacceptable!" he blared like a fog horn. His moist lips blew droplets of liquid onto her face. She pulled further away by using her heels and hamstrings to crawl backwards until she felt the sumptuous, oversized pillows hit the headboard of the bed. She was stuck. There was no more room left. She faced him.

"I'm sure it is," she explained, trying to stay calm. "But it's my choice. Even in my contract, I can—"

Whack! Her hand automatically covered the cheekbone he'd just ripped open. She felt her fingers get sticky. She was bleeding.

You dirty motherfucker.

Like the splinter. He'd drawn first blood. She may be a Legacy Girl fraud but Eve would not tolerate abuse. Her back straightened. She had trained herself to fight pain, to cut off its capacity to affect her. He didn't know that she had broken both ankles on the soccer field. That she'd been diagnosed with three concussions but had probably had six more. Her wrist sprained when the goalie's entire body weight dropped on it during her headfirst rush to crash the net. Hey, you old fart, have you ever dislocated a shoulder? Well, she had, and this rat-faced *ancestor* was absolutely not going to hit her again! He thought pain would diminish her.

It *fortified* her!

She used her leg muscles to pop up on both knees. She was right-handed, but his face was closest to her left. Balling her fingers into her fist, she unleashed her arm and connected an uppercut with his nose. Blood spurted loose

226

from one nostril. He fell back onto his naked rear end and groaned like a baby cow.

"Oh my gawd …" He bayed in pain. "Goddamn you, you little bitch!" He swore and sniveled, as he rolled from his side into a fetal position, using the comforter to catch the torrent of red. Red on red. The comforter absorbed the blood without notice. Maybe that was why it had been ordered in such a bold color.

Legacy Girls weren't supposed to fight back. They were paid to be pliable, docile, and *Jesus Christ*, ready to go at it all night long! He'd taken an extra Viagra just to make sure he was up for the challenge. He had plans for Number 14. Good plans. He'd take her to places she'd never seen, he'd make love to her on the beaches of Capri, and dress her in the finest clothes made by designers he had on call. When he snapped his fingers, they jumped. They *all* jumped. Why was this one trying to ruin everything?

His eyes went black. Shock became rage. He came at her again, his skinny legs strained and lunged, but then precipitously buckled when she swept her shin below his thigh. He went down hard again.

Eve ripped the belt from his bathrobe and wound it twice around his arms, then knotted it four times around the bedpost. He screamed obscenities at her but he was breathing heavily and losing strength. He was not physically equipped to match her endurance, or her brawn. She plopped down heavily on his shrunken pec muscles. He heaved and bucked but then began to beg for her to move.

"I … can't … breathe …" he wailed.

She moved off him. He wheezed and growled at her but she ignored his insults. Part of this was her fault and she allowed him to express his outrage with this unexpected turn of events. He'd wanted sultry and erotic and here she was making it all about pain—and not in a good way. She just wasn't cut out for what he expected from her. She'd thought she could do this.

But she couldn't.

"Listen to me," she told him pointedly. "Stop it and listen!"

He rolled his head back and forth. His wrists pulled at the knots but they held. His feet tried to kick but couldn't. His ab muscles were no longer tight enough to support his back. It slacked and rounded. Everything in his seventy-one-year-old body collapsed and threw up the white flag of surrender.

He scowled at her.

"I know you're disappointed but you never should have hit me." Eve looked down at him with pity. "Who hits girls? That makes you a coward."

He rolled his lips but couldn't speak.

"I made a mistake," she continued. "I thought I could do this. I thought it would be easy. I've worked my ass off my entire life, and I …" she sighed and shook her head. "Why am I even explaining this to you?"

He seethed. He wasn't interested in her confession. All he cared about was what had been lost to him. A sexual playmate, a casual girlfriend who looked pretty in a dress, and a companion whenever he wanted one for as many years as he had left on earth. She'd blown it! And now she wanted to blabber on about how hard she worked?

"I will ruin you," he frothed with fury.

Eve rolled her back molars. He wasn't getting it. She'd offered an apology—of sorts—and he wouldn't accept it. Fine. She'd finish this once and for all. And she'd hardly be the one who was ruined.

"Where's your phone?" she demanded.

"Fuck you!" he howled. Eve skirted her bottom back over his stomach and hopped up and down a couple of times. Her firm butt cheeks rammed his gut until he screamed in agony.

"Sto … *ppppp!"* he begged.

"Where's your phone?"

He hesitated again but could no longer take the torment. His heart hurt, the blood rushing through its timeworn chambers throwing off its already choppy rhythm. He could not sustain his role; the ingénue was now the master.

"Pants. Right pocket."

She jumped off the bed and found the folded pile of clothing he'd intended to change into later. After they'd had their proper first meeting. Eve tried to forget about that part. She dug into his pocket. She pulled out his iPhone.

"Password?" He blinked in fast beats as though she'd just spoken in Mandarin.

One … two … deep breaths later … he'd stall some more.

"Password!" she demanded again.

"7840," he chucked the numbers at her like grenades. "What are you doing?"

She entered the four digits. "Just giving myself a little insurance."

She hit the phone icon and then scrolled through recent calls. While there were no contacts named "Honey Bunny," or "Babe," there were several calls to "Gayle."

"Who's Gayle?" she asked him.

He wildly objected and tried to whip up a mild tempest, but there was no energy left and it swiftly blew out of him. Then he begged and pleaded in indignant bursts of childish sobs. Eve nodded. Good. That confirmed Gayle was a significant other who likely had no idea where he was spending this frosty winter night. Where did she think he was? Business trip? Hunting excursion with the grandkids? Shopping … for her?

It was disgusting. But she had almost been part of it. Eve felt hot shame trickle down her face in the form of regretful droplets of salty tears. She wiped them away. She would not *cry*.

She placed a call to Gayle. Three rings later, a brittle voice greeted her. Gayle listened in silence as Eve confessed. For both of them. Her Messiah's eyes were closed, though his head swung slowly back and forth with racks of his own tears shaking his shrunken anatomy as though it were a paper doll's.

When she hung up she returned the cell to the pocket it had come from. She untied the knots and let his hands free.

He was a humiliated heap of bitterness but the vehemence had subsided.

"Gayle knows who I am," she told him. "She knows where I go to school and where I live. If something happens to me, she'll know it was you, and right now, she doesn't like you very much. Cheating on your wife is one thing but harming … *or killing* … a teenage girl is another. That would be unforgivable. Wouldn't you agree?"

He shot daggers at her, despising every muscular inch of her, but most of all, loathing the indomitable courage that had just earned her a big win. The Legacy Girl had outmaneuvered the Messiah.

Now onto the Governor.

And, then, Mother.

She had no idea how she'd get back to campus in the cold dark of night. She just knew she had to. She climbed back into her clothes, slammed the bedroom door behind her and ran full bore down the hallway, almost colliding with the English butler who'd stoked the fire in her room, and left a tray of chocolate drizzled cookies, and two small tea cups with delicate slices of lemon on the side. His eyes widened in shock.

"He may need some medical attention," Eve told him.

"Number 14 …" he gulped, still so deeply jarred by her sweaty and disheveled appearance he didn't know what else to say. *Was she bleeding?*

"Don't call me that!" she instructed. She cut around him effortlessly, just as she would a defender trying to block her run to the net.

"Don't ever call me that again." She was at the door, her statement disappearing like fog into the crisp night air. No one heard it but Eve had the final word as she put The Heights behind her for the last time.

CHAPTER TWENTY-SIX

She had a low battery and no service. Jaycee threw her phone onto the passenger seat. She needed Barton's counsel. She longed to hear Van's voice. Los Angeles felt like it was a million miles away. Marcy was probably pacing her tiny kitchen in fear that now she'd lost not just her daughter, but her niece, too.

Shit!

Time felt like it stood still in the house but it was already the next day and the roads were desolate and empty. Her phone was useless, Eve was still missing, and now Jaycee had a Governor to worry about, too.

Of course, Cecilia hadn't moved on her own. She had worked in concert with an advisor to identify a potential Legacy Girl. She may have coaxed Eve, but the Governor was in on it at the very top. Was it the money or the glory of being invested in a secret society? Some people were so starved for power they would do anything to keep it. She considered the mafia. They were criminals yet so devoted to family they'd do whatever it took to keep it safe. Theirs was a world of conflicting priorities. Commit murder, extortion, or blackmail but assume absolution because your heart was in the right place.

Family. How far would she go to protect Van? Eve? It was a hypothetical inquiry. She'd do whatever it took, exactly as she always had. She absently touched her neck. Her own scar showed how far she'd go when someone she loved was in trouble.

Her headlights illuminated swirls of opaque white near the center line of the road. It was snowing again. She backed off the accelerator and reminded herself she'd be of no good to Eve or Marcy if she wound up down an embankment.

WWBS. It was what she asked herself regularly now, how she and Van joked when they watched the news together and a police official made a far less remarkable on-camera statement. Come on, they'd laugh, that sucked! No comparison whatsoever to their favorite cop and his sneering yet dead-on analysis. They even finished each other's sentences at times with it: WWBS. What Would Barton Say?

Jaycee sighed angrily. If she couldn't have him by her side, what was her next best option? She'd *think* like him. Start in the eye of the hurricane and work her way to the outer bands. Jaycee blinked rapidly. She put him right there next to her in the front seat. His hazel eyes would quickly prowl for clues. She imagined him rolling his palm over the mutilated finger stump that still hurt like a sonofabitch no matter how vehemently he denied it. Humid heat from the air vent trickled through her nose, in and out, until she could feel her mind allowing his presence to arrive.

"I'm in the shit here, Barton. Total blackout darkness all around." She spoke out loud, to herself, and the Barton in her head.

"Come on, kiddo, even Mason's not afraid of the dark anymore. You have to feel your way out." She knew he would say that. Yes, I get that. But how? Help me!

234

"Where do I start?"

"What about Eve made her so vulnerable? To Cecilia, and to this Governor piece of shit."

Jaycee nodded. A good start. She knew Barton would wrap all nine of his fingers around the throat of a man who participated in the desecration of a teenager. What about Eve or any of them had triggered the evolution from schoolgirl to kept mistress?

"I can't see that clearly yet. Money? Yes, or at least maybe, but it's different here, Barton. In L.A., ambition becomes shapeless and needy. Pretty young girls arrive by the hour. They've grown up as beauty nobility in their small towns, the Princess of the Peach Fair, or the senior prom queen. Everyone told them they had eyes like Cameron Diaz, or a body like Gisele. They would totally take Hollywood by the gonads on day one!"

"We're surrounded by them," Fake Barton told her. "The models-slash-actresses who have their confidence shredded until their rent is due and the only jobs left are at Lens Crafters, or the Cheesecake Factory."

Jaycee gave a throaty reply. "Right," she uttered. "Maybe a few of them ran home to the broken-hearted high school sweethearts they'd left behind. But, Barton …"

"Yeah?"

"Those aren't the only jobs left. What haunts me are the girls who give in to their dark sides, who think there's no way out. They believe those greasy-haired photog types who promise if they show a little nip, agents could book them into movie roles right away. We know those are the roles that send them to clinic every month to test for STDs."

"So if Hollywood eats pretty young women for breakfast, why not all of them?" Barton wanted her to lift the tarp. Dig in. Figure out why some of these girls were capable of pulling the rip cord before they splattered onto the ground?

"Make this a special report you're about to put on TV," Barton told her. "You'd be working on the ending, right? You've followed the trail, your sources have leaked out some juicy deets, and you got the green light from the cops to go with it. How would you tag this story, Jay Jay? Tell your viewers why Eve was a prime target."

Yes, plug in the components and let the formula churn out the results. Jaycee's stories were never told without an ending. Even if it took months, or years, a suspect was brought to justice and a wrong was righted as best the system could provide.

We have an update to a story we first brought you last month, last year, ten years ago.

It was the line that led newscasts almost nightly. Viewers longed for closure. They, along with the reporters, grew attached to the story. They walked together to the bitter end. But in Legacy Girl world, she wasn't sure she'd ever get there.

"Okay," she started. Wrap this up. "Now that I can assume Eve is probably Number 14, daughter to Number 13, I need to nail down the rest of the family to find who adopted her in the first place."

Her hot breath was fogging up the windshield as Jaycee deconstructed her puzzle with pretend Barton.

"Holy United Academy is the corner office for the Governor." She drew the picture, thinking in images as she always did with Ben and his camera by her side. *No!* That was wrong. Ben wasn't there anymore. But why could she see him so clearly? Because he had been her trusted partner in the field. Ben rolling up on a scene, his torso permanently tilted to one side like a lazily scrawled number seven as the bulk of his camera sunk into his collar bone. Ben muttering, "All right, Jay Bird, where my freaks at? Let's find 'em." He then zoomed in and focused on the people or landscapes that would hit the news that night.

"Don't!" voices growled. "Don't do it. Don't let him in, Jay Jay." Barton, and her own dismay roared inside her head. She was disgusted with herself for letting him slink through her locks. When she returned to Los Angeles, Jaycee still had serious work to do. He was always just a thought away.

Focus!

"I am, Barton, I am."

She bore down, booting Ben, and revealing blank space for a new persona. Let him take shape. Who was he? She called up physical traits, added a lumbering long-legged gait, an arrogant incline to his head. The Governor was becoming a shifty-eyed small business owner who ran a tidy legal store from the front while he dealt a bootleg stash through the back. Stealthy, secretive, and profitable, with the goods coming in from preexisting sources and then shipped straight to The Heights.

"The books stay legit," she whispered.

"How?"

"The products on the shelves are real so the good people pay at the cash register." Jaycee pictured the exchange.

"And the bad people line up in the back," Barton supplied.

"All those plain white envelopes they pass along are stuffed with cash," Jaycee confirmed. "But those sales never hit the books."

"But he keeps track," Barton carried the scheme. "The Governor knows about every single sale, and exactly where all those envelopes come from."

Legacy Girls were merchandise and yet Holy United remained storied and unsullied. Students graduated, went on to achieve great things in their lives, and then sent their kids back for more of the same. A continuous circle built upon tradition, success, and ultimately, lots and lots of money. Ironic really, given those were the same intangibles that also kept Legacy Girls dedicated to their Messiahs.

Jaycee built from there.

"Okay," she told Barton. "It's all disguised as commerce, business, but it involves human beings. Hearts and emotions are in play."

"So damage is inevitable," he added. "Although it may take a while to reveal itself as the fucking monster beneath the bed."

'Scuse my mouth, Jaycee said to herself, adding that absentminded apology Barton always did when his narration became colorful. The monster was near, that hissing, supernatural fiend that sabotaged happiness and self-confidence. The menace that destroyed lives.

"Your past is present in your future." His spectral message carried itself on wispy wings, fluttering just behind her reach. *What?* She'd heard him say that before. But how did that apply to Eve? Jaycee churned ideas and concepts. Your past is present in your future. Her past. It was loaded with interviews. So many interviews. Use that to bridge this together.

"I've interviewed adults who were damaged when they were young," she said. "They get that jolt one day that breaks through all the protective layers of their memory."

"They flash back to it. The event, the hurt, and the shame." Barton trucked her along.

"Yes," she confirmed. "It may be decades later, but they see it all over again. They *feel* it."

The cycle of a victim. Sometimes, it was an inexplicable slide into depression, or an inability to hold up one half of a healthy relationship. Jaycee had seen their anguish. The hunters who had pursued them wore disguises like a patient sixth grade teacher who offered half of his peanut butter and jelly sandwich, and then caressed the child's knees while they studied state capitals in the empty classroom after school. Or, that of a stout little league coach who offered to drive the lanky first baseman to practice because his parents worked. He was so kind when he paid the registration fee, just because he knew the family couldn't scrape together the forty dollars. It was more than fair that he'd expect a little payback.

Jaycee had the past and present, but she had to frame the future. That would reveal the insidious beast who had wound his way in by the same kind of trickery. How he lured his girls. Holy United Academy housed the biggest fiend of all, worse even than the slob who caressed the quiet boy in the back of the movie theater, or the little girl as she slept in her foster care family's extra bedroom. He found the scholarship girls at boarding schools, and reminded them of how fortunate they were to have him on their side. He provided them a taste of the good life, just a droplet, until they realized how easy it could be to have it all the time. Drinking it up forever. He knew there was no central authority to report to, no investigative resource, no hovering parent, and certainly no homey kitchen table to confess at. He used the fortunate fact that what they would do at The Heights remained the most underreported crime of all, cunningly banished away to become the nightmares of the future. The future. *Their futures*. When the Legacy Girls would stuff it away like a bad report card in their backpack, hiding beneath shame and trauma they would never fully understand.

"But even if one day the torment comes," she began aloud. "No one will believe them anyway."

"Hammer against the skull, Jay Jay. Slammin' them upside the head. These girls are fighting the statute of limitations, and everyone else's doubt. They'll drive themselves crazy, and sometimes justice is just too slippery to hold onto."

"Because even if they do report it someday, it won't matter?"

"Nope. Children are notorious for making shit up."

"Or for forgetting things."

"We let them down all the time," Barton reminded her. "The system isn't set up to seal all the cracks. They fall through and we lose them."

Jaycee's eyes were slits. *We lose them.* No, that was unacceptable! She refused to lose Eve through the cracks of Holy United Academy. Even though life allowed far too many victims to remain victims, she had to reveal the abuser. The Governor could not emerge whole. The spotless storefront could not prevail.

Pop rocks bubbled behind her brow. Jaycee rubbed her face, it felt sweaty and slack. So much to untangle and yet she was so drowsy. And why could she suddenly hear Van, too? Her small rental car was filling up.

"Here, Jay Jay, drink up." He handed her a martini glass brimming with his high octane specialty, reserved solely for the nights she had a fancy work event to attend, but preferred pajamas and a movie on the couch: his finely mixed espresso martini sprinkled with the flakes of nutmeg he added just for her.

She smacked her lips as the hallucination carried the liquid down her throat and into her stomach, remembering how it always ignited her auxiliary engine. Thank you, Van. Her team was here.

Even though it wasn't.

"What have you seen?" Barton sidestepped around Van and returned her back to her time on campus.

"I've seen them," she told him. "The students. I've been among them." She'd watched them in the intimate setting of their shared existences. The raucous swap of grabs and giggles with their headmaster, the awkwardly inappropriate placement of a teacher's fingers and hands on their bodies, and the slithering sensuality of early womanhood encased in uniforms ordered two sizes too small.

Without knowing fully at the time exactly what she was dealing with, she'd watched the indoctrination up close. The ruse. The closeness that was promised to parents when they abdicated control over their youngsters. How wonderful was it that the headmaster and the teachers lived on campus right there with their students? They learned, laughed, dined, and *slept* … under the same roof.

We're family here at Holy United Academy. No one ever leaves. They always come home.

Veiled truths and sickeningly sweet bonding experiences. A casual, unorthodox leader, larger than life in both stature and personality. A magnetic figure with charisma so potent it made you feel *sooooo* good about what you knew was so bad.

"Dirty fuckers are sometimes motivated by a sick friendship they build with their victims," Barton was in her head again.

"They touch and coerce a child," Jaycee added. "They want them to feel safe in that. Like, hey, we're mature here, we're different, and it's special. Just for us to enjoy."

Was Eve enamored by the fondness, and accessibility? Did this family feel more like one she fit into? Did she buy the headmaster's pitch that he was always available, his door wide open, his lair warm and inviting?

"How do they lure them, dominate them, and then ship them off to The Heights? How do they get them to go, Jay Jay?"

Motherfucker! Jaycee felt her fingers pulse with scorn. She recognized the person she had just built. His features morphed until his brown eyes danced with the provocative prowess of an assassin.

"What did you expect from a man who calls himself Biff?" Barton demanded.

Biff! Jaycee's hands clenched the wheel. She remembered the cold schoolyard standoff. He had balked at her audacity, that cheeky irreverence for the family that he had found insulting and unwarranted. His gigantic boots had been uncomfortably close to hers. Threateningly close. No one ever leaves Holy United Academy, my dear sweet girl, they always come home.

Barton was right again! What *did* she expect from a man who called himself Biff?

Jaycee's foot tingled as she kicked at the accelerator. Her destination was predetermined. But before she confronted Governor Biff on his own territory she needed an ally. It couldn't be the soccer coach who shunned her in

243

a huff of antipathy. This had to be someone who could inspire a holy awakening within a darkened heart. Eve must be released, her Messiah ordered to stand down, and her innocence restored. If Jaycee could accomplish anything at this point, it had to be that.

Snow fell steadily upon the highway. The purity of each unique flake reminded her that a storm always passed. It may shake the tree limbs and knock out the lights, but eventually it rolled out to sea so the cleanup could begin. What was injured or impaired could then be built back stronger than it was before.

"Hang on, Eve," she heard Barton say before he vanished into the empty space of the front seat.

"Hang on," Jaycee repeated. "The storm's almost over."

CHAPTER TWENTY-SEVEN

Dawn was breaking in exquisite gold over the forest canopy when Jaycee pulled back onto campus at Holy United Academy. Lifting her chin to reveal her face in the rearview mirror, she nearly gasped. It was almost bone-white. She had beaten up her already fragile body, taken it from the steady climb out of the dark well of her recovery back to sheer exhaustion. Her healing neck ached and her recently banged up knee throbbed. She shoved it all down. No way could she approach this as the dark horse. She had to bring everything she had to this battle.

There wasn't much time left before the empty walkways filled with uniformed students scurrying their way through another school day. A few lights were coming on in resident halls and she could see twirls of steam rising from the smokestacks of academic buildings.

This was go-time. End game. Her all-or-nothing offensive. She hadn't bothered to change back into Eve's uniform. At this point, it didn't matter what she was wearing, only that she came to win. Jaycee set out toward the Chapel. She had to get there before the rest of the students arrived. It was her only chance to beg in private for Pastor Anthony's assistance.

She knew she couldn't take on Biff alone. She had to appeal to whatever sliver of righteousness remained, with the most virtuous figure she could find. Pastor Anthony was literally her Hail Mary pass. Sure, he was somewhat smarmy in his rose-colored simplicity, and she'd questioned if he truly lived with the effervescence he had tried to display to her, but Jaycee had to hope God's graces were at work, too. Even though she had lied to him first, somehow Jaycee had to make him see her for what she really was: a faithful servant who may have come to him under false pretenses but was, in truth, trying to save the forsaken. It had to be all about Eve. Pastor Anthony knew Eve. He'd told Jaycee he'd watched her games. He'd suggested that Eve wasn't perfect, no, she had simply cultivated herself. Like everyone else at Holy United Academy, Eve became a spiritually superior, "self-nurtured" person.

But Eve was also Number 14. Pastor Anthony had to help release Eve from her sinfulness.

She was limping. She didn't feel her knee glitch midstep until she tried to trot down the freshly shoveled brick pathway. Adrenaline shoved her along. Jaycee hopped twice on her other leg for every one stride on the bad. She started to sweat in spite of the raw sting of the air as it hit her nostrils. Her jeans clung to her backside like icy hot man hands. She was a dirty mess. It would be an alarming look she brought to Chapel.

The bells tolled on the half-hour. Only thirty more minutes before the entire Holy United Academy student body poured through the Chapel doors and into the pews to celebrate the arrival of another day. Pastor Anthony was probably earnestly preparing another lesson for his young flock. One that was drenched in gratitude and the value of service. How did he not know the Governor was waiting …

like a fortune-hawker … to pounce on the very philanthropic vulnerability he preached?

Please God, she whispered through her fractured footsteps. *Please let him see through my nasty hair and tired eyes. Give us the strength to walk forward together for Eve. Carry us safely away from the danger and into the light.*

Amen.

She rarely spoke to God, but in this setting, about to seek assistance from His holy servant, she'd damn well better try.

Jaycee skipped down the final pathway that led past neat lines of white-covered evergreen shrubs trimmed to waist height. She put one hand on top for support, her fingers sinking fast through fresh snow. She steadied herself and caught her breath. Through the nose, out the mouth. The stairs were next. She climbed up twelve steps, and then stopped. She kicked her knee out once, twice, moving the joints until the motion became fluid. This time, she didn't bother with a high bun, glasses on her nose, or the garb of the faithful youngsters. She came as herself. Gripping the long handle of the front door, she pulled back the panel and stepped into the vestibule. It was empty. Jaycee lurched down the main aisle. She listened for movement in the back, where Pastor Anthony would be finalizing his daily missive to share with his eager litter.

She was halfway down the row of pews. The classic wood altar with a grapevine trim displayed a bold brass cross in the center. Its legs were carved and decorative.

Although clergy living quarters were traditionally built away from the sacred chapel or church, here at Holy United they appeared to have been built right into the back. Jaycee passed around the altar and discovered a half-open door that led to a dark hallway. That hallway then widened into what looked like an apartment, complete with decorative wreath and welcome sign. The lights were on inside and Jaycee could hear movement.

She listened closely.

A male voice sounded like it was underwater. She could make out noise but the words had no shape. She leaned her head through the molding of the door trying to get deeper into the airflow. Yes, she could hear him. Pastor Anthony's stubbornly southern nasality rose into the empty living room and over the back of the plaid couch that faced a small plasma TV mounted on the paneling above a brick fireplace. Three separate entryways were on the left side wall, while another was straight back behind the fireplace. She could see a tiled floor that she assumed was the kitchen. She walked quietly around the side of the couch and poked her head in. Four chairs were neatly tucked into a dining table in the middle of the room. A row of oak cabinets led to a stainless steel fridge, stove, and a dishwasher below. A coffee maker gurgled near a compact window shaded with plantation shutters in the closed position.

It held all the trappings of someone starting his busy day, but the kitchen was empty.

She crossed back into the living room and chose the first entryway.

Suddenly, one voice became two. Jaycee's mouth dropped open in wide-mouthed gulps as she realized that interspersed with the pungency of Pastor Anthony's accent was a decidedly flat northern lilt. And it was female!

Oh my God, could it be? It was a long shot. A one in a million chance that somehow Eve had come to the same place seeking respite and consolation. Was she confessing to her own lurid participation in Biff's detestable enterprise?

This was it! She had to help Eve. She was her family and someone had tried to hurt her.

Jaycee threw herself through the doorway. *I'm here, Eve! I'm here ...*

But then, she wasn't anymore. Even though she saw shadowy forms and colors, her eyes faded with a peculiar feeling that she'd suddenly been dropped through a hole that had opened in the earth beneath her feet. She was falling and then the voices stopped.

CHAPTER TWENTY-EIGHT

Her head was somehow caught in a catcher's glove. Every few seconds a fastball connected with her chin. Jaycee struggled to lift it out of the way but the pitcher kept firing.

Boom, boom, boom!

"Hey, hey …" words came at her from behind in flutters. Like a mosquito in her eardrum, they buzzed and zipped around but she couldn't swat them away. Her chin was pulled sharply out of the glove. Something hard landed on her cheek.

Ouch, she thought. Stop it! *S…t…o…PPPP!* She jerked her hand to her face and caught the offending hand. It fit into her own for only a second before whomever it belonged to jerked it back.

She opened one eye. The room spun. A flowered lampshade was next to her on the ground. She must have grabbed it as she fell. But why had she fallen? Why was she on the ground?

"Wake up," the voice was back. The hard slap to her cheek became softer. Fingers grabbed her chin and shook. "Wake up!"

She heard only a woman's voice. Jaycee tried to slide onto her shoulder but the back of her head jolted her brain with a blinding bolt of pain. She moaned. What the fuck had happened?

"Come on, get up." The voice was persistent.

"I ... can't ..." Jaycee protested. She tried to persuade both eyes to open. She focused on a painting in the distance. Jesus was reaching out a robed arm to a child by his side. She encouraged her aching eyes to attach to the image. Like she told Van to do. Memories were images. Find the image first so the brain can connect.

"Get ... up!" the female voice was right there in her face. And it was pissed!

Jaycee had also taught herself to function in spite of discomfort. First, on live television when technology failed and she was on screen when her video should've been. More recently, that was how she'd channeled the strength to climb out a broken window the size of a shoebox to save herself and Van. How she had tried like hell to bring integrity back to the Throw Away Girls. She had to put the pain away until later. There was still work to be done. Right now, she had to deal with that goddamn voice.

"Get ..." it told her again.

"I'm trying!" she finally yelled back. Shards of white hot pain wrapped around her forehead but then started to release. They pulsed with her heartbeat. That was better. She could deal with that.

Find the image. Let the brain come back.

Dark hair. Flushed face blotchy with exertion, sweat, and ... crusty blood? She was hurt, too. Her eyes were like an angry cat's. But below the irritation was a discernible sorrow. She wasn't just hurt, she was ...

What was she? Jaycee scurried around her own void. Find the image!

She had the eyes of someone who knew of life's hardships because she had lived them. Eyes like Eve.

Like Eve.

Eve!

Jaycee slipped under a dark wave again. It took her back. *Way back.*

* * * *

The image of a child, feet flying free from a wooden plank connected by two braided ropes to the fattest branch of the backyard oak tree. Jaycee saw the eyes. Watchful, hooded, deliberate instead of casual.

"Eve, come here," she'd told her. "Try this, it's the spicy mustard." She held a grilled hot dog bun out in her right hand. "Come here!"

The little girl dragged one foot through the dirt to slow the swing. When it was safe, she stepped off and walked to the back deck. Jaycee was sitting on the lowest step. That made them the same height. In the sun, the eyes looked almost gilded. They were startlingly golden and bright.

She reached hesitantly. Her small hands tried to grip the bun but the hot dog came free. It crashed to the grass, depositing chunks of spicy mustard-infused relish across Jaycee's lap on its way down.

The eyes clouded over and the tiny fingers curled back in contrition.

The wave was cresting. That damn voice was back.

"Move it!" it was hostile, infringing on her flashback to another time when they were this close. Eye to eye.

NO! Jaycee rolled her head. She remained locked on the child from her past.

* * * *

"Come here, Eve," she'd told the little girl. "It's okay."

Jaycee reached over and lifted the quivering chin. Her hand looked so large against the petite curve of Eve's lower jaw. She lowered her nose and met Eve's forehead with her own. Skin to skin, and eye to eye. Jaycee locked onto the feeling. Hold it, she told herself. Feel it. Let this child filter right through her skin and around her heart.

"Get up! Get …"

The female then hushed. As Jaycee opened her eyes, she could see the young woman was close. So close to her. Forehead to forehead, skin to skin.

"It's all right, Eve. Trust me, everything's going to be okay." The much younger Jaycee had hugged Eve tightly until the trembling stopped and her quiet cousin had embraced her back. It was much more than a dirty hot dog and some splattered condiments. It was the reaction of a person who expected perfection. Eve could never stand for a blunder.

The eyes of the little girl had become those of a woman. They blinked rapidly and then filled with awed recognition. She covered her mouth and took a loud breath of air. Jaycee's heart told her their fusion had held.

"Jay Jay!" she whispered. "What the hell …" the voice was clipped.

Jaycee knew how that felt. She nodded because her own throat was cropping her voice, too. Emotion rushed through her. Eve was alive! She had ridden out the storm. Jaycee couldn't stop the liquid relief flooding her field of vision. Eve's face moved in and out of focus.

"Oh my God, Jesus, oh Lord, oh Christ. I'm so sorry," she was babbling apologies and non-words. Gently, Eve pulled Jaycee into a sitting position against the wall. She settled her legs and then brushed the matted hair from her face. She studied her face, rediscovering who she was.

"What the *frig* are you doing here?" she asked her once she was certain Jaycee wouldn't keel over.

"I came for you," she told her honestly, simply.

"But … but … how …?"

"Your mom. She is so worried. She called me and I rushed back here. I've been trying to find you …"

The eyes became dull again. Jaycee couldn't let her get away. Not this time.

"No, Eve, don't," she told her. This time her fingers found a fuller chin. She tugged on her cousin's face, lifting it back to where it was. "I just want you to be okay. I don't care about …"

Eye to eye. Jaycee knew Eve was already punishing herself more than any Messiah ever could. "… about any of that. I just care about you."

Eve nodded. The two cousins smiled at each other and the hug that followed was warm and natural.

"But why'd you smack me?" Jaycee asked after pulling out of their embrace. Her hand rubbed the side of her head. Everything was still tingling. "So goddamn hard, too."

Eve wiped a hand down her face and shook her head. "I'm so sorry," she started. "I heard someone coming and then saw blonde hair, tight jeans …"

Jaycee knew.

"You thought I was someone else," she said softly. Cecilia. *You look exactly like her!*

"Yeah, how'd you know that?"

"Oh, Eve, when you're ready, we have a lot to talk about."

A scratchy snivel from across the room took them both by surprise. Two heads whipped around simultaneously, one having totally forgotten about the man in the room with them, the other, entirely stupefied by what it saw.

"Jay Jay," Eve said, straightening up to her full height, which was now nearly equal to her older cousin's. She moved toward the man angrily writhing in a chair, whose authority had been neutered with the help of some weighted pew rope around his chest, and a pocket-sized Bible stuffed into his mouth. It would be comical if it weren't so ghastly. He lamented his situation in raspy, guttural shrieks and whimpers. "I'd like you to meet someone who calls himself the Governor. I, however, have my own name for him—"

"Pastor Asshole," Jaycee interrupted. Her anger blazed red hot. She'd come to him in pursuit of aid and collaboration. She'd needed him to take on Biff. She stood up, her knee stiff and her world swimming. Two mighty arms steadied her.

"You okay?" Eve looked into her face.

"Yeah," Jaycee's entire weight was supported in Eve's care. "Damn Eve, you've grown up so strong."

"Jay Jay, you have no idea."

CHAPTER TWENTY-NINE

Pastor Anthony was about to celebrate his eleventh year at Holy United Academy. He'd spent nearly his entire life administering the tidings from his higher power, having been uniquely blessed with a message straight from the Lord above. He was one of the fortunate who received his instructions early. And boy, they were crystal clear! There was no mistaking what he was put on this earth to do.

Pastor Anthony's purpose in life—and, more importantly, in service—was to help spread God's message of love.

He'd been about fourteen years old when Wendy Styles had taken him by the hand before Sunday services began, and led him out to a mossy patch beneath the leafy, tall trees that shaded their wooden church from a blazing southern sun. She'd shown him how heavenly a girl's hands can feel when they knew where to go, and what to do. The good Lord had created them just right: strong enough to squeeze but gentle enough to fondle and stroke like a kitten's tongue. It was the first distinct memory he had of a pleasure so intense he knew it must have been inspired by the big man upstairs.

It was a rapturous epiphany. A holy miracle. Pastor Anthony had just been hit by a celestial lightning bolt right between the …

Eyes.

Once services were over and their families mingled near the buffet table that held plates of homemade chocolate chip cookies, blueberry muffins, and his mother's famous lemon squares, Pastor Anthony felt compelled to find Wendy. She had shared her gift with him so unselfishly and completely, he must give something to her. But what? He had no skills of his own; he was just starting to learn how to return gratification of the flesh.

His hands wrung in thought. He thrust both into his pockets. His fingers on the right side moved against a folded piece of paper he'd forgotten about. His mother must not have emptied his pockets when she did the laundry. There it was, the ten-dollar bill that had been change from his movie ticket the weekend prior. Folded up, faded by detergent and the spin cycle, it had become crispy and dry. But more importantly, it was available for deposit! He took it out and stared at it as though it were a shiny block of gold.

That was it! A favor for a favor. Even the Bible told him that *in all toil there is profit, but mere talk tends only to poverty.*

Wendy had toiled and thus, she deserved to profit. It became the first deposit he made in the Bank of Bliss.

The teenage boy became a man, his body grew strong and his sexual experience vast, but his mission remained his top priority. He developed comprehensive youth ministry programs that brought the word of the Lord to every child, but only the special few received his sacred message in all its unblemished glory. Like Wendy had done for him, Pastor Anthony sought to do for others. After all, it was his duty to spread the message of love. God had spoken.

'Course there were those who tried to disrupt his delivery of God's word, so Pastor Anthony had learned to be selective about those who entered his hallowed circle, or his own version of Wendy's moss beneath the trees. Because he had much outreach to do, Pastor Anthony never settled in one spot too long. He developed exceptional rapports with members of his congregations who were as deeply inspired as he to administer God's will. Once they had strengthened their core competencies of organization, careful selection of exclusive members, behavior techniques, and motivational outreach, Pastor Anthony moved on. His quest for independence eventually brought him to the enticing world of boarding schools. His first position in Florida had been perfectly executed. Prudently chosen recipients heard God's message through him, and then, despite their young age, became as sophisticated in its delivery as he had been that first time with Wendy Styles.

Because they were all God's chosen messengers.

And He said to them, 'Go into all the world and preach the gospel to every creature.'

Pastor Anthony was as fulfilled as a man could be. But then, he became aware of an opportunity richer than his wildest dreams. He could not only support his members to function at their highest levels, he would be welcomed into a circle so covert, so entirely devoted to his mission, it only clarified to him that God was again leading him by the hand to bring forth an even fuller, more spectacularly immaculate mindfulness few humans were ever granted!

The four-term United States Senator from Colorado had heard of the notable work Pastor Anthony had been doing. He requested a meeting. He sent a private jet. Pastor Anthony boarded the Lear 60 with the proud understanding that this was part of his own reward for being such a meticulous vessel for the Lord's work. A favor for a favor, he never let his hands stop toiling or else the devil crept in.

The Bible told him so.

The cabin held six seats made of the finest leather he'd ever felt. Pastor Anthony sat facing the cockpit, the only passenger onboard, and delighted in the view he had of the attendant's toned legs. She waited until they hit a comfortable cruising altitude, and then approached with a tray loaded with fresh fruit, flaky croissants, and long glass flutes that had come alive with the hiss and fizzle of a hundred-dollar-a-bottle champagne.

He had indulged in two glasses by the time the jet dropped its landing gear and touched down. Only this wasn't a busy commercial plane terminal, it was a strip of pavement connected to the largest estate Pastor Anthony had ever seen. He stepped down the generously wide steps and onto the ground where a limousine driver dressed in a formal black suit swept open the door with a flourish and invited him to make himself comfortable.

It was a three-minute drive to the main house. He was dropped off at an elaborate entrance next to the six-stall garage. Another man wearing a dark secret service-style suit greeted him with a firm handshake and invited him inside. The home was breathtaking yet lived in. A gaggle of dogs raced toward him.

"They're all friendly, just give them a kick if they jump," the man told him.

Pastor Anthony had a deep fondness for all God's creatures. He'd no sooner kick a dog than he would an infant. He spent time scratching and greeting every last one. From an unseen door in the bowels of the enormous living quarters, Senator Chuck Langton strode toward him. He wore pleated khaki pants and a striped button-down shirt with the collar open one button too low. He was an aging man who mistakenly thought he was still virile enough to pull that off. Pastor Anthony smiled. In his experience, God's directive was often delivered by men just like Senator Langton.

They retired to the library where they shared Macallan scotch in tinted glass tumblers, each sip leading them to a greater sense of shared responsibilities. They not only connected, they transcended. Pastor Anthony learned of even more enlightened hands, doing God's work exactly as he was, by spreading the message of physical euphoria and earned reward. He was proud to become involved with the noble senator and to learn how his own life's work was being used to clear channels in government, business, and entertainment. A guaranteed pipeline of funds that ensured re-election campaigns were funded, loans were approved, civic centers were built, and female counterparts prepared to collaborate. No man delivered to this world with such esteemed work to do should be stymied by financial distress. An affiliation with the senator, and those like him, safeguarded Pastor Anthony's central objective. He felt God's guidance as he accepted the six-figure check, and a brand new position as spiritual leader at a small private boarding school in the Rockies.

"You will teach and inspire, but most importantly, you will govern for us." He was told. The senator was quite explicit in his expectations.

Hmm. I am the Governor, he thought, liking how that gruff word rumbled his throat.

It had been a rewarding experience for three joyful years. But when the senator called him back to his sprawling residence for another fireside chat with the same tinted tumblers in their hands, he was instructed that it was time to move along. He was needed elsewhere.

The senator told him of an impending retirement. How did he feel about a move north? Almost as quickly as he'd stepped off the plane with a single suitcase, Pastor Anthony fell under New Hampshire's spell. The luxurious smells of the forests, the gray cascade of slick granite plunging into valleys sprinkled with lupines tickled his creativity. He felt as one with the rolling hills and meadows. When the skittering, noisy birds rode the winds without a care where they took them, Pastor Anthony could hear their joy. New Hampshire was so close to God, he allowed his roots in the rocky soil to grow deeper, stronger. He felt love.

The chilly lake waters were stocked with trout that cooked up on a hot grill like flaky pastry. On weekends, he organized a prayer group that hiked the trails in Franconia State Park. They set out in darkness to experience the magical colors of day breaking from the top of the world.

For the first time in his life of ministration, he'd prayed that God would allow him to pacify his wanderlust, even temporarily, to extend his residency in this exquisite rural paradise. His accommodations were enchanting, and his daily work took on a tranquil regularity. The Lord continued to bless him with the gift of discovery. He could see so perfectly beneath the pubescent shells, straight into the essence of his chosen few.

His Legacy Girls.

As their Governor, he meticulously matched them by both their looks and their dispositions with their affluent Messiahs' preferences. He trained their Mothers to carefully raise them from birth in their new family, developing their aptitude and handiness with a skillful eye that would help them gauge the perfect time to set them free to enrich their own terrestrial existences. Only then were they ready for their inaugural visit. Only fully indoctrinated Legacy Girls would be sent to The Heights.

Eventually, his established and proven Legacy Girls took on their own Daughters. He felt such vindication as his circle of life was carried out in a consistently perfect delivery of satisfaction for all. A favor for a favor.

Pastor Anthony had been a fully satiated member of God's kingdom. He served with distinction and appreciated his endowment. But then, as if Satan himself had cast the role, a witch named Eve emerged in his Garden of Eden.

He glowered at her with all the hatred of a compromised deity rudely heaved from his throne.

His divine utopia, so flawlessly constructed with the Lord's own blueprints, was being burned to the ground.

CHAPTER THIRTY

The betrayal was bewildering. He was aghast at what had unfolded in his living quarters. First, a violent ambush. Manhandled by a … a … *she-wolf*, who assaulted him with her fists, and rendered him incapacitated and voiceless. That had been followed by the appearance of an outlier who had misrepresented her way into his inner sanctum. Now, apparently, an ally to the enemy. Another of the devil's loathsome field workers.

He had failed. Pastor Anthony had allowed the beast to pervade his family and now it was turning on him!

The two assailants sat facing him, each having been wounded yet proven conclusively superior over whatever force God had employed to block their passage to his refuge. He didn't blame God; he knew He had tried to defend his honor. It was never His fault. He had designed His creations with all they needed. It was man who always let Him down. Intention had fallen to sin, yet again.

"Tell me how it works." He heard the blonde perjurer ask, as she sat on one of his wooden backed chairs with a pink satin cushion. He blinked fast. How had he not seen it before? When she had been alone in his pew, pretending to be in need of his support. How had he not seen the remarkable, uncanny resemblance? When she'd spoken in hyperbole, how had he missed it!

A fool's mouth is his ruin, and his lips are a snare to his soul.

The devil had descended in disguise. He'd snaked his way in, hidden inside his most beautiful, most devoted Legacy Girl of them all.

Cecilia.

* * * *

Jaycee sipped from a mug of water Eve brought her from Pastor Anthony's kitchen. He had stopped fighting the invasion. Eve had removed the Bible from his mouth. It left small bloody cuts where laugh lines had sunk into his skin.

"Shall I?" Eve directed at him. "Shall I begin? Or do you want to tell my cousin here what a shitty human being you are?"

He sat stone-faced, and silent.

"All righty then," Eve said. Sunlight broke through the slanted wooden panels of the room's shutters. Jaycee could see dark etchings around Eve's eyes. She looked so old for being so young.

"We're marked. Like the runts in a litter. Certain girls here at Holy United Academy are identified as the poor slobs who toil and labor under the stress of scholarships. They know we come from nothing, our families are broke, so we work our asses off to be here. They use that." She hadn't taken her eyes off Pastor Anthony. He slumped into his own misery, his handsome features slack and overcome.

"When did it start?" Jaycee asked her softly.

"Right away," she told her. "That very first day. I should've seen it coming. I didn't ..."

"You couldn't!" Jaycee corrected. "You're a child, Eve." Even though she looked like a woman. "You couldn't have known."

Eve offered a grim smile at her cousin's attempt to sway blame away from herself. She appreciated that but had already accepted her own degree of responsibility. "Well, I didn't."

"Cecilia?" Jaycee asked. The beautifully rotten apple that had charmed Eve. The mention of her name forced Eve to recoil in surprise.

"How do you know …"

"I'll explain that later," Jaycee told her.

Eve nodded. "Okay. Yes, Cecilia. She's good, worked me over like a pro, knew how to hit all the pressure points. I've never had anyone tell me I was working *too* hard. It was always, 'Come on, Eve, work harder. Be better' …" Eve waved a fist, having adopted the authoritative tone of a teacher, a coach, a principal. The people in her life who had relentlessly pushed and burdened her with ridiculously high expectations. She had to be perfect. She couldn't drop the hot dog.

Enter Cecilia, who slithered in like well-timed therapeutic relief.

"She showed me a way to make it stop." Eve met Jaycee's eyes. Her pride had been dinged up but not totaled. "Of course at first it sounded totally gross, like, how does a girl do that?"

They do it because they have to, Jaycee thought. She considered the actresses who saved their babysitting money to pay for the plane ticket to sure-fire stardom. No one was more surprised than they to realize all the creative ways to pay the rent for one more month. Just until that juicy role came their way. Sure-fire stardom was what you made of it.

"Cecilia does that?" Jaycee asked, but she already knew. The spa-crafted eyebrows, the Tiffany bracelet, the visits to The Heights, the Messiah who may or may not pay the insurance bill on her car. The confession to Kendra.

Number 13.

"Yes," Eve told her. "She's my Mother. More like mother *f'er*," she scoffed. "It's all a big happy family full of sex with old men, money, mansions, and trips on private planes to exotic places, and … and …" Eve paused. She knew she had skipped the crux of the story. Her reason for giving herself a pass for the first time in her life.

"And, taking a moment to not be perfect," Jaycee supplied. Now she could see all the reasons why Eve had been the ideal mark.

"Sort of," she agreed. She looked again at Pastor Anthony, who remained quiet. "And this one," she pointed at him, "this one knows which girl goes to which guy, and when. He helps the Mothers find and train them until they're ready to become …"

"Legacy Girls," Jaycee finished.

Eve looked at her in shock. "Jesus Christ, Jaycee. How much do you already know?"

"I've been sniffing around."

Upon hearing that, Pastor Anthony erupted from his noiseless protest.

"She's a liar!" he declared. "A false witness. The Lord tells us that lying lips are an abomination! Those who act faithfully—"

"Shut up!" Eve and Jaycee shouted at him in unison. Pastor Anthony sneered, but swallowed the rest of his Bible verse. It tasted oddly sour.

"As I was saying, I have poked around here," Jaycee clarified. "I pretended to be a student. I figured I had to worm my way into your life, at your level, to figure out if you were really in trouble. Or worse." They locked eyes again then moved back to Pastor Anthony. "I have met this idiot before but I wasn't me, I was more like all of you. I even borrowed your uniform."

Eve was open-mouthed. "You wore my uniform …" she said again in disbelief.

Pastor Anthony huffed. The two women glared at him.

"On loan from your mom," Jaycee told her.

"You've been to my *house?*"

"That's where I went first."

"Oh, God. My poor mom. She thinks I'm missing …" Eve put her face in her hands and sighed. "But, I just talked to her …" Hadn't she? When was that? Eve couldn't remember. Days ran together. Sometimes she forgot to even call her mother back.

"Ramona called her. She's been worried, too. She said you wouldn't just stay away like other kids do. It wasn't your style."

"You know Ramona?!" Eve stared at her cousin. "Ramona was worried? About me?" Eve was talking more to herself, and she seemed astounded. Jaycee wondered why. Why didn't she think people in her life would care about her well-being?

"What the hell, Jay Jay, what are you? A CIA operative?"

Jaycee laughed. "No, I'm just a family member trying to help. A long-lost family member," she added sheepishly. "But still, someone else who cares about you. There are a few of us, Eve."

Eve remained dumbfounded and awed by the underground maneuvering that had been going on. She stared at Jaycee. Her oldest cousin. She'd grown up thinking she looked like the princess of a faraway land. Golden blonde, stunningly well-proportioned, with a presence that had you asking if she was mortal or a video game ball-buster brought to life.

She must've been staring. "Eve," Jaycee said sharply.

"I heard you," she said. "I guess I didn't think anyone would even notice. Kids here, they can just not show up for a couple of days. I assumed everyone would think I was just doing that."

"Self-nurturing," Jaycee provided.

Eve again stared at her in consternation. "Again, CIA? Or practicing psychic?"

"No," she shook her head. "Just a TV reporter by way of Los Angeles."

The cousins eyed each other with ample admiration. Two willful young women who finally understood what it meant to have a family, a real family, not one built upon sex, lies, and cash, but the drop everything and just show up kind. Not because it had to, but because it couldn't imagine not being there.

Jaycee stood up. Pastor Anthony didn't deserve to hear about her life, or her concern for Eve. They told him to keep his mouth shut. He pouted like a toddler in a time-out. She directed Eve back to the kitchen area where they sat together at the table, and began the process of reconnecting. Jaycee told her what she'd been doing since they had last known each other, where she'd been, and why she'd come back.

"L.A.," Eve articulated each letter. "From New Hampshire all the way to Los Angeles. What a cool life you have, Jay Jay."

"I do, but I almost lost it all, Eve." Jaycee told her. "But that's a story for another time. The important thing is that we get you home. Your mom needs to know you're okay."

"But how did my mom even get your number? How did she think to call you? How the hell did she find you?" Eve asked, brimming with obvious inquiries.

"Who cares, the point is, she did."

Eve seemed to feel remorse for the anguish she'd unintentionally brought. "My mom," Eve half-laughed. "She tries so hard," she told Jaycee.

"You're more like her than you think," Jaycee replied. She didn't want Eve to ever feel the resentment she felt for her own useless mother. It wasn't healthy or productive, and at her core the two sisters were nothing alike. Eve was loved, while Jaycee was more tolerated.

"Actually, I'm starting to think there's another family member I take after most of all."

CHAPTER THIRTY-ONE

Eve had started to open up about her visit to The Heights. The long ride, Cecilia's candy apple red Rover, how she'd thought she could handle it. Until she couldn't.

"You're Number 14," Jaycee confirmed finally.

Eve nodded. "I was. I'm not anymore."

"Cecilia's your Mother."

"Yeah, she's Number 13," Eve told her. "She told me how great it was, that if I closed my eyes really tight it wasn't even that bad to screw old men, and they didn't even want that half the time. Her Messiah is, like, wicked old. He's tired a lot, and many of the nights they're together all he wants to do is brush her hair while they watch romantic comedies and take bubble baths. He brings her Vogue magazines from all over the world. All the places he travels to. It's crazy, actually." Eve smiled. "She told me she could never afford to buy Vogue on her own, it's too expensive. So now, she keeps every copy and rereads them cover to cover."

"She's a cold-hearted bitch, Eve," Jaycee reminded her. "She's not your friend."

"Oh, I *know* that," she said firmly. "She used me. But my point was that she made it seem easy. All of a sudden, something in my life could be easy."

Jaycee watched her. Life had barely begun and yet it had already worn Eve down.

"Cecilia knows what it feels like to be poor. Like us. Like how you and I were raised. We didn't have shit, Jay

Jay. Everything I had, so far, I had broken bones for. I've sweat buckets on the soccer field and in the classroom, and I knew it was just beginning. My entire life was laid out in front of me and I knew every second of it would be spent working."

She was right. Jaycee could understand how the unthinkable became probable for her. How Eve could do unspeakable things because she felt she had no choice. It was the only way for her to escape the relentless pressure. Jaycee sat in agreement. It had been her life, too. Every second of it spent chasing a big job in a bigger city, working overtime, answering the call, and shunning everything in favor of a reward that was never satisfying enough. She'd learned the hard way that love mattered most. The lesson had almost killed her. Her love for Van had forced her to survive.

"I know none of this ever would have happened if Cecilia hadn't lured me in. But, Jay Jay, no one forced me. I made the decision on my own."

Jaycee automatically tried once again to defend her cousin, but Eve shook her head. "It was my decision." She looked Jaycee straight in the eye. She owned every bit of her choices. That kind of bravery couldn't be taught, a person either had it, or never would. Eve had it. Jaycee had it.

"And it was my decision not to go through with it," she added. "Although obviously," she paused, touching her injured cheek, "that didn't go over very well."

"So you never …" Jaycee lowered her gaze. She almost couldn't bear to ask.

"Did the nasty?" Eve answered pointedly. "Nope, just in the nick of time. But, the poor old guy had come to party so he was not happy with me. Not one bit."

"He hurt you?" Jaycee felt the relief that Eve's virtue had been preserved give way to the pounding of her anguished heart. An old man had struck Eve. Had *hit* a child! She shuddered. Which was worse? Hitting her or having sex with her. Good God!

"He did," Eve told her, but there was a defiant glint in her eye. "But trust me, I gave a lot better than I got. Just not in the way he expected."

Jaycee thought of Cecilia's Messiah, how he may be plotting to strip her of the fine things she'd amassed. "But, what will he do to you?"

"I've leveled the field a bit," Eve said evasively. "He has bigger fish to fry at this moment. It's in his best interest to leave me alone."

"Cecilia may not be so lucky."

"Oh, you can bet on that. She's a shitty Mother. I have officially taken away her parental rights."

"Who is he, Eve?"

Eve supported her chin on her right knuckles. She sighed slightly. "Some rich old guy, Jay Jay. We're not allowed to know their life stories. I've heard many of them are politicians, some in the movie industry. Every year, several Legacy Girls score invites to the Cannes Film Festival, and none of them are actresses. They're hugely successful men and we are hand-picked to match their preferences. All I know is that he liked that I could play the piano, and that I had dark hair. He chose me. Before I met him, Cecilia had me practice. Like, how to not get grossed out, how to fake it, and pretend that I liked him. Doing that alone in front of my mirror was a lot different than actually doing it …" She twisted her mouth.

"Did you ever sign anything?" Jaycee thought of the lawyered up contracts and overwhelmingly detailed agreements threatening ruination that would surely scare a minor into thinking they were legal and binding.

"I did, but I know it's just paper. Most of the girls, however, they think it's real. It's part of what keeps them under their spell. Can you imagine? They actually think they'll be sued." Eve's shoulders rocked.

"Exactly," Jaycee agreed. Because they're babies! "He'd control how often he saw you?"

"Yes. I don't know where he lives in his real life. But, the plan was for him to call for me when he came to The Heights. I would get my own cell, like Cecilia's, and his would be a number I responded to immediately. No matter what I was doing, I would drop everything and rush off to meet him. Forever. Like, even when I was old myself. We were theirs … forever."

"But otherwise, you could have a life of your own?"

"Yes," Eve confirmed. "A family, a job, whatever I wanted. As long as I knew that I was his first."

"The money?"

That made Eve's lip turn in. She battled a fresh rush of shame. Her head dipped, forcing Jaycee to sit on her hand to prevent it from rushing to her chin to lift it back up.

"A shitload of money," she said quietly. "And stuff, although I didn't care about the stuff."

She looked into Jaycee's face, ready to share her heart. It poured out like a torrent of secrets finally unleashed from their hiding place.

"My mother is an empty woman," she began. "Like, her *soul*, Jay Jay. Does that make sense?"

Jaycee nodded.

"Between them, she, my dad, and my brother work five jobs. Five! You know why? Because I'm the smart one. They work until they drop to keep me here at Holy United Academy and then, at the next exorbitantly expensive learning institution I'll pursue in my high-achieving life. I'm the only one who stands half a shot of making something of myself one day. Getting the fuck out of here!" Eve's eyes welled. "My dad and my brother, they're simple men. They get up every morning, and they go to work. They may grumble but they don't know any better. My mom, though, she knows there's a bigger world. She knows I don't fit in with them so she makes them work." Eve choked. "Work for me." She shirked her head sharply back. "How could I do that to them even a second longer?"

The pressure to be perfect. She'd felt it every single day of her life.

"It had to stop." Eve elevated her eyes. Her final declaration. The only time she would explain why she had been ready to immolate herself in exchange for a truce. A deal with fate. She would give, but the taking from her family *had ... to ... stop!*

She loved them. It struck Jaycee completely. She and Eve were indeed alike, but Eve was better. She was not only capable of the forgiveness Kendra had encouraged Jaycee to seek, but she already lived with love first. She may not show it, but Eve loved her family so dearly she would do whatever it took to protect them.

Like flying out of broken glass to protect Van. To save her own family, Jaycee had finally acted with love. It had just taken her longer to realize what truly held her heart. It wasn't a promotion at work, not a brand new purse or a condo in the most desirable Los Angeles zip code. No, love for someone else had been the only thing that mattered.

Jaycee reached for Eve's hand. Unusual for her, because she wasn't a demonstrably mushy type of person. Maybe she just needed to confirm to herself that Eve was physically still in one piece. Emotionally, Jaycee couldn't tell how deeply she might be scarred. She knew quite well how trauma seared a person in places you couldn't see.

"Your mom is not empty," she told her. "She is so full of pride for you ..." she had to clear her throat, her voice was fading. "She loves you so much, Eve. They work for you because they love you."

Eve nodded. Jaycee pushed quickly, she feared she was shutting down. There was so much more she still needed to know.

"He'd come to party," she returned to Eve's earlier point. "Your Messiah. You mean at The Heights, right?"

Eve nodded. "Yes. I would describe it to you but I have a feeling you already know what it looks like."

She smirked. "I've been there."

Eve got up and walked to a cabinet. She extracted another mug and filled it with water from the faucet. She took long gulps. She refilled the mug and returned to her seat. Eve plopped down like her bones were collapsing. Her smooth face was dewy, that delicious tinge young skin adopts when its sweats.

"How did you find out it even exists?" she asked Jaycee. "This is not something they put in the admissions packet. It's like, super secret society type of stuff."

"It's not quite as secret as you think."

"It's way north, like near Canada, in that wild back country where your dad used to take his snowmobile."

Where Goose had rescued her after her father got shitty drunk.

"There's a diner nearby."

"Yeah, Cecilia wanted to stop there but I begged her not to. The smell of food would've been too much."

"She has a friend there," Jaycee started. Kendra, with the baggage of her own past, telling Jaycee that forgiveness can act as glue for a crumbled life. Don't hate the blonde girl for what she had done to your family, she'd told her, understand why she did it.

"She's opened up to her friend at the diner about what she does at The Heights."

Eve looked at her. It seemed to surprise her to hear that. Eventually, she lowered her gaze. "Maybe she had to confess to someone before it ate her up on the inside. It's not just us girls, Jay Jay. This goes beyond just the Legacy Girls."

Norm and Molly knew, too. Officer Wheeler. Clint, the town manager—he may know of the helicopters circling above, but he kept his eyes firmly at the ground. The pristine fire trucks. Chief Solomon. The community center about to enter Phase Two once the snow melted away. The annual town bash, the happy residents content to cut checks for taxes that stayed manageable. The Christmas party for the police department down the road from Holy United Academy. It featured name brand alcohol, prime rib and roasted duck when it should, by all accounts, be a potluck dinner with cans of Bud Light and boxes of wine.

Jaycee felt that old anger return. Now that she knew Eve was safe, she felt that undeniable—almost desperate— need to fix it. To bring justice and satisfaction. To ensure her report ended properly, with vindication for the wronged and total decimation for the savages. It was how she tagged every story she told. The final report was all about the perfect ending.

"Eve," she rose from the chair and hobbled in thought around the kitchen. "We have to blow this wide open!" Her hands wrung tighter until she was squeezing them so soundly the tips of her fingers turned white. Barton! Time to bring in the real Barton, not the one she'd cooked up in the car, but the one who could call all his old police buddies and have them race up here to pull the noose tighter … *tighter* … until they clipped the head of this devil right off!

"I can find a good reporter up here. And, I have this cop friend. I trust him. He's helped me before, and he's just what we need. He can start making calls, he's totally connected in law enforcement … he can help us right now … I just need to call—"

Strong hands gripped her by the shoulders and pulled her around almost in a full circle. Forehead to forehead, skin to skin, her baby cousin was now in control.

"Jaycee," she spoke her name firmly. She looked entirely like an adult fully capable of making her own decisions. It forced Jaycee to do something she rarely did in her life, that thing she repelled like it was a poison that could kill her. She backed down.

And it hadn't killed her at all, in fact, it had barely hurt. She was still standing.

"Thank you for caring about me and for dropping your life to help find me. But I was never lost to begin with," Eve stated. "And from here on out, we do this my way."

Jaycee sighed until all that hot air came out of her. Well, how about that? She felt a new sensation rising up from her core, a feeling she had—up until that moment— reserved solely for her own use.

Pride. For another.
Pride for Eve.

CHAPTER THIRTY-TWO

They had to move fast.

"Chapel starts in fifteen minutes." Eve led the way out of the kitchen. Jaycee followed.

Eve moved quickly back to Pastor Anthony. She stood before him like the captain of a sinking ship directing his crew on the roles each had to play to keep it afloat. She had turned the mutiny back onto him. The Governor was about to be released from the bunker but with an updated set of marching orders.

"Here's what's going to happen," Eve told him. "Everything I was promised will stand. My Holy United tuition … whatever isn't covered by my scholarship, I want paid in full. Any extra expense will be covered. The college of my choice … again, paid. I also want you to further persuade my Messiah to forget he ever knew me. Make sure you tell whoever else needs to know, too. I want this straight from you. Your orders."

Pastor Anthony yanked at the ropes. Eve further winnowed his options.

"Chapel is now …" she looked at the slim watch on her left wrist. The only regulation jewelry they were allowed to wear. She didn't try to hide Tiffany bracelets like Cecilia. Eve didn't care about the *stuff*.

"… twelve minutes away. If you don't agree to do what I tell you to, I'll open the doors to the entire student body and invite them in here for a look. I can hear them now. 'Oh, Lord almighty, Pastor Anthony, what happened to you?' They'd be so worried about you that I would be forced to tell them everything. I'd start with my little excursion north, and the benefactor waiting for me inside the mansion. And then Biff would have to ask who pays for that mansion, because we all know how expensive it can be to run a house like that. And, I just know he'd be thrilled to hear what some of his precious girls are really doing during their 'self-nurturing' adventures. And why the police never, *ever,* worry about where they've gone. Right, Pastor Anthony? Because somehow, they know we're all one big happy family here at Holy United Academy. And all your little Legacy Girls always come home."

Jaycee watched her with a mixture of admiration and horror. She thought she might have to save Eve. Well, clearly Eve was infinitely capable of saving herself. Pastor Anthony, though, didn't stand a chance against the fire power coming off her.

"Anything else?" he asked defiantly.

Eve considered that. "Now that you mention is, there is one more thing."

Eight minutes until Chapel. Pastor Anthony had no bargaining power, and zero ammunition in his holster. He'd expelled his final missile and she'd simply sidestepped around the explosion.

"Coach Whalen," she stated. Jaycee rubbernecked yet again. That odd soccer coach who had become fed up and repelled by her suggestion that Eve was off somewhere "self-nurturing." Was Eve demanding action against him now, too?

It went the other way. Jaycee felt Eve's admiration for the tough-nosed man.

"He works too hard. Did you know he watches tape year-round? Breaks down plays, analyzes our shots, even the most minute shit like how we pass with our left foot, or whether we're squaring our hips when we shoot. Did you know how much extra he does for us?"

Jaycee nodded. She knew. She'd seen him mumbling to himself, fast-forwarding, rewinding, planning tweaks and shifts to his approach. He cared. He wanted to be the best he could be for his girls, not the other way around.

Pastor Anthony didn't respond.

Five minutes until Chapel. Until Holy United Academy saw him for what he really was.

"I asked you a question." Eve's face had gone dark. She was really pissed about something with that coach.

"No," he fumed. "I didn't know that."

"That's right!" she stormed back. "You didn't know that because all you cared about was when he went to Biff to talk about how ridiculous it was to let kids, *teenagers*, miss school and answer to no one. Coach Whalen wanted kids in distress to come to him, or Biff, or their parents and talk about it. You know, how normal people work their shit out. He told me running away was a failure of leadership and it reflected poorly on him and everyone else here. And you, Governor, wanted him punished for that."

Three minutes until Chapel.

"Three minutes. You have three minutes to decide what your legacy will be."

285

Like the gutless sham of a man he was, Pastor Anthony considered her offer.

"What do you want!" he cried.

"Coach Whalen rents some crappy apartment two towns over. I know that because he was late for practice one day and explained to us that his tire blew and he had to jog. He had to jog to campus!"

Two minutes until Chapel. Eve circled the room, opening her arms wide.

"I think Coach Whalen would do wonders with this place. I can see all those state championship trophies fitting nicely on that shelf ... right ... over there ..." she angled her hands like a viewfinder.

"I also think he deserves a big fat raise. Something in the neighborhood of what you make. Later today, you'll tell Biff you've decided you need to move off campus. You will explain that it best fits your desire to live a more unpretentious, God-fearing life. If he argues, you will insist. Then, I expect Coach Whalen will quickly share the happy news with me, and the rest of my team. He'll never be late for practice again. Got it?"

Eve didn't wait for an answer.

"And finally." She stood over him, tall and proud against the cowering villain. "You will have no more contact with me for the rest of my time here. You won't look at me, or speak to me, or even think of me, or any of my friends," she pointed to Jaycee, "ever again. So, if you promise you'll do all of that, everything I just told you, then I'll let you go. But make it fast. You have thirty seconds until Chapel."

Pastor Anthony closed his eyes in prayer. He begged the Lord for the wisdom in that moment to carry on his important work, his life's purpose. He would never know why he was being tested, only that if he trusted in his purpose, God would never abandon him.

Trust in the Lord with all your heart, and do not lean on your own understanding. In all your ways acknowledge Him, and He will make straight your paths.

Amen. He knew what he had to do, the Bible had told him so. Again, God was speaking directly to him.

Pastor Anthony agreed to her outrageous ultimatum. And if there was one thing he could guarantee this wicked sorceress, he would never so much as look at her indecent face again.

He began Chapel that morning looking slightly tired. But, as he led them in a common prayer Pastor Anthony did not ask God for forgiveness. After all, in his enlightened heart, he had never done anything wrong.

CHAPTER THIRTY-THREE

"Eve," Jaycee was having a hard time keeping up with her as she tore out of Pastor Anthony's rear door and onto the frozen path that wound around to the front of the Chapel. "Eve, slow down."

The younger, fitter girl paused. "Sorry," she muttered, but instead of slowing down, she simply linked her arm through Jaycee's so she could pull her along at the faster pace.

"Where are we going?"

"There's one more person I need to talk to."

"Can't that wait?" Jaycee was huffing with exertion. "We need to tell your mom you're okay. She's so worried."

"We will, Jay Jay," Eve pronounced. "But when I say so."

She didn't like it, but Jaycee hurried along with Eve until they reached the tallest residential hall on campus. Only residents had key access to the front door, so Eve waited until a group of students exited their dorm and ran toward Chapel, already three minutes late. She slipped through the open door with Jaycee on her hip.

"Wait here," she told her.

"No way!" Jaycee responded.

Eve looked at her. "Fine then," she told her. "But let me do the talking."

Jaycee nodded. They boarded the elevator. Eve hit the button for the fourth floor. Jaycee looked over at her focused face. Eve was staring straight ahead, expressionless. Jaycee wasn't positive who lived on the fourth floor, but she had a strong inkling.

The acidic fertilizer that had grown the most secretive of gardens was about to get neutralized.

The elevator doors opened. Eve took off like a shot on a trajectory to its target. She stopped at the last door in the hallway and planted her fist on the door. She pounded out three sharp raps, then another two when the first round was ignored.

"Open up!" she yelled. Eve knew the occupant inside was the only Holy United Academy student who dared to skip Chapel. The Legacy Girl who had ensured she would be permanently excused.

"Fuck off!" came the scratchy voiced response.

Eve sputtered a fed up chuckle. "I said, open up, Mother!"

There was no haughty retort. Jaycee didn't even realize she had been holding her breath until the door swung open and Eve swept both of them through it.

Cecilia gaped at her. She tried to speak in bursts of nonsensical vowels. "Uuoo, ooo … I … aaa … I …" she was flummoxed, shocked from sleep by a ghost. The Ghost of Legacy Girls Past.

"Hey, Mom!" Eve greeted her with a hug that rattled her bones. Cecilia groaned. Her high ponytail bobbed as Eve slapped her open palm between Cecilia's shoulders … hard … several times.

"So, yeah …" Eve started. She let Cecilia go, but had done so by chucking her backwards onto her bed. The beautiful blonde hair was disheveled, hanging in long pieces across her sweaty forehead. Despite wearing only a sports bra and pajama pants, Cecilia was panting. She watched Eve expectantly.

"Let's get a few things straight, shall we?"

Her bewildered eyes twitched as they finally found Jaycee for the first time. Cecilia sneered at her, suddenly understanding she was the same loser transfer who had interrupted her at lunch. Only then could she find real words.

"Fucking balls!" she bleated. "What do you want?"

"Not much," Eve began. "Just a few things I've been thinking about on my long, like wicked *lo… nnn … ggg* trip back here. There I was, freezing, exhausted … all alone on the highway … trying to figure out how the hell I would even survive. You know that road, right, Mother? The one with no houses to stop at. No cars at night. Remember that road?"

Cecilia dropped her head and stared at the tops of her knees.

"So anyway, just when I thought I couldn't move another step, each foot literally icing up inside my boot, I saw headlights coming down that road. Headlights! Of course, it could've easily been someone who slit my throat and left me there to become a fossil, but it wasn't."

Jaycee had wondered how in the world Eve had made it back from The Heights. It was a part of the story she hadn't heard yet. She watched her cousin, feeling her ice-cold fear like it was her own. It crept from her stomach, over her heart, and into the back of her throat. Eve could've survived the wrath of her Messiah only to succumb to that of the elements.

"Did you know how all those bags of potato chips get from the manufacturing plant in Maryland, to the hungry people of Vermont?"

Cecilia was blank. She sat, miserably immobile.

"Well, that's okay, I didn't know either. So, there's this one route. It runs straight up through western Massachusetts, and into central Vermont. Then, it's a short jaunt to the northern warehouse where all the chips are offloaded. That's when Pete, the guy who drives the chips, decides whether he'll run that same route back home again, or if he'll take the scenic drive through New Hampshire. Wouldn't you know it, Mommy dearest, he has a place on Lake Winnipesaukee that he checks on year-round. Can you imagine the sheer luck?"

Again, Cecilia listened silently. Jaycee was also paralyzed by Eve's story.

"So, there I was, all cold and tired, hobbling along about fifteen miles down that road, and here comes Pete! I can't even think about what would've happened to me if Pete hadn't decided to check on his lake house. Can you, Cecilia? Can you even imagine what would've happened to me out there on that road?"

Eve sighed. She was almost done.

"Anyway, turns out Pete has a son about our age, so when I told him I'd had to leave a party nearby because I didn't like what the kids were doing, he was all sorts of

happy to help me get home. In fact, I heard all about the
policy he has with his own kids to call him anytime they're
out with their friends and something happens that makes
them uncomfortable. Booze, drugs, sex, whatever, he didn't
care where they were or how late it was, he'd come pick
them up. No questions asked."

Jaycee wanted to wrap her arms around Eve and hug
away the awful torment she must have been going through.
So young, so brave, and now, so lucky to have made it out
alive.

"Pete's truck was snug and warm. He gave me the hot
chocolate his wife had packed in his Thermos. I ate six
bags of chips from a box in the back. Sour cream and onion
flavored. They were delicious."

She smacked her lips. That was it. How she'd made
her great escape from The Heights, and the Mother who'd
brought her there, and then left her behind. This family
meeting, hastily called as it was, would involve some
sacrifices to make things right.

A favor for a favor. An exchange of goods for services
rendered.

"So, here's what we're going to do," Eve told Cecilia
firmly. If she thought about objecting, the steely
determination in Eve's eye stopped her. She gulped. Being
a mother was so much harder than she'd ever expected.

CHAPTER THIRTY-FOUR

The two cousins sat in the driveway of Eve's house. She had insisted that showing up in person was the best way to alert her family that she was alive and well. And, she hadn't wanted to blow the big surprise she had for her mom.

She beeped three times. Three loud honks.

Jaycee watched the front door for signs of movement. Finally, the wispy curtain was pulled back and curious eyes squinted into the cold morning air. The door cracked open. Jaycee could see thin legs, already wrapped in their khaki uniform pants, start to tentatively step down onto the stairs that led to the driveway. Marcy's face squinted and then contorted with glee once she recognized the girl sitting behind the steering wheel.

Jaycee's eyes welled. She had brought Eve home. Well, Eve had really brought herself home, but she had helped. A little.

Eve burst out of the driver's door and threw herself into her mother's arms. They cried, laughed, and just soaked up the physical sensation of knowing each of them was okay. No matter what had taken Eve away, she had returned, and all that had been so desperately wrong was shifting back to right.

Finally, Jaycee stepped out of the red Range Rover. She walked around to the hood and leaned against its warmth. It felt good against her back. She watched Eve and Marcy sniffle away tears of relief and then stepped into her aunt's open arms. It was the tightest hug she'd ever felt. Jaycee knew the strength behind the embrace was fed by gratitude. When she pulled back and looked at Marcy, she no longer saw the ruptured husk of a broken-down woman. No, what she saw was pure elation. Aunt Marcy had never looked more beautiful.

"Let's get you two inside," she said, with a smile so genuine it gleamed brighter than the sun reflecting off the clean white of the New Hampshire snow.

* * * *

"It's this thing we do at Holy United," Eve was explaining to her mother as they all sat around the kitchen table. Marcy had told them that both Eve's dad and brother had already left for work.

"We're allowed to take a few days off and just catch our breath." She was writing the script for the only story she would ever share with her mother. The only story she could handle.

"But where did you go?" Marcy asked. She had made coffee but hadn't touched hers. Instead, she held onto the mug so tightly Jaycee thought it might shatter.

"To a friend's cabin. It's one of those ski-in, ski-out places built right into the side of a mountain. You can literally pop out of the front door and ski down to the chairlift."

Eve was good, Jaycee thought. She made her lie seem reasonable and genuine.

"What mountain?"

"Oh, Mom, that doesn't matter," Eve dismissed her question. "It's not like you'd know where it was." She looked at Jaycee as if to include her in the family joke. "She doesn't even ski."

Jaycee smiled. She never liked to lie, but sometimes, like now, you had to. The truth of what Eve had been through was something no *real* mother should ever have to hear.

"So, now you'll just go back to school and it will be fine that you missed a couple of days?" Marcy was trying to understand this odd policy. It certainly hadn't been explained in the paperwork she'd signed.

"Yeah," Eve smiled. "And now I feel reinvigorated! All it took was a couple days of rest and I'm good as new."

Marcy looked keenly at her daughter. What did she see? Eve looked about the same, despite that little nick on her cheek she told her came from a branch hitting her face while she was skiing. No, it was something else. What was it?

"I called the school, Eve," she told her. "I even called the police. But you're right, everyone kept telling me that when you were ready, you'd come back." She shook her head.

"They *were* right, Mom," Eve told her softly. "When I was ready, I came home."

"I even called you," Marcy turned to her niece. She was still partially caught in the whirlwind they'd been swept into. "Your cousin here dropped her entire life and … and …" she couldn't go on. It was too emotional again.

295

When she had finally stopped to think about the lengths
Jaycee had gone to, it was overwhelming. How could she
ever thank her enough? She tried, but then stopped as she
noticed the two cousins had exchanged a knowing look.

"What?" she asked them both. "What are you not
telling me?"

"Nothing, Mom," Eve hushed her. "I swear."

"You know everything," Jaycee assured her.
"Everything you need to know, we've told you." It was a
half-truth that made her feel better.

Marcy may not have believed them entirely, but she
allowed herself to try.

"So, you'll be heading back to school, then?" she
wrapped her palm over Eve's hand.

"Yes," she told her. "I have some work to catch up on.
After Jaycee found me back on campus, she told me how
worried you were. That you'd called me but my stupid
phone was dead again—I really should think about getting
an upgrade—and I didn't know how upset you were. Right,
Jay Jay? Didn't you tell me how worried I'd made my poor
mom here?" Eve looked at her.

Jaycee nodded. "I did."

"Once I knew that, I wanted to come here in person so
you could see for yourself that I was totally fine." She
smiled in a way that lit her face from the inside. It struck
her mother how beautiful she was. How grown-up she
suddenly looked. Eve seemed to glow, to *beam.*

That was it! Marcy knew then what the difference was
in her brilliant, focused, hard-working daughter.

She was happy.

A fresh round of tears filled her eyes as she watched two cousins who had, until recently, not seen each other since they were both children. That had changed, too. They'd grown up. Marcy knew in her heart that in addition to getting her daughter back, she had just gained another.

"Please, Evie," she said finally. "Don't ever do that to me again. Promise me."

Eve reached over to hug her mom at the table. "I promise," she whispered into her hair. "I'm so sorry I put you through this."

Jaycee smiled. She felt a sudden, deep longing to feel Van's chest against hers. To tell him how much she'd missed him. To tell him she was sorry for leaving. She couldn't wait to tell Barton how she'd uncovered the sewer and helped her cousin climb out before it, and the spider's web, swallowed her forever. Even though the warmth of this kitchen made her feel like she'd come back to a place where she was welcomed all along, Jaycee wanted to go home.

"I'll need a ride to the airport," she told them finally.

Wink wink, nudge nudge.

"And, I'll need a ride back to school." Eve grinned at her mother.

"Oh, gosh, of course," Marcy said. She jumped up to grab the three mugs and place them in the sink. "And I have to get to work." Even though she'd just experienced the most joyous moment of her life, there was still her job to worry about. Her crabby boss yelled at her if she showed up even five minutes late. Damn! Did she have enough gas in her car to get both Eve to school, and Jaycee to the airport? Well, wait a minute, she thought, coming back around to look at the two girls, who were looking at her like they'd just swallowed something that got stuck on the way down.

"Jay Jay, don't you have to drop off that rental?"

"What rental?" Jaycee asked innocently. The real rental was still parked at Holy United Academy, waiting to take her back to the airport.

"That red one in the driveway," Marcy pointed out the front door.

"Oh," Jaycee said casually. "You mean that red Range Rover? Oh no, that's not mine."

"It's not?" Eve asked her.

"Nope," Jaycee shook her head.

"Then whose is it?" Marcy jumped in, watching their bizarre ploy with narrowed eyes.

What now?

They both sat there waiting for it to sink in. Finally, Eve got up and walked to her mom near the sink. She took her right hand, opened it up, and plopped the keys inside her palm.

"It's all yours."

CHAPTER THIRTY-FIVE

Jaycee handed over her own set of keys to the attendant at the desk. With the rental returned, she set about getting herself home. Manchester-Boston Regional Airport could deliver her almost immediately to Chicago, but then she'd have a two-hour layover before she could pick up the next flight back to L.A.

Who cares, she thought. Just get me there. She had grabbed the first route offered to her at the United Airlines desk. "That's fine," she told the girl at the counter. "I'll take it."

The flight was leaving in forty-five minutes, which gave Jaycee just enough time to power her cell phone back up. She plugged the charger into the station conveniently provided for passengers and fed some life back into the dead screen. She put her head back, lowered her back onto the chair, kicked her legs out, and closed her eyes for what felt like the first time in days.

It had been days.

Days since she was summoned back to the place she'd worked tirelessly to avoid. But why? Now, she realized how important New Hampshire had been in making her who she was.

She could come here again, with a fuller understanding of those she had left behind. In their own way, they were good people.

Hugging Eve goodbye had been more difficult than she'd expected. When they promised each other they'd keep in touch, they meant it. Jaycee knew that third bedroom in her condo would work perfectly for an extended visit. She couldn't wait to see what Eve would become.

"Holy shit, girl," she'd told her as she kissed her cousin's cheek the last time. "Together, you and I could take on the world."

"I feel sorry for the world." Eve had smiled that grin again that told Jaycee all the scars she couldn't see would heal nicely on their own. Eve was going to be just fine.

Cecilia would be, too. Once she'd gotten over the fury of losing the one thing she loved most of all, her fire-engine-red Range Rover, she had retreated to her bed, pulled the downy comforter over her head, and screamed into her pillow as they'd walked out the door.

It had been a joyous thing to behold. Jaycee had hoped for a more thorough decimation of the teenaged wasteland that was Cecilia, but Eve insisted they had punished her enough.

"She's not completely evil," she told Jaycee, who tried to argue that yes, in fact, she was.

"No, Jay Jay," she explained as they rode the elevator out to the back lot where the Rover sat in its own special space near the door to the laundry room. "She's not."

Eve told her Cecilia's younger brother had been born with cerebral palsy. Her Legacy Girl payout had supplied a motorized wheelchair, and a team of specialists to care for him. Even though Cecilia had orchestrated a series of events that could have left her irreparably damaged, or even dead, Eve had already forgiven her.

Like Molly and Norm had forgiven Kendra. She called it a gift she hadn't deserved.

"We all had our reasons for doing it," Eve told Jaycee. "That's why I could never take the entire operation down. There are people involved who depend on it. You see that, right, Jay Jay? Their lives, their families, their towns, and all the people they love, depend on us keeping their secret. I can't remove the top and expect the bottom to remain self-sustaining. One half feeds the other."

It explained her resistance when Jaycee had started talking reporters, police, and a nuclear exposé. It went against her grain but she had promised to keep the secret, too. And when she'd asked, incredulously, if Eve wanted to stay at Holy United Academy, her answer had been swift and decidedly final.

"There are other schools, Eve," she'd tried to tell her. "You can get into any of them. If you're worried about the money, I can help you. Let me help you get a fresh start—"

"No, Jay Jay," she'd shut down her argument. "Do you know how lucky I am to be here?"

Jaycee's face must have registered shock.

"It's world-renowned. I am getting a first-class education here. I love my soccer team. Coach Whalen won't be mad at me once I explain that I wasn't 'self-nurturing,' I'll tell him I was sick. It's all okay. There are really good people here. Even Biff. I know you thought he was somehow involved, but he's not at all. He wants what's

301

best for us. I don't just want to stay here; I *have* to stay here."

Jaycee threw up her hands and told Eve she trusted that she knew best. Another first. Jaycee Wilder never threw up her hands to trust anyone.

She climbed up from the darkness of her mind. She'd almost fallen asleep. She heard the voice over the intercom that her flight was starting to board. She gathered her things, and unplugged the phone. She looked at it. It had been on vibrate, so she hadn't felt it buzz. And buzz, and buzz some more. She had never seen it register so many missed calls.

Barton. Van. Barton. Van again.

Oh, no! Her stomach rolled as her seat was called. She had to board.

What was happening!

She threw her bag around her shoulder and quickly decided on who she had to call back first.

She loved them both, but Van came first now. It was always Van.

She had to hear his voice. Come on, Van! Answer the phone. Pick up! Talk to me!

One ring, two, three rings.

"Jay Jay!" he said finally. Jaycee's legs almost buckled with relief. At least he was alive.

"Jay Jay, where are you?" his voice was tinny, like the connection was bad. She couldn't hear him.

"Van, I can't really hear you ..." but then there were two voices. Van had her on speaker. Who else was talking?

"Jaycee, where are you?" It was the same question but this one was loaded with force, like when the operator at the White House informs you *the president* is on the line.

Barton?

"Barton, is that you?"

"Where are you?" came the same question. "We've been trying to get ahold of you!"

"I'm sorry," she explained. "My phone died, there's so much that's happened. Barton, you were right—"

"Are you still in New Hampshire?" he interrupted her sharply.

The boarding agent was beckoning to her. She really wasn't supposed to be on her cell when they were trying to load the plane. She had to go!

"I'm leaving. Like right now, I'm about to board my flight. I was going to call both of you once I got to Chicago."

"What time do you get into Los Angeles," he asked.

Jaycee struggled to recall when she landed. Eleven o'clock, midnight? She had to check but her ear was on the phone, the agent was staring at her, she had no time for this.

"Uh, tonight. Late tonight. Barton, what the hell is going on?"

Tell me! Something was wrong. Why was Barton with Van, on speaker?

"Jay Jay, listen to me." She held up a finger to the agent, who was now getting pissed.

One minute, I'm so sorry, she mouthed.

"Hurry, Barton, I gotta jump on this plane."

"He's back."

Jaycee couldn't hear him. Or maybe she did hear him and she just wanted to pretend she hadn't. The angry face of the attendant swam in front of her. Her ticket fell from her fingers to the dirty carpet below. Her feet shuffled forward but she never felt herself falling.

The attendant grabbed her shoulders. "Ma'am, do you need medical attention?"

"No," Jaycee thought she responded. Did she speak?

"No," she said again, but this time she was talking to Barton and Van.

"How?" she asked. She didn't recognize her own voice. "How do you know?"

Van's voice was back. "I got the mail a little while ago. I opened an envelope addressed to you. I didn't think you'd care."

"I don't care, Van, you know that." She leaned against the attendant for support. If she went down again she'd prefer not to land in the crud collecting near her shoes. "What was in the envelope? Van?"

"It was an I.D. badge from a hospital in St. Helena."

An I.D. badge? Jaycee knew she'd been to St. Helena at least once before. It was a sleepy little community in Napa County. She'd done some story about the downtown architecture being featured in a planning board presentation. She'd also learned no one could use those noisy leaf blowers without prior authorization. Yes, they governed that. It was that kind of place. Residents loved it for that very reason. Had she ever been to a hospital there?

No. She hadn't. She was sure of it.

"Well, it's not from anyone I know," she tried to tell them. "I've never been to a hospital in St. Helena."

The attendant was now telling her she either had to board or take the next flight.

Please, she told her, one minute!

"Are you sure?" It was Barton.

"Yes, I'm sure. I have to go—"

"Jaycee, it's the I.D. badge of a young blonde girl. There's blood on it. She resembles you."

Jaycee swayed again. No, Barton must be confused. It had been Cecilia who had resembled her. Cecilia. In New Hampshire.

She was so overtired nothing registered. Until suddenly it did. She moved the mental puzzle she'd just completed for Eve, and opened up an empty one.

She swallowed hard.

An empty one, for herself.

"What does it say?" she gulped into the phone, although she already knew. It wouldn't be the same, but it would be sickeningly close.

"Natalie Thorpe, part-time nursing aide, twenty-six years old, five-foot-eight—"

"No!" she screamed into the phone. Maybe she wouldn't even be allowed on this flight.

"What does it say, Barton?" she demanded once and for all.

"It says Swing Girl," he told her finally, bringing the full weight of what that meant straight into her heart. She jumped like she'd just been hit with a jolt from a wire torn loose from its connection. It seared her with the same red-hot foreboding she had first felt when she'd seen past his charade and into his incurable disorder.

The attendant could wait no longer. Somehow, Jaycee disconnected the call, found her legs, and used them to board the plane that would bring her home. Now, she knew Barton and Van weren't the only ones waiting to welcome her home.

Swing Girl.

Another innocent girl. Another targeted murder. Jaycee walked to her seat and felt the frigid fingers of dread wrap around her body. She shivered. She'd known all along that one day, he would come for her again. When he was ready, he would return to finish their story as he had wanted to tell it all along.

The jet's engines roared as the plane took off and headed west.

Jaycee was going home, but it seemed her former photographer and best friend in the entire world was already there. Waiting for her.

Ben was back.

The End

Epilogue

Natalie Thorpe usually preferred a thicker build to her men. Football stocky, or jacked like a firefighter. She wanted to feel bulky arms holding her so tight she could time out the rhythm of their owner's heartbeat. Unforgettable. Firm. Hot and hard. That was when she felt safest. After a childhood spent dodging the clenched fists of an alcoholic stepfather, feeling safe was the first check on her list when she decided whether she wanted to see a particular man for a second date. A third. Maybe even a fourth if he was really special.

This guy was special. She'd known it right away. Maybe it was the way his eyes crinkled at the corners when he'd greeted her in the OR just before the surgical team cracked open the knee joint of the patient about to get a brand-new one. She was nervous. It was the first surgery she'd been invited to view and she should've been laser focused on the bone crumbling away from the deteriorated ligaments made flimsy by overuse and age. Instead, she watched him move. He entered his space with fluidity and elegance, so unlike the raw, athletic energy she typically aligned with. His languid body mesmerized her with that tantalizing, slippery feeling in her stomach that had nothing to do with the gore spilling out through the gloved hands of the surgeon and onto the table.

When they had coffee two days later, Natalie felt comfortable enough to tell him that the swing shift at the hospital was just about killing her. She didn't want to complain, especially to a guy, but she was self-conscious of the purplish stains beneath her eyes, and the dour tone of her skin. Her body was struggling to be alert when it should have been sound asleep. He'd smiled when he told her she was beautiful; he was sympathetic to her fatigue. When he touched her hand, lacing his fingers between hers for the first time, she felt a syrupy pulse of desire. They were thin, those fingers, but just masculine enough to stoke the hunger within her. His knuckles were soft but she could feel vitality throbbing within him. She gripped his hand, and rotated her thumb to stroke the inside of his hand. Sure, he may be narrow of body, but his spirit was stout. Natalie was smitten.

But was she safe?

Well, not for long. A week later she learned in excruciating fashion how much damage can be inflicted by wiry arms and slender fingers. Just before her eyes closed for the last time, she looked down upon her body, and noticed how similar her insides were to those she'd recently witnessed flowing over the puckered ridge of the incision inside the operating room. But this was different. In the OR, the blood flow had been carefully controlled and mopped away. Here, it was haphazard and imprecise. Why wasn't he trying to keep this sterile? Didn't he know that hospitals could be fined, or worse, shut down, for improper handling of bodily fluids? This was going all wrong. And why was he calling her a jaybird?

Why?

Natalie Thorpe never had the opportunity to answer her own delirious question. While her muddled mind stayed in the phantom OR of her flossy consciousness, her lungs were being swamped by a paralyzing torrent of blood. Air was stuck either out, or in, she could no longer control its route. She left the world along a garbled thread of gratitude that an imaginary anesthesiologist had made everything go dark just before the hammering anguish turned to unobstructed agony. How many times had she heard the doctor tell a grieving family that a dead loved one had gone quickly? It was a blessing, really, like that jaybird he kept mentioning, guilelessly cruising away upon a prevailing wind.

"Jay Bird," he breathed out again, enamored with the sumptuous way her nickname curled around his lips. He could never resist her. He missed her humor and her candor, but mostly, he missed the thrill of her fear. His most precious adversary would soon know he was close. He gently kissed the young nurse who was not quite as blonde, sharp, or profoundly exceptional as the real thing. None of them were.

"Thank you," he imparted a proper acknowledgment to her lifeless corpse. He rose to leave her.

Her killer took two things from Natalie Thorpe: her very essence and the hospital employee identification badge he would need to make contact. To let his Jay Bird see just how much he'd been thinking of her.

Acknowledgments

My deepest thanks to my go-to source for all things criminal, twisted, and sinister, Detective Sergeant John Sonia of the New Hampshire State Police Major Crime Unit. Your insight into law enforcement practices, boarding school culture, and the psychology of a predator was invaluable in telling this story. To Los Angeles Police Detective II Kristin Merrill, we're heading back your way for the next installment! I can't wait to pester you for location, scene, and investigative details. Thank you for your service and friendship.

To the Waldorf Publishing team. Barbara Terry, Danielle Vann, and Beth Stifflemire, couldn't do it without you! To Mark Isaac, thank you for taking our cover image ideas and carrying them across the finish line. To editors Carol McCrow, Elisabeth Pennella and Holly Park, I appreciate your careful attention to my details.

Lastly, to my precious family. Everything I do begins and ends with you. I'm the luckiest girl in the world, and I know it.

Author Bio

Jennifer Vaughn is a longtime member of the award-winning news team at WMUR-TV, in Manchester, New Hampshire. As the evening anchor, Jennifer has lead coverage that has earned Edward R. Murrow, Associated Press, and New Hampshire Association of Broadcasters Awards.

She is also the recipient of multiple Emmy nominations, the Red Cross Sword of Hope Award, and had her debut novel, *Last Flight Out*, featured in the Swag Bag at the Daytime Emmy Awards in Beverly Hills, CA, in 2013. Jennifer has had prominent roles in internationally televised presidential debates alongside CNN, ABC News, and FOX News, has anchored election night coverage for both national and state contests, and provided political analysis for several radio and television news outlets.

She's interviewed every sitting president and presidential candidate since 1999, supporting WMUR's extensive first-in-the-nation presidential primary coverage. Jennifer has covered everything from Super Bowls, world championship parades, ABC's *Extreme Home Makeover*, deadly natural disasters, and exciting medical breakthroughs.

Alongside her husband, Brad Dupuis, and children, Brody and Darby, her family is proud to support charities that direct financial assistance to cancer patients. All proceeds from the sale of *Last Flight Out* were distributed to local organizations. Jennifer is also the author of *Throw Away Girls*, Book 1 in the Jaycee Wilder Series, and *Echo Valley*. Learn more at www.jvwrites.com.